THE WRONG STORY

L J JENNER

CRANTHORPE
—MILLNER—
PUBLISHERS

Copyright © L J Jenner (2023)

The right of L J Jenner to be identified as author of this work has been asserted by her in accordance with section 77 and 78 of the Copyright, Designs and Patents Act 1988.

All rights reserved. No part of this publication may be reproduced, stored in a retrieval system, or transmitted in any form or by any means, electronic, mechanical, photocopying, recording, or otherwise, without the prior permission of the publishers.

Any person who commits any unauthorised act in relation to this publication may be liable to criminal prosecution and civil claims for damages.

This book is a work of fiction. Names, characters, places and incidents are either products of the author's imagination or are used fictitiously. Any resemblance to actual events or locales or persons, living or dead, is entirely coincidental.

First published by Cranthorpe Millner Publishers (2023)

ISBN 978-1-80378-110-5 (Paperback)

www.cranthorpemillner.com

Cranthorpe Millner Publishers

To Richard, Ben and Alex – the three amazing men in my life who inspire me more than they will ever know.

Prologue
1989

I have no idea how long we've been here. Five minutes? Half an hour? Longer? It's still dark outside. I glance, unseeing, around the room as I move again, finding another chair to sit on. I've tried most of them now, unable to settle for more than a few minutes, sitting, getting up, pacing then sitting again. The room is impersonal, two large tables with orange plastic chairs, reminiscent of school. Around the corner, hidden in the short edge of its L-shape, are a sink, kettle and fridge. Chipped mugs hang on a wooden cup stand. I washed one that someone had left in the sink earlier just for something to do, scouring its inside to remove the old, dried ring of tea.

A woman came in a short while ago, dishevelled and pale in old tracksuit bottoms, baggy t-shirt and a scruffy cardigan. She glanced at me and half smiled, nervously, not knowing if a smile was appropriate. I smiled back, or at least that was the signal my brain tried to send to my face. I wasn't sure what expression I actually managed. She got a Tupperware box out of the fridge and left. She didn't speak. Nothing of consequence could be said here. And it wasn't a place for anything inconsequential.

I don't know how long we've been here. I only know that time is slowing down, each second lasting longer than the last. I know this because the only sound in the room is the loud ticking of the clock on the wall and the gaps between each tick are definitely getting longer. I'm glad. Each tick is taking me inexorably towards something I don't want to know and the cold dread of it is growing with each passing second.

I move away from the only other person in the room. He hasn't moved since we arrived but I know he's feeling it too. I know we should comfort each other, but I need to move away from him. If I increase the distance between us, then I won't be infected by what he is trying not to know too. I am a black hole, collapsing in on myself so that I can avoid what's coming next. If I can disappear altogether I won't feel it.

Footsteps. Getting louder. A door opening. A face. I try not to look at it but my eyes move of their own accord and I know. Instantly. The face tells the whole story, immediately communicating its dire news as though someone had plugged me directly into its owner. My body knows before my brain catches up. The black hole explodes and I silently shatter into a million fragments. The floor rushes up, first to my knees, then my forehead, as my body folds. I hear but don't feel the impact. There's another sound; animal, guttural, tortured, a long way away. Arms grab me, lift me, hold me tight, but it's too late. No-one will ever put the pieces back together. Some of the fragments are lost forever. I am gone. I will never be back.

PART ONE
1996

Chapter 1

I was expecting someone called Robyn. That was all I knew about her, a name and a phone number. Anticipation was making me fidgety. What would she be like? What would she be bringing? Did I have the skills needed for her to trust me? Or would some unconscious incompetence on my part leave her isolated in whatever suffering had brought her here?

I listened to the rain on the glass and the ticking of the clock, which always seemed incredibly loud as I sat there alone before clients arrived. Gradually my breathing and heart rate slowed.

Robyn-with-a-y. That's how I'd already come to think of her. At about the age of thirteen, I had wanted to be called Robyn-with-a-y. I'd thought it sounded so exotic. I used to picture myself as Robyn-with-a-y: tall, slim, elegant and very definitely non-conformist. Robyn-with-a-y cared nothing for the opinion of others.

In contrast, my slightly chubby thirteen-year-old self had been brought up to be too afraid of adults to be non-conformist. I was the original mousey 'good girl', so obedient and rule-driven that fitting in with my peers had been virtually impossible. I'd longed to be Robyn-with-a-y and be cool enough not to care about any of them.

The sound of a car door opening and then closing, followed by the soft squeak of trainers on the path, gave me ample warning of the knock on the door. I stood up to let her in.

The Robyn who entered looked nothing like my fantasy version of Robyn-with-a-y. Far from the striking, exotic being of my imagination, she looked quite ordinary, yet strangely familiar. In her early twenties at a guess, she was understated in blue jeans and pale pink sweatshirt, underneath a now rain-splattered waterproof jacket. Although reasonably slim, she didn't have the model sylph-like figure I had just been picturing.

She looked nervous, as most new clients did to be fair. Who wouldn't feel nervous coming to tell a stranger their deepest thoughts and problems? What Robyn didn't know was that there were usually two scared people in the room in any first session.

She met my eyes, shook my hand – surprisingly firmly – and smiled a polite rather than genuine smile. I gestured to the seat and offered her a glass of water. I noticed that she didn't remove her coat.

Therapy, when you thought about it, was a strange enterprise; two strangers sitting in a room, one hoping the other has all the answers and will rescue them from something, the other secretly hoping the same thing.

I tried to make it easier, to be friendly and approachable, to normalise a distinctly abnormal situation. I asked about her journey and whether she had found the place easily enough. I tried to persuade myself that this was OK; that it was really Robyn I was putting at ease, rather than myself. Even so, I worried about imaginary other therapists judging me, those who preferred the 'therapist-as-a-blank-screen' approach. The faceless imaginary 'others' who still seemed to haunt me despite all the money I'd spent on my own therapy.

Robyn smiled back, playing her part in the social ritual, but remained very nervous and clearly felt a bit awkward. She accepted a glass of water and fixed her eyes on mine; big, round, terrified eyes, staring expectantly at me while the rest of her face tried valiantly to smile politely and join in the societal game. Did she even blink?

She waited patiently for me to finish the obligatory spiel outlining the limits of confidentiality and when I might break it. I sensed that she just wanted to get on with it and I wasn't sure how much of what I was saying she was actually taking in. She was smiling and nodding while her eyes seemed to be pleading with me to hurry up. I felt pressurised to finish; she didn't want to hear this stuff.

Finally, I asked her if she had any questions. Unsurprisingly, she didn't.

"So, can you tell me what brings you here? And why now?"

She finally averted her gaze. After a pause, and still without looking at me, she said quietly, "I'm here because I think I'm going to have to leave my boyfriend."

I was intrigued by her choice of words: *going to have to leave*. Not, 'want to leave' or even, 'am thinking of leaving'. My heart sank. The old stay-or-leave chestnut; choose between following a need to be more authentic, more true to oneself, or a need for familiarity and security. There's never a right answer and both options bring pain, at least in the short term. I didn't think that I was very good at working with this issue and I knew myself well enough to know why.

"Going to have to leave him... but you don't really want to?" I paraphrased, making the implied explicit, but doing so tentatively.

"I love him so much! He's my soul mate."

I waited.

She glanced at me and quickly looked away again, visibly struggling with what she needed to say. "He really is a great guy – kind and considerate, the life and soul of the party... the life and soul of my life." Her voice was quiet, almost a whisper. She needed me to know this about him first.

"But?" I gently nudged her towards the rest.

"But..." she echoed, making brief eye contact before visibly deflating.

The sadness was palpable, the internal battle clear. She needed to do this, but really didn't want to. After a pause, she stole herself to continue.

"But, he gets angry." She sighed and continued to study her hands as she intertwined them in her lap.

She clearly wasn't going to elaborate without a prompt and I noted a subtle flash of irritation in me, there for a second and then instantly gone.

"Angry?" I reminded myself that having to drag everything out of her was a warning light. I knew to be careful and guessed what might be going on; Robyn seemed to be ashamed. She didn't want to tell me her story because there was something shameful in it. With a sinking feeling, I guessed what it might be.

A brief flashback: An open hand on the edge of my peripheral vision, too close, too big. Just a small echo of a somersault in my stomach.

Right now, in the present, my heart beat a bit faster for a moment. *Stop it!* My need to be with her through this, to ensure she didn't feel alone, intensified.

"It scares me... I get... really anxious, try to make everything OK again... then two weeks ago—" She stopped abruptly, evidently struggling to speak.

"It's hard to talk about," I gently acknowledged. In training, we were told that this was the therapist's most valuable tool; focus not on the content but on *how* the content is expressed.

She looked relieved as she finally met my gaze again and simply said, "I just feel so stupid!" before her skin blotched, the tell-tale give away that a strong emotion is being felt. Something shifted ever so slightly between us.

Robyn didn't cry, but gradually started to tell me about Andy's temper, how he would blow up and storm out, kicking things and slamming doors. Later, he would come back, silent and sulky, and she would always end up apologising, trying to win him round, smooth it over, fix it. And that usually worked. Finally, she got to the episode two weeks ago.

"He really lost it! I was telling him he had to do something about his anger after he stormed out of a meeting with his boss. He accused me of being on his boss's side, said I didn't understand, that I was just like his mum, always assuming it was him who was wrong. Why couldn't I just take his side for once? Why couldn't someone just for once be on his side?"

I waited again for her to continue. Sometimes it's best to just stay out of the way when a client is trying to tell a painful story.

"I tried to wheedle him around, saying that I *was* on his side, but that he couldn't keep behaving like this. I said that I loved him and I was always on his side, doing what I always do, trying to calm him down… and I went to put my arms around him… and… and he hit me… he hit me across the face with the back of his hand. He said something like 'get away from me'. But then instantly his hands flew up to his mouth and he was apologising and trying to check my mouth – it was bleeding – and saying he was sorry over and over…" Her demeanour changed abruptly. "But it's such a bloody cliché, isn't it?"

She looked directly at me again, really wanting me to validate what came next.

"You hear about this all the time and they're always sorry… always sorry until the next time!" She spat out the last sentence bitterly. "I can't be one of those women! I just can't! I won't!" she added vehemently.

"But part of you wants to stay anyway." My instincts told me this was the part more in need of validation.

A long pause. "The stupid part wants to," she said more softly. "But I know it's not right. I know it'll happen again. I don't want to be that woman who keeps going back because he says he's sorry, while everyone whispers behind her back no matter how many lies she tells about the bruises; I can't be that woman, it's not who I am." The words sounded firm and decisive but everything else about her told me otherwise. The words had no energy in them and there was a tangible weight of sadness surrounding her.

"Tell me about the stupid part. What does that part think?"

Another pause. "The stupid part thinks he'll change – that I can change him." She laughed bitterly, "Oh God, what a fucking cliché. The stupid part thinks that I can love him better!"

"Try for a moment to not judge that part of you. It might be a cliché, I don't know, but I think that part of you is sad. I'd like to hear about that." *Careful Maggie, don't steer her. Don't let your own stuff get in the way. Keep it neutral, stay curious.*

"It is sad. But it's also so angry with him, so angry with him for ruining it. It was so good between us – apart for his temper obviously – but now he's gone too far and I have to leave. He's ruined it!"

"So now you have to lose all that was good between you because he couldn't, or wouldn't, control his temper."

"He says he 'couldn't' but I refuse to accept that. We all make choices, even in the heat of the moment. It's called free will. We make our own lives through the choices we make, I really believe that." Robyn suddenly seemed to run out of steam.

"Is there a 'but'?" I wasn't sure.

"I don't know… maybe. Part of me wonders if I'm naïve. I believe in free will and choice because I get fed up with people telling me I'm lucky when my so-called luck is actually about hard work, choices and sacrifice. But then I wonder if it could be true that he couldn't control it. Could it be that something happened to him that – I don't know – wired him differently? And if that's true, is it permanent or can it be undone? What if he is actually a really good guy with just a little bit that's screwed up, and I just abandon him and screw him up some more? What kind of person would that make me?"

"It sounds like you feel responsible."

"I don't feel responsible for the fact that he hit me, I

know he's totally responsible for that. I do feel responsible for not giving up on him though…" She shook herself and then changed tack again. "But then I look at this from an outsider's perspective and I see how it looks, how obvious it is."

"Is it obvious?"

"Like I said, it's a bit of a cliché, a man hits a woman, the woman thinks that he'll change, that she can change him, and keeps going back for more, while everyone outside the relationship can see the stupidity of that."

"You're not on the outside though."

"No, no I'm not. It would be easy if I was."

"And it's not easy at all, is it?"

"I feel like it should be though. I must be stupid to even be considering staying."

I genuinely wasn't trying to encourage her to stay, though I was acutely aware that I was getting dangerously close to the possibility of her inferring that. I just wanted to bring the complexity of her feelings out into the open. She feared judgment around the part of her that wanted to stay and didn't hate him, but those feelings were there. I wanted to welcome the whole kaleidoscope of feelings she had about this, but that didn't mean I thought she should stay. Or at least, I hoped it didn't. My own history had been hovering around in the ether for the last half hour and I was very consciously trying to avoid contaminating her experience with mine.

"And nevertheless that's exactly what you are

considering."

"Yes I am. Stupidly, idiotically, madly, I actually am. So, what do you think? Can you cure me of stupidity?" She half smiled sheepishly at me, but at least she looked a bit more relaxed than when she came in. And she had owned the shameful part of herself, the part that she called 'stupid'. I knew we could work together.

I smiled back. "I don't know about that, but I can help you to explore all the different aspects of this so that you can understand what's driving you. You talked about choice earlier. Well, self-awareness increases choice."

As I sat cradling a cup of tea after she left, I wondered how it would end for Robyn. What decision would she make? And would she too always regret it?

Chapter 2

After Robyn left, I had two more clients, one after the other, and then dashed round the now sodden fields with the dogs. It had been raining solidly for two days but had stopped for a brief lull partway through my last session. As I tramped through the mud, I watched the two dogs weaving in and out of each other in a mad game of chase. Not for the first time, I marvelled at the way they ran just for the sheer love of running. I envied their energy and zest for life, their ability to be totally in the moment and to run for no other reason than because they wanted to. I couldn't imagine such joy and abandon – not since that day – but how I wished I could.

The fields were always the tonic I needed after a day full of clients, a punctuation mark between work and home. Even on days like today when the sky was a dull monotone white and the trees still barren, I loved the peace. Birds cawed and trilled, mixing with the distant hum of traffic, and I focused on the sounds to empty my head of the stories I'd heard that day. It was a brief respite before the school run, family life and domestic chores took over.

Sam was as chatty as ever in the car when I picked him up from school, and I struggled to focus on the minutiae of his day. I had spent the afternoon with two heart-breaking clients: a suicidal teenager and a woman who had terminal cancer. I only learnt much later of how I carried these kinds of stories with me – physically as well as mentally – for hours, if not days, afterwards. Back then, I didn't have the self-awareness to notice how affected I was by the trauma and despair I absorbed every day. Listening to Sam's chatter about his maths test and his outrage that Henry Roberts had cheated by copying him, I found it difficult to empathise or even sympathise with him. His dramas felt small and trivial. I had to consciously remind myself that if I didn't listen to him when he talked about the small stuff, then how could I expect him to talk to me about the big stuff? I forced myself to listen, and felt the familiar flutter of guilt that seemed to hover permanently around my parenting these days.

I forgot about clients, apart from the niggling feeling that I'd met Robyn before. Throughout the evening the thought that I knew her kept popping into my head, taunting me with its not-quite-a-memory, not quite *déjà vu* quality. In between, I supervised homework (homework in primary school, how ridiculous), cooked a healthy meal (spurned purely because it was healthy), washed Sam's sports kit (which seemed to be an everyday requirement these days), and tried valiantly to listen to Mathew telling me about his day.

In the twelve years that Mathew and I had been married, I had never really understood his attitude to work. To him, work had always been a means to an end. He was good at what he did but he had no passion for it at all. In fact, he hated it. Having embarked on an accounting career to please his accountant father, he had proved to be very good at it and had risen through the ranks to finance director. It had never occurred to him to do anything different, and especially not now his 'golden handcuff' salary meant we had a very comfortable lifestyle. But he hated everything about it: the people, the tasks, the politics, and the lack of any sense of progress or making a difference – everything. He lived for evenings and weekends and just put his head down and got on with the rest, driven by a strong sense of responsibility, but without any real joy or ambition.

These days I couldn't possibly spend every day doing something I didn't really care about, not anymore. Now, I'd rather have no money and live in a caravan. I'd never tell Mathew that though; he took pride in his ability to provide such a comfortable lifestyle for his family. He made sure we had everything we could possibly need, and enjoyed doing so. I was grateful for his dedication to me and Sam; I just wasn't as interested in money or fancy holidays as he seemed to think I was.

When I stood back from it, it was hard to listen to someone who was just going through the motions.

Mathew didn't ever seem to stand back from it though. He didn't seem to consider whether what he was doing was something that actually mattered to him, or even whether he enjoyed it. He just got on with it. I didn't want to hurt him or, God forbid, be rude, but the truth was I felt disingenuous listening to him these days. Just like I felt with Sam, compared to what I dealt with every day, quite honestly what Mathew did was trivial. I caught myself; *how arrogant you are Maggie!*

Mathew was a wonderful human being, I reminded myself. I had no business judging his choice of work and anyway, for most people work is simply a distraction; it provides a structure and a way of filling time. It gives an illusion of meaning when, in reality, there is no meaning.

The problem was that I spent my working life with many people for whom that illusion had been shattered by tragedy. They had had their eyes opened to the reality of the human condition: we are born and we die, simply filling in the time in between as best we can. They now saw in psychedelic high-definition what the rest of us successfully avoid seeing: that we are *all* just going through the motions. We somehow achieve the mental trick of never thinking about how transient it all is, instead focusing on vainly trying to minimise the inevitable suffering that seems to be part of the package.

Oh God, that sounded so depressive! I didn't feel depressed, I felt wise, as if I knew something most people didn't. In the past, this kind of thinking was considered among the wisest of philosophical musings. These days, if you said something like that out loud, people would look at you oddly and want to prescribe Prozac immediately.

Did I see it all so clearly *before*? I did a long time before, when I was Robyn's age, but I couldn't remember later on. Why is it always so hard to remember who I was before? It was as if I'd died that day and someone else took my place. I was a new person, never the same.

Once Sam was in bed I ran a steaming bath. Listening to the gloop and then tinkle of the water as I repeatedly dunked and then squeezed out a sponge, I tried desperately to focus on the present. I concentrated on the sound of the water, felt the heat of it against my submerged skin, the relative cool of the exposed parts. It was hopeless. My thoughts drifted back to a time before, a time that I didn't want to remember and, cruelly, one of the few times that I apparently couldn't forget. It didn't plague me daily, but given my session with Robyn, it was inevitable that tonight the memory would resurface again.

*

I am twenty years old and madly in love. He is at uni with me and is the lead singer in a popular local band. Everybody loves him but he only loves me. Being his chosen one makes me popular by default and I bask in his reflected glory. Everyone sees the fun-loving, adventurous Andre, but only I see what's behind that. Andre has a life force that compels me. It's completely irresistible to me because it is me. Andre brings me face to face with myself. The only difference between us is that Andre isn't afraid. Andre hasn't had his life-force crushed by a crippling inner people-pleaser; the product of a screwed-up depressed mother and an aggressive, controlling father. Andre is free in a way that I have never been free. And he is alive in a way that I have always yearned to be. Truly alive! Everyday! Always! Andre has taught me not to fear. He quotes The Dead Poets Society *line: 'I don't wish when the time comes for me to die, to discover that I haven't lived.' We agree that is the only thing that is truly scary; the idea that we won't consummate our lives. It's not all about hedonism – that's just the Andre who everyone else sees – it's so much deeper than that. Andre wants to experience everything, fully, openly, willingly. That includes suffering, sadness and despair if necessary. He epitomises what it means to be authentic and fully present. He wants to know himself and the world completely. We plan to travel the world together in a few months when we graduate.*

*

It's late, very late, nearly morning in fact. I'm curled in a ball on the bed facing away from him. He is pleading with me to forgive him, promising to make it up to me, that he'll never do it again, that it was abhorrent what he just did and he has no idea where it came from. I am in shock. It all seems surreal, like it didn't really just happen. I curl up tighter, trying to block him out. We've been like this for hours. I want to sleep. I need the oblivion of sleep. I can't take it in, and I don't know how to be.

*

This is the way the memories go, backwards and forwards instead of chronologically like a film. They hover around the moment, circling it, landing on it only briefly.

*

The hand by my head, open, flat, not curled in a fist. The back of his hand in the corner of my eye, coming towards me fast, too big, too close. His face, ugly with anger and menace, instantly changing to opened-mouthed shock, a parody of Pierrot, comical in any other circumstances. Holding my head, turning it towards him, checking my mouth. "Let me see." Wiping the blood with his thumb. Get away, don't touch me.

The next few weeks, a daze, more pleading. What to do? I don't know. The grief! Where is Andre? What happened to the man I loved? He would never have done this. Never! Who is the person in front of me, pleading, apologising and yet saying it was unforgivable? It was unforgivable. It's always unforgivable!

And yet I can still see Andre. I can still see him in the man standing in front of me. He's still the man who thinks violence is abhorrent. He's hurting too. He's hurting so much. He is feeling deep, deep shame, I can see that. Sweet, funny, beautifully alive Andre. And I can't lose him. I can't go back to being too afraid to live. I need him.

Telling my mum. Why do I do that? I need advice, but I know what it will be. Dad furious. Why did she tell Dad? He wants to kill him. His rage is blinding, primal, someone hurt his baby. He bans me from seeing Andre and, although he no longer has that power, old habits resurface and disobedience feels almost impossible. Mum crying, what am I thinking?

"You can't stay!" she sobs. "Do you really think it won't happen again?"

I need a more objective view. I tell Miranda. She knows Andre nearly as well as I do. She'll see the other side of this. I believe he's truly sorry. Miranda will too. She doesn't. She thinks I'm mad and gets on a feminist soapbox about the oppression of women. This isn't about feminism. It's about Andre, Andre and me. She tells me that's a cop out. We all have to individually stand up to oppression and violence against women. I know she's right. My heart breaks and I feel it physically. A clichéd hole in my chest – that's genuinely how it feels. Bizarre. I have to end it, but moving physically hurts, my limbs are aching and heavy. I sleepwalk through the next few days, weeks and months.

*

The bath had gone cold. I briefly considered adding some more hot water but my extremities had shrivelled and I still had ironing to do for tomorrow before I went to bed. Having towelled myself dry and put up the ironing board I continued to reflect on Robyn. How could I not subconsciously steer her? How often had I wished that I'd known then what I know now? That life is not so black and white. That it wasn't inevitable that it would happen again. Maybe Andre was exactly the man I thought he was. Maybe he just also had a darker side that made him the complex, flawed human being that he was, that we all are. We're all capable of terrible mistakes – as I'd later discovered – and we all have a darker side.

I wondered again what happened to Andre, wondered for the billionth time what would have happened if I'd made the other choice. Had he turned out to be the violent monster that Miranda and my family had predicted? Or had the shame and regret he clearly felt after he hit me, stayed with him and kept his subsequent partners safe?

It was so unacceptable 'out there' to discuss this. I found it difficult to word it in a way that didn't sound like I was condoning violence. I didn't in any way think violence was acceptable, it was always unjustified and abhorrent. I just also believed that people make mistakes and that we shouldn't judge anyone forever on one mistake. Criminals serve their sentence and then are given a second chance. Some do manage to reform, vow never to go back and succeed in changing their lives. Men who hit women are assumed to have an irredeemable character flaw and are written off as evil. And often that tragically proved to be true. I knew that, I wasn't naïve. But not all of them. I just didn't like judgmental pigeonholes. I hoped I wasn't naïve, but I also knew that I would never exactly be objective about this either.

I had tried valiantly to hold onto the person I was with Andre, tried desperately to be the free spirit he had unleashed. I went travelling alone to the places we'd planned to see together and had some real adventures by not letting fear get in my way. I had climbed mountains in Nepal, bought a black-market ticket on the trans-Siberian railway and had even been smuggled into Burma illegally under a tarpaulin on the back of a truck. I had stayed with the Karen Freedom Fighters for two weeks, listening to their stories and watching truckloads of young boys, some only fourteen years old, leave for the font lines. I still had a photo hanging on a bedroom wall of one young boy, his eyes haunting me whenever

I looked at it. Somehow, he managed to look both defiant and terrified at the same time, like he knew he was going to die.

I never spoke of it now. Most people I knew now had never met that Maggie. *I* didn't know that Maggie; I didn't recognise her anymore. She certainly wasn't the same woman I was now. If I told the story of Burma, it would feel as though I was talking about someone else. I admired that Maggie though, the Maggie I was before fear and people-pleasing and rule-following squashed her back down. I yearned to be her again. If I'd stayed with Andre, maybe I still would be.

Instead I had returned to England and the graduate scheme job I had lined up before I left. In corporate-land I'd held onto some spirit for a while, challenging the status quo and why things had to be a certain way. It was a precocious way to behave that was always going to get me fired or promoted. I was lucky! At some point during my ascent through management grades, I re-absorbed the 'right' way to behave and became like everyone else. I did my job well, I had vision and pushed my area forward, but I didn't really take risks.

I accepted things that weren't right and stopped fighting everything. I went to pointless meetings and stuck to meaningless agendas. The things I would have wanted to change were too big, too impossible anyway, and so I gave up.

I met, fell in love with and eventually married Mathew, attracted by his kindness and calm energy. He helped me tolerate the last vestiges of frustration I felt with organisational bureaucracy and I let them go, accepting the senseless rituals of working life. I let go of my yearning for adventure and instead accumulated promotions and rooms full of useless stuff. I banished Andre from my thoughts and my heart and laughed at how silly and immature I'd been.

But a small part of me missed the youthful passion. I knew that I had become like everyone else, sleepwalking through meaninglessness. In the process, something important, vital – in every sense of the word – became deadened. Deadened and yet still there, dormant, deep inside me. Not totally banished, so that I could just sense it. I wished it were gone completely rather than being just out of reach. It would have been easier. As it was, I felt like I'd sold my soul.

Thinking about all of that again, I felt a mixture of sadness, shame and anger; anger especially towards myself for deep down being such a conformist.

Instantly that thought was swamped by a tsunami of guilt, as though I was wishing a different life for myself, a life without Sam and Mathew; Mathew, who I loved with all my heart. Mathew, who had held me as my whole world fell apart and stopped me doing the same. Mathew, who fed me and bathed me when I was unable to do those things for myself. Mathew, who held the empty shell that I was and slowly, patiently, tenderly led me back to life. Mathew who, when the time was right, gently nudged Sam towards me again, knowing instinctively that it was only for Sam that I would ever find the will to live again. Mathew to whom I owed my life.

Mathew – kind, sweet, loving Mathew – who deserved so much more than a wife who secretly pined after a lost love. A destructive, violent love at that. What was I thinking?

Chapter 3

"I still can't believe that this is happening, that I have to make this decision! I'm just so angry with him for putting me in this position!"

Robyn was in full flow midway through our second session. Having told me the shameful truth in the first session, it seemed much easier to talk now and we had already got in touch with her anger. The intensity with which she felt it was now rushing her words and the more she talked, the more enraged she became.

"I don't think he really knows what he's done! What was he thinking? I want to scream at him for ruining it. Actually, I just want to scream! I really don't think he knows what an impossible position he's put me in. I'm actually more angry about being in this position, about having to make this choice, than I am about being hit! It's so unfair." She came to a sudden halt as she tried to make sense of the words that had just tumbled out of her mouth. "I mean... I know I'm in this position because he hit me, but... it's being in this position that makes me furious. That sounds all mixed up I know... I can't explain it…"

"I think I understand." Boy, did I understand. "If he'd hit you but there was no choice to be made, say if he'd hit you and then he'd left you, then you'd be angry maybe, but not like this."

"Yes exactly! Then I'd be angry… and probably sad too, I'd miss him… but I'd also get a lot of sympathy wouldn't I? That sounds very attention-seeking when I say it out loud. I don't know if that's what I mean, but people would be different towards me."

"Different compared to if you choose to stay?"

"If I choose to stay, then they'll judge me."

"And will you judge yourself?"

"Probably. That's why it's such an awful choice. I have to choose between losing everything we had or keeping it all but feeling like a total loser! And it's not fair that it has to be me who decides to end it, that I would have to feel responsible for that, when it's him who's absolutely responsible!"

"And you don't want that responsibility. That makes you even more angry with him."

"Yes it does! It's not fair that I have to decide!"

"And if you decide to stay, you'll feel like a loser?"

An image of Sam rolling his eyes popped into my head. Adults using words like 'loser' sounded stupid apparently, and at the grand age of eight it was evidently very easy to be embarrassed by your parents. It did feel a bit wrong coming from me, like wearing someone else's clothes, but I was trying to make her reflect on the feelings she'd just expressed. Using her exact words seemed appropriate.

"Totally!"

She unexpectedly ran out of steam and didn't seem to want to go any further. We were on a roll one minute, and then suddenly she looked lost and sad and I was momentarily thrown. Instead of reflecting her apparent sadness back to her, or even just waiting, I changed tack slightly.

"And if you decide to leave?"

Robyn was obviously thrown by the question. She looked up from a brief reverie, as if waking up, and took a second to understand the question. I'd interrupted a busy silence, one where she was reflecting on something, the kind of silence a therapist should never interrupt. *Damn!*

"If I decide to leave..."

She fell back into reflecting and this time I left the silence. Her eyes became unfocussed as she turned her gaze inwards, looking for the answer. When she finally spoke, it was almost a whisper.

"If I decide to leave I might as well be dead."

My heart sped up fractionally and our already tenuous connection was lost as I panicked. Was she talking about suicide? Instead of simply being with her in the moment, checks and safeguard procedures flooded through my mind, unhelpfully leaving a total blank in their wake. The 'therapy police' were suddenly metaphorically in the room, watching me, making sure

I picked up on vital clues concerning her safety. I hated the therapy police! Just their invisible presence watching over my shoulder always broke the connection anyway.

"Might as well be dead?" I allowed my surprise to show in my tone but deliberately used her exact words. If in doubt, reflect back the client's words.

"He brings me to life. That's the bit that no one gets. I was literally only half living before I met him. Less than half living. If I decide to leave, I'm deciding to go back to a living death." She had been talking to herself again but now she looked at me directly, sighed and deflated. "I can't explain it."

Oh shit, this is way too close to home!

"Say a bit more Robyn, I think I'm getting it, but say more if you can."

"I don't know how to explain it. It's like I didn't know how to live before I met him. And not just live, I didn't know how to be me. I feel so totally accepted by him, I don't feel I have to try to be something I'm not. I've spent my whole life trying to be what I thought someone else wanted me to be… and most of the time it felt like I'd got that wrong anyway and what I thought they wanted wasn't actually what they wanted, so I was still wrong."

"Like you spent all that time pleasing other people, not yourself, and yet still being wrong?"

"Yes, but I didn't know what I wanted for myself either. Eventually it felt like I just went through the motions, doing what I was expected to do whilst yearning for something else, but not knowing what that was. Just knowing I wanted more... and then along came Andy and he felt the same way but he was way ahead of me. He could articulate it, and could explain why everyday stuff all felt so meaningless. We spent hours just talking about it and he knew about loads of philosophers who'd said the same thing and, I guess, just knowing that all these great thinkers had thought this way too, and so did Andy, made me feel OK about the way I felt. For the first time ever, I felt OK about being me; that it was OK to want to really live rather than to simply exist. That I wasn't mad because I didn't just accept it all like everyone else seems to. And for the first time I do feel like I am actually living! I feel alive."

OK to want to really live rather than to simply exist... be careful Maggie!

"And if I leave Andy... if I leave him, I go back to being an alien again, different to everyone else, going through the motions again, yearning for more."

"It sounds like Andy brought something out of you that was already there. He didn't create that it in you, he liberated it." I wasn't sure if I was talking about me or her now but I wanted her to own some of this stuff and not give Andy all the credit. "That part of you will still exist whether you stay or leave, won't it?"

"Absolutely! He did liberate me! But I will go back to being trapped again if I leave him."

"You sound very sure."

"I couldn't be me and really *live* before Andy. I won't be able to after Andy. And part of me thinks why should I have to anyway?"

"OK." It was more of a 'tell me more' comment.

"I mean, everyone will assume that hitting me is who he is. But everyone makes mistakes. This really isn't who he is, I know it isn't… or… I think I know it isn't. Part of me is so sure… I know him better than anyone and he isn't like this. I don't know what happened but it's not him. I get angry at the thought of everyone judging him, and then judging me for not having leaving him. He's a good guy, he really is… I sound deluded don't I?"

"Tell me more about Andy the good guy." *Careful, Maggie, don't lead her. Andre is too present as well right now. Hmm Andre… Andy… curious…*

"He's kind, he is really kind. He goes out of the way for people, all sorts of people, strangers as well as friends. They don't have to ask him, he's just incredibly good at noticing when someone needs something and then just doing it. He's attentive to everyone. He listens like you're the most important person in the room – in the world – and like what you have to say is the most interesting thing ever. He doesn't put it on, he really is interested in people and what makes them tick… and toward me he's… I've never felt more understood in my life. Actually, I've never felt understood before full stop, but somehow with Andy I don't even have to say anything and he just gets me. We catch each other's eye sometimes when something happens, or someone says something and we just know what the other's thinking because we're both thinking the same thing. I feel like I'm basking in a kind of glow just being near him. He makes the world feel like such a good place to be. Sometimes, when I don't know he's there or I hear his voice, my stomach literally flips. Just his voice does that to me. It's crazy!"

She hesitated, as if she almost couldn't bring herself to say the next sentence out loud.

"He tells me that I'm beautiful." She blushed and continued in a whisper. "No one has ever called me beautiful… I know I'm not really but…"

"You don't think you are?" I interrupt.

"I know I'm not. But I believe that Andy genuinely thinks I am."

I made a mental note to explore her own view, not just physical but in general, of herself. Robyn stopped and gazed at a spot on the floor. She was lost in her own thoughts and this time I was aware enough to leave the silence and not interrupt her.

"He makes me feel really special… just because I know that I'm special to him, to someone so amazing." She slowed down again, spacing out the words and sentences, remembering, reflecting as she spoke, and gazed at the same spot on the floor. "Up until this, I would have done anything for him… I literally would have died for him… without him I couldn't live anyway so I really would actually die for him. I still would." She met my eye again, hers glinting with suddenly threatening tears. "I still would, I know I would. How mad is that when I came to get help to leave him?"

"Is that what you came for?"

The mood shifted, like she had just shaken herself out of a train of thought.

"Oh I don't know. Maybe I didn't. I can't think about it anymore to be honest with you, it makes my head spin." Robyn looked at me and smiled a polite, incongruent smile. She'd had enough. It was only the second session and she'd been unusually open. It wasn't surprising that she would need to pull back. Or maybe it was just that she'd got too close to tears and that's why she suddenly felt uncomfortable.

We needed to change direction and it looked like she was giving me the responsibility for where we went next. A process observation would have been good at this point but I was too involved in what she had just been describing, too moved and a little too awed by the intensity of her feelings to be that clever.

"Tell me what you mean by really living versus meaninglessness." This was undeniably a question from my agenda not hers. I was curious to hear whether this meant what I thought it meant, whether it echoed the thoughts that had plagued me for years too.

"It just seems to me that most people don't really *live* their lives. They get up, go through some tasks that fill the time but that ultimately don't really matter, like cleaning the fridge, or adding up some figures and reporting the answer to someone. And then they go to sleep. And repeat that daily until they die. None of it matters. It's all futile."

She was describing my life and Mathew's perfectly and I caught a sliver of shame quickly followed by defensiveness. My thirty-seven-year-old self instantly wanted to explain that cleaning the fridge did matter, that it was a question of germs and looking after your family. How much I'd changed.

"All of it?" I asked.

"Yes, all of it. If you zoom out from our planet, we're all like ants, scurrying around for no real reason. Even stuff that looks meaningful like, I don't know, medicine or something. It keeps people alive but to what end? Why does keeping people alive even matter from a zoomed-out perspective? I can't explain it very well. Does any of that make sense?"

"Absolutely! And many famous philosophers would agree with you and struggled with the same questions."

"That's what Andy says."

For some reason I really didn't like Andy.

"And really living?"

"That's much harder. I've known the meaningless for much longer than I've known really living. I just know I don't want to get up, go to work, go to sleep. I want to do the things Andy and I do now for the rest of my life. I want to carry on sitting up all night talking about important stuff. I want to make love under the stars. I want to travel. I want to drive through the night to see a sunrise on a beach and say to hell with being on time for work the next day! I want to seize every opportunity!"

"*Carpe diem*," I mused without thinking.

Robyn looked confused.

"It means seize the day."

"Exactly! Seize the day. *Carpe diem*? I like that. Before Andy, the futility of it all felt depressing, pointless. Now it feels liberating. If nothing really matters then I'm free to do the things I love, to experience everything. I don't mean it as irresponsibly as it sounds... or maybe I do. It's this misguided sense of responsibility that gets in the way, this idea that we all have to get a house and a mortgage and lots of stuff, but stuff doesn't make people happy, does it? Not really."

I glanced at the clock. *Damn! Five minutes over!* I didn't want to stop there. I was simultaneously intrigued and impressed by her. She reminded me of values and ideals I'd buried a long time ago and I felt ashamed and saddened to think that I'd lost them.

"No, often it doesn't. But we're running over Robyn. We need to stop there even though we're obviously in the middle of something really important."

"Part of me wishes I didn't think like this and then I could just get on with it and you know, be normal. And another part hates the idea of being normal. Normal is dead!" Robyn was obviously not quite ready to finish so suddenly and I didn't blame her. I didn't want to stop there either.

"Normal is dead?" I echoed. "Well that's quite a thought to end on until next time. Are you OK to stop there for now?" It was a rhetorical question!

*

I sat in my chair ruminating on that one sentence for a long time after Robyn left: *normal is dead*. It could mean a myriad of things. It could mean there is no 'normal' anymore, that 'normal' is finished and, the world is crazy. But I was just playing with the words. I knew what she meant.

For a moment, I was transported back to a dark play I'd seen years earlier. *Equus* was about a boy in hospital being treated by a child psychiatrist. The psychiatrist is struggling with what his profession means. He is starting to believe that by curing the children he treats, by reshaping them to fit in with society's norms and rules, he is also killing them, robbing them of their passion and everything that makes them vital and alive, sacrificing them to what he calls the God Normal.

I had always identified strongly with the psychiatrist's struggle and now Robyn brought it all back to me. I had chosen a counselling model which emphasised that people *always* make the best decisions for themselves with the experience and knowledge they have. Even decisions that appear self-destructive make perfect sense when you truly understand that person's experience and knowledge (which is not the same as saying that they're objectively 'good' decisions). There is no universal 'normal'. Every person's unique reactions can be seen as 'normal' given the unique life experiences that led to that reaction.

How could anyone listen to what Robyn had said and not understand why she would struggle to leave Andy? It might look self-destructive if someone were to only consider the fact that he hit her. But to her it also felt self-destructive to leave him. 'If I leave, I might as well be dead' she'd said. It was so understandable when viewed from her perspective. Did that mean she was right though?

Suddenly, the faceless others were crowded into the room judging me, telling me I should steer this child away from such a monster. And she was a child. I knew from the form she'd filled in the week before that she was only twenty, almost still a teenager. The faceless others reminded me that at twenty she was naïve, that she knew nothing of life, and that I had a duty to enlighten her.

"You know what it feels like at that age, everything is so intense," the faceless others tutted, as though the intensity was wrong and the muted, realistic, grown-up version of love was right. But what if reckless abandon was actually the right way to love? And who am I anyway to kill that passion, to sacrifice Robyn to the God Normal? Quite honestly, I didn't have the heart for it and, with Robyn, I knew I probably couldn't even if I tried.

I was captivated by her youth and was very aware that I envied it. I loved being around teenagers. I loved the energy of their youth, the way they lived life to the full, the way they said yes to everything and worried about the consequences later. I know that some would call that irresponsibility, and point out that they lack certain neural pathways that connect risk to reason. I called it living.

Not for the first time I wondered if that was why I was a therapist. Did my clients' stories and emotional rollercoasters give me a sense of really living without me having to leave my cocoon of safety?

I didn't want all of that vitality of youth to end for Robyn, and I didn't want to be part of killing it. I knew that she had probably lost a huge part of it when Andy hit her, but I wanted to wrap what was left in tissue paper and keep it safe. I wanted to protect Robyn's passion, her yearning for more, and her ability to love with abandon.

And I knew that this was more about me than her. It was about my grief for something lost.

Normal is dead! I knew exactly what Robyn meant. 'Normal is the good smile in a child's eyes' says the psychiatrist in *Equus*. 'It's also the dead stare in a million adults'.

That's what she meant.

Chapter 4

John's three-storey terraced house was halfway up a steep hill in the middle of a small hamlet overlooking Stroud. To get to the room where he saw clients and supervisees, you had to go up two flights of stairs to a study-like space in the eaves. As I traipsed up behind him, I always hoped that I would be able to peer into some of the other rooms we passed and glean something of his life. It never happened. The doors to the rest of the house – and to his personal life – were always scrupulously shut. I knew that was entirely appropriate, but I still felt shut out. It was strange to have been in someone's home once a fortnight for over two years and yet to know so little about them.

What I did glean was that John, despite his eminence in the field, didn't seem to be a particularly rich man. It made me glad for Mathew's ample salary and the fact that I didn't need to worry about money in the same way most counsellors did. Although I didn't really want or need some of the material stuff he provided, I did really appreciate the absence of worry. No one makes a lot of money from counselling except for the few at the very top, who maybe make money from spin offs, books and workshops, that kind of thing, but not from just counselling. Even John, with all his books, didn't seem very wealthy. Without Mathew, I wouldn't have been able to do what I did. I couldn't have even paid for my training.

The house was nice enough, fashioned in a hippy style (at least in the corridors that I was allowed to see), but it felt small and dark to me. The counselling room had a sloping ceiling with a roof light allowing plenty of light in, but the space was pokey and you had to duck your head to get to the seats. I couldn't imagine how his taller clients managed.

I was trying to explain to John how I felt about the work with Robyn. "I'm getting in my own way, I know that." I was cradling the glass of water he had poured for me earlier.

"How so?" John responded in his soft American accent. I suspected he knew but was trying to get me to explore it and articulate it. John knew enough of my past to make the links with what I had now told him about Robyn.

"She reminds me so much of me. I don't want her to make the same mistakes. I have an agenda for her rather than being neutral."

"Is that true?"

The question surprised me. Yes of course it was true. Wasn't it? I considered it for a long time before answering. I didn't want Robyn to give up on Andy, or the part of her that he had set free, but another part of me feared her staying in case this was the beginning of a pattern of domestic violence.

"No, I guess it's not," I finally said. "I'm actually as stuck as she is. That feels worse than having an agenda."

"Why worse?"

John was a man of few words. I often thought he was a caricature of a successful businessman rather than a psychotherapist. Or maybe an actor. He was still very good-looking, in that very distinguished silver-fox way that some aging actors are. Clean-shaven and very tall with incredible white hair that was still thick and shiny, I could easily imagine him as 007 in a tuxedo and bow tie. Maybe his looks and charisma were why I seemed to lose several brain cells when I was around him. My mind often went blank and I felt de-skilled and totally incompetent. He insisted on asking probing questions and trying to make me think, but sometimes I wished he'd just tell me what to do rather than making me do all the work! Obviously I knew that me doing the work was the whole point and that clients often feel just as frustrated with the same process. Knowing that didn't make me like it any better though.

"I hate feeling stuck! I think that I should at least have an opinion and the courage of my convictions! I can always see both sides. That's the problem. I suppose it's less of a problem professionally in reality.

At least I can empathise with clients whichever way they go. But in the rest of my life it's a real problem. I'm always on the fence. It feels like I can't be strong on any issue."

I was thinking of a discussion Mathew and I had had the previous evening about Sam getting into trouble at school. Sam believed the teacher hated him because he had been singled out when others had also been misbehaving. It was that hurt that caused him to behave even more badly, and empathising with that hurt made it impossible for me to discipline him for the worse behaviour that followed. Mathew thought he should be punished while I thought we simply needed to talk with Sam about it. I felt weak and ineffectual as a parent compared to Mathew, yet somehow right at the same time.

"And professionally? How does *stuckness* feel professionally?"

John gently brought me back to what we were supposed to be talking about and avoided the potential tangent. Gentle or not, I bristled slightly at the implied rebuke.

"Frustrating! Like there should be an answer that we can both find. Also, when I've worked with clients who have been stuck with a stay-or-leave decision before, it's gone on for ages, and so I suppose I'm concerned that this will too. Then it's felt like the counselling isn't achieving anything at all and I feel de-skilled and like I've failed."

I suddenly remembered the client who had stormed out two weeks earlier, the anger she'd expressed and my doubt that we were accomplishing anything.

"In fact, I sometimes wonder if I'm just chatting rather than counselling and I think about what other counsellors would think if they could watch me working. I don't think it would be very positive and—"

"Maggie, Maggie, Maggie! You really should be past all this self-doubt by now! 'Not accomplishing anything'? 'Failure'? You really do get in your own way! How can you possibly connect with clients when you're so self-conscious?"

I felt the tell-tale flush of heat rush up from my collarbone and over my face. Recognising that I was blushing instantly made it worse and even the tops of my ears were suddenly burning. John's frustrated tone catapulted me back decades to my father's perpetual annoyance with me. I felt small and wrong and stupid, and in the process completely missed his meaning.

"I know I'm getting in my own way. I identify too strongly with Robyn. That's what I said," I mumbled resentfully.

"It's this crippling self-doubt that gets in the way Maggie," he corrected me firmly. "I so wish you could let it go! You're thinking too much about all the different ways you could go wrong, all your imagined failures in the past. Why don't you try *using* your experience in relation to Robyn instead of criticising and discounting it?"

He was exasperated with me and I felt again the burning shame that was an echo of repeated childhood incidents of paternal disappointment.

"Let's turn this on its head for a minute," he said more gently. "You said that your identification with Robyn was getting in the way. You thought you had a strong agenda and then realised you didn't, that you were stuck. Let's see if we can use your reaction rather than trying to get over it or push it away. Let's look at why you're stuck and see if it helps us with Robyn's *stuckness* in some way."

"OK." I tried to push the petulant, chastened child and the shame and embarrassment away, but I was flustered and found it difficult to think straight. My vision blurred as I hurriedly blinked away the tears that would only add to my humiliation. I knew that John believed in me and that his irritation came from me not believing in myself, but his frustrated tone was wholly counterproductive. I was back in the midst of some unhelpful childhood feelings and struggling to find a way back to adulthood.

"Tell me everything you know about your own *stuckness* and let's go from there," John said, trying to help.

"I envy her I guess. That's one side of it. I envy her vitality and passion and... *life force*. I don't want her to throw that away, I want her to hold onto that forever. And Andy seems crucial to her holding onto that... and her love for Andy is on that side of the equation in another way too. There's beauty and purity in a love like that – it's elemental, all encompassing, and soul-to-soul. I'm scared she'll leave him and become a hollowed-out version of herself."

Now the defensive wall had been breached, all sorts of feelings were threatening to run amok. A lump instantly formed in my throat and my voice cracked as I realised I was talking as much about me as about Robyn. I quickly changed tack to talk about the other side of my *stuckness*.

"On the other side, I'm scared that if I encourage her to stay and he does turn out to be a violent monster, then I will be responsible for that." I hesitated, aware that I was on dangerous ground again, my own lack of confidence coming to the fore.

"It's OK, just say whatever comes into your head for now." John seemed to be backtracking and I wasn't sure what was the right or wrong thing to say anymore. A moment from the session with Robyn jumped into my head where we talked about exactly this: this sense of trying to please someone but still being wrong.

"I picture her parents asking what on earth her therapist was playing at." I plunged in, still incapable of thinking clearly enough to do anything else. "They'll think me irresponsible and unprofessional and feel very let down… I even imagine them putting a complaint in and me being one of those disciplinary sanctions they report on in the back of the professional magazines, my incompetence there for everyone to see." I held my breath. Would he dive in with another attack on my overzealous inner critic, my catastrophising?

"So, on the one hand, you want Robyn to hold on to something that feels very important to you and her, something that you lost. And on the other hand – well, the other hand doesn't seem to be about you or Robyn very much, it seems to be about what other people might think."

"Yes, I suppose so. The therapy police again." I smiled sheepishly at John in a feeble attempt to build a bridge between us. We'd talked before about my disproportionate fear of being in the professional sanctions section of the magazines. It was John who'd coined the term 'therapy police' and we'd discussed how they get in the way of the courageous work necessary in the business of counselling relationships.

"So, go back to Robyn's *stuckness* now."

"Thinking about it, it's the same as mine: what she wants to do versus what other people will think."

"A parallel process then. And if *you* weren't worried about what people would think of you as a therapist, if there were no consequences for you whatsoever, what would you do?"

"I would encourage her to trust herself, to believe in her own instincts about this."

"The way you do with most of your other clients actually. So, what is different with Robyn do you think?"

"Her age I think." The adult was back in control and

John's questions were helping me to reflect. "She's on that cusp between childhood and adulthood and so I feel a responsibility to other people, such as her parents, as well as to her… and her instincts aren't based on much experience so they could be wrong. This love could be that heady, infatuated, blind version. The 'love as psychosis' version."

"And if that's true and he does then turn out to be a violent monster, how do you imagine Robyn then?"

I pondered that for a few moments. "Actually, I imagine her being OK. She has a strength about her. I don't see her being stuck long-term in a domestic violence situation."

"OK, so you encourage her to trust her own inner-knowing, and then what else do you notice if you imagine yourself doing that?"

Another pause. "Actually, I worry about something else: I worry that she has Andy on such a pedestal that she doesn't see herself… I believe that she can hold onto that vitality and life force with or without him. She sees him as amazing but doesn't see that she is too."

"So how would you deal with that?"

"I'd work on her relationship with herself. I'd explore why she says she can't be herself without Andy, and I'd do that without any agenda one way or the other about whether she should stay or go. Actually, that whole decision seems like a side issue now. This isn't about me killing Robyn's love for Andy, or about Andy at all. It feels much more about Robyn being OK with expressing who she is and making decisions based on what *she* thinks, not other people. That includes Andy but I guess that will be important in all her relationships, won't it? With Andy, with her parents, people in her future."

John nodded subtly, encouraging me to continue.

"It's about her being able to be different and yet still *fully* present in her relationships, about knowing that difference doesn't sound a death knell in a relationship... maybe, thinking about it, there's something in the conforming part of herself that she needs to value too... yes, I think that's it. My goal for Robyn would be for her to own the free spirit part of herself rather than attributing that to Andy, and to accept the parts of her that need safety and belonging too rather than judging those parts of herself."

I sat back, pleased with myself. John smiled too and I got the impression he'd known right at the start where we needed to get to, though of course would never tell me directly. Would I ever be able to see things for myself as clearly as I did after a session with John? Would I ever be so wise?

I didn't notice any of the journey home as I reflected on the supervision. It seemed so clear now that this was more about Robyn's relationship with herself than her relationship with Andy. I remembered other details from Robyn's first session that were suddenly obviously relevant: the way she soothed Andy's temper and apologised even when it wasn't her fault because she couldn't stand the tension and conflict; the way she had always been a people-pleaser, desperately trying to find the right way to be and yet feeling wrong anyway.

My mind flitted to that same sense of not knowing what was right or wrong in the session with John. I'd felt very young in that moment and it had been impossible to be rational or objective in any way. It was so agonisingly familiar. I had felt like that constantly before I met Andre, always wrong, always a disappointment. When others were around, the wrongness was often accompanied by the same blind panic I'd had just now in the session, like I had to find the right answer, but didn't have any idea what it was. With others around I was acutely aware that I wasn't sure how to be. When I was alone, I'd soothed myself by deciding that other people simply couldn't see reality as clearly as I could, that they weren't as wise as me. I felt judged by them, but I judged them just as much. I felt superior and yet inferior at the same time, longing to fit in and yet clinging on to my difference.

Did Robyn feel like that? Was it as painful for her? 'Part of me wishes I didn't think like this' Robyn had said. 'Part of me wishes I could be normal'. Underneath the ache of her love for Andy and the unbearable decision she was facing, was Robyn as conflicted between who she was and who she felt she needed to be? 'I didn't know how to be me' she'd said. I'd forgotten the agony of that feeling, its crushing hopelessness. Underneath Robyn's story of conflicted love, maybe this was actually about two opposing primal needs: the need to fit in and the need to stand out.

I realised that I hadn't felt that torture of wrongness for a very long time. If I envied Robyn's youthful passion and zest for life, I didn't envy her that feeling! Not one bit! It occurred to me that, although Robyn reminded me of an aliveness I felt I'd sold out on, I hadn't lost it totally. It was still there, protected and safe, in some secret place deep inside me. What I had lost was the overwhelming torment of feeling wrong. That had morphed into relatively inconsequential self-doubt. It wasn't a 'crippling' self-doubt, despite John's assertion. At least, I didn't think it was. I still felt different to many people but I had also discovered that a lot of people think as I do. These days I still felt different but fundamentally OK (*apart from the one obvious exception, but that was nothing to do with this, don't go there*). What if I could help Robyn to feel fundamentally OK at her tender age? What if I had been able to shake off that sense of wrongness at her age? What would my life be like now?

And the bit of me that wasn't lost but was hidden, deep inside somewhere? I realised I could suddenly touch it again. It felt familiar and welcome, like coming home. Robyn had reminded me of something vital and alive, as though just spending time with her had already started to unlock the box where I had concealed a part of myself. I had no idea what it meant, only that I felt lighter.

Chapter 5

February slipped into March. The red rug and cushions in the counselling room were swapped for versions that were a jumble of spring colours: various shades of green, teamed with daffodils plucked from the garden to transform the room. Marking the season's transitions by changing the colours never failed to at least marginally boost my permanently sagging energy levels. Despite my reluctance ever since *that* day to feel anything as inappropriate as optimism, the cusp of the new season always seemed brimming with prospects. Spring signalled renewal, sunshine, warmth and a return of colour. Summer was full of holidays and barbeques and evenings sitting outside drinking wine by a fire pit. Autumn brought amazing colours and crisp walks crunching through leaves, whilst winter heralded Christmas and cosy nights in, curled up by the fire.

I could still appreciate the miracle of all those things, despite the fact that wonder and gratitude would now always be stained with sadness and regret. It was as though I experienced anything positive from inside a glass jar, like I was permanently surrounded by a thin casing of melancholy.

Maybe it was just boredom. Maybe I spent so much time in here that I just needed a change. Whatever the reason, I always loved walking into the room after a recent colour change. Seeing bright, yellow daffodils on the coffee table was a favourite feature though; Not only did I love daffodils, it also seemed amusingly appropriate to have a flower from the narcissus family in the room where people often came because they needed to learn to love themselves.

With Robyn that was slow work so far. She had been coming weekly for four weeks and we had explored her relationships – both with Andy and with herself – from several angles. I had told her explicitly that my hope for her was that she learnt to value and appreciate all the aspects of herself. Transparency was always important and I didn't want to be covertly working on something other than what we had agreed. Trust and collaboration were essential.

Although she went along with it and it didn't alter the content of our sessions at all, I didn't get the impression that Robyn shared my view that her relationship with herself was key. I don't think she really understood it: the concept of appreciating and valuing herself and trusting her own wisdom was so alien. So, we had settled into a strange but not unusual partnership, whereby she was interested primarily in deciding whether she could trust Andy, whilst I was interested primarily in her learning to trust herself. I often reflected on the irony that if she were ever to disagree strongly with me about something, then I would have achieved my aim: when she could trust her own opinion and wisdom over mine and argue with me, I would have been successful.

I didn't know much about her childhood as there was usually too much happening in the present to reflect on the influences from her past. I was aware that this was a gap, but it never seemed to be the right moment to steer her round to talking about it. Mostly when we talked about her parents, it was about their reaction to her current situation and their opinions about Andy. She worried particularly about her dad thinking she was stupid or weak, so she kept the complexity of her true feelings hidden, only giving him the headline that she still loved Andy. He had reacted so aggressively to this that she instantly clammed up and retreated in shame. Her parents had no idea of the joy and vitality she had felt with Andy, and still yearned for.

It was tricky work. I wasn't trying to push her into telling her parents about how Andy made her feel. In fact, I didn't want to push her into anything at all. I wanted her to experiment with expressing herself, but even that had to come from her. If she was to learn to trust her own decisions, giving advice wasn't going to help. I also had to be mindful of the possibility that, just as she feared, they would indeed reject the parts of her that she had so far kept hidden. And I knew that there was a very real chance that they would. After all, Robyn's instincts had suggested as much, and we were working on the assumption that her instincts were accurate. Being true to yourself doesn't automatically mean universal acceptance, and acceptance by others is never the aim anyway. Accepting yourself is the aim. Learning to self-soothe, if and when that rejection and judgment happened for Robyn, would also be important.

Early on, apparently desperate to stop Robyn making a kneejerk decision to leave him, Andy had suggested they put the relationship on hold temporarily whilst she worked out what she felt. They still talked and met for coffee regularly but there was no physical contact at all. I didn't know whether this meant Andy was sensitive and caring or deliberately manipulative. Robyn was firmly in the first camp and in the spirit of what I was trying to achieve, I encouraged her to trust that instinct too.

I had also learnt though, through experience with other clients, that there are often other instincts – quieter, darker, scarier instincts that people push away. People admit to me long after the event that deep down they knew something else, something not right, that there were niggles in the background that they chose to ignore. I was watching closely for any hint of those intuitive doubts with Robyn. So far, her expressed sense of Andy was that he was wholly good and her doubts were intellectual rather than something she felt. They were based on caricatures of men who hit women rather than based on Andy. I wondered if there was something else, something about Andy that she wasn't yet admitting to herself. I wondered if her yearning for life and passion required her to block out certain instincts. True wisdom only comes when we listen to all our intuitive knowing, including the bits we don't want to hear.

Andy had so far seemed remarkably patient and hadn't pushed Robyn for a decision or for a return to a physical relationship. He was keen to see her as often as she was willing and repeatedly expressed huge remorse. He provided no reason for me to doubt Robyn's instincts about him. Neither of us knew how long she could reasonably vacillate for though; the current arrangement wasn't going to be tenable for long.

On the day of our fifth session, Robyn arrived looking different. Although there had been emotional times in several of our sessions, after that first session she generally arrived looking relaxed and comfortable in anticipation of our conversations. Today, however, she looked decidedly tense.

I poured her a glass of water and adjusted my own demeanour to be more in keeping with hers. Once Robyn had removed her coat and we were both seated, I waited. She wasn't looking at me but instead examined her hands that were fiddling with a button on the coat she'd strewn over the armrest of her chair. My mind raced with speculations but it was pointless to guess; it could be anything.

"He got angry again," she eventually volunteered.

"Oh." My tone implied *'oh no'* and she quickly realised what I might be assuming and rushed to correct me.

"No, no, he didn't hit me."

"But he got angry?"

She made a disgusted face. "Yes, he got angry. And I made it all OK again, as usual… and I'm furious with myself!"

Whoa, this is different!

"With yourself?"

"Oh, with him too, don't get me wrong, but I'm furious with myself because I didn't do anything wrong yet I was the one who soothed him and grovelled when actually he should have been grovelling to me!"

She'd been speaking with a real strength and energy, looking me in the eye, but suddenly she sagged and played with the button again.

"I feel pathetic!"

"Why don't you start by telling me what happened?"

Robyn explained that she and Andy had planned to meet for coffee but she'd been held up in traffic caused by a bad accident on the main route into town.

"I knew he'd be waiting and wondering what had happened. I ran all the way from the bus stop to the café and rushed to apologise. He was stony; a look that I know so well and find literally unbearable! The thing that really gets to me now is that he didn't even want to know why I was late at all! It was like he *wanted* to be affronted. He must have been able to see how hard I'd tried to get there as quickly as possible – I was sweating and panting like a dog! Any normal person would have been relieved nothing had happened to me and wanted to know about what had kept me. Not Andy! He sulked. When I tried to explain, he said it didn't matter but made it very clear that it really did matter! He wouldn't look at me. He wouldn't listen to me. I went to get us both a drink hoping he would calm down a bit but he was just as stony when I got back."

She paused, took a deep breath, then noisily blew it out in a frustrated sigh.

"Eventually I just said, 'Look, it really wasn't my fault you know, I couldn't do anything about the traffic.' And that was it! He said it summed up how I felt about him, that he wasn't worth the effort. All this 'needing time' – he made air quotes with his fingers – all this 'needing time' was just my way of stringing him along, punishing him and getting my own back. There was no chance of me going back to him so I might as well admit it!"

Andy no longer sounded like the patient, remorseful man she had described over the last few weeks. I noted my own anger towards his unreasonable reaction and my fear for Robyn.

"I was stunned! Stunned and scared. I thought he was making the decision for me and I guess I reacted from that fear. I was stroking his arm like I used to, telling him that wasn't true, that I couldn't imagine life without him. I more or less promised him that I would be going back, that I just needed a little bit more time. I said that I loved him, that he was the best thing that ever happened to me. And for a very big part of me that was true. But there was also a small whisper inside me that was still frustrated with him, that thought he was being ridiculous! I got stuck in traffic for God's sake! Once!"

"But you ignored the whisper and listened to the other bit?"

"As always."

"The whisper has been there before?"

"The whisper is always there but the fear is always a lot louder! I can usually see that Andy is in the wrong. Well, not completely in the wrong, but there's always another way of looking at it. The problem is I can see his perspective so clearly too and I never stick by my own opinion. It's like in this case, I can really see how Andy must've been feeling. He's been very patient and understanding about me working through this – and yes, I know that's the least he can do – but if he really does love me as he says he does, he must also be very scared and insecure too. He'll be looking for evidence of what I'm feeling all the time, trying to second guess what I'm going to do. And if he is as ashamed as he says he is, it's likely he'll be expecting rejection because he probably rejects himself."

I was struck by what great insight she had and by just how similarly I would have reacted in those circumstances: stuck on the fence or privileging the other person's position. That wasn't hypothetical either, it wasn't just how I imagined I would be in her shoes. It was familiar. That's exactly how I had been with Andre, too busy empathising to hold onto my own opinion! I'd forgotten that side of it. My empathy for him meant that I'd always soothed Andre's moods away too, whether I'd caused them or not. I'd learnt some stuff since then though.

"So, you see him very clearly, his motivations, his insecurities. You know all the different sides of Andy."

"Yes, I..."

"But you don't give him the chance to see you in the same way?" I deliberately interrupted her.

She looked a bit shocked, but I hadn't finished.

"You only allow Andy to see part of you, the part that loves him and is completely empathic and forgiving. But there's another part isn't there? A part that gets frustrated, that is strong in its own right, that has opinions that are different to his. A side of you that sometimes sees a different perspective. You don't allow Andy to see that side."

"I'm scared he won't like that side, that he'll leave."

"I can see that. But can you see that by holding back the bits you're scared he'll reject, you're not fully in this relationship with him anyway? Only a part of you is actually in the relationship. He doesn't really know you, not all of you anyway, so how can he really love you?"

I was aware I was taking a huge risk and that it was a very challenging thing to say. But I also believed in the paradox that couples first need to be separate individuals in order to be truly close. I was irritated that music and films often perpetuated the fusion myth of 'true love': the idea that couples should think and feel like they are two halves of one body. She was only showing Andy the aspects of herself that he would approve of and my earlier fear for her now morphed into frustration.

As I continued to lecture, my frustration leaked via my tone.

"We all have things we don't like about ourselves and it's understandable that we might want to hide those bits, or try to change them. But in this case, we're not talking about a part of you that you don't like. Or at least I don't think we are?"

"No, no. It's not a bit I don't like." Robyn looked a bit thrown by my sudden change in approach.

"So why hide it then?"

"I don't know, I..." She started to say something and then apparently changed her mind. She visibly sagged, like she'd given up. "I don't know," she said despondently.

So much for being client-led. So much for trusting her instincts. So much for not being directive or giving her advice. I had no business being frustrated with her, after all she had arrived frustrated enough with herself. *Damn, Maggie! You're just as bad as John.*

I frantically tried to think of a way to pull back from the potentially shaming avenue I had just started down.

"Do you want to try something a bit different?" I asked her, grinning in an attempt to change the atmosphere.

"Okkaayyy," she replied, exaggerating her wariness but catching my mood.

I pulled a jar containing buttons of various shapes and sizes towards me. It always sat on the coffee table but wasn't used as often as I would like.

"There is an exercise that can help us think about the different parts of ourselves and whether they are expressed or not. It goes like this..." I proceeded to explain to Robyn how she could select a button to represent each of the different parts of herself that she could identify. We would lay them out and think about what each part needed, whether it was hidden to others or not, and how she expressed that part to the outside world. Clients were invariably sceptical, it sounds such a bizarre thing to do, but most were willing to give it a go and, so far at least, it had invariably led to insight and learning.

As we started, Robyn was obviously still shaken. She was extremely compliant, trying to be a 'good' client, obedient rather than relaxed and authentic. *Shit, what made me slip into judgement and frustration? It was a stupid thing to have done!*

She started predictably with the parts of herself that we had already talked about: the free spirit and the people-pleaser as she referred to them. Her parents saw the people-pleaser and Andy the free spirit she said. I encouraged her to think about that some more, treading carefully now to avoid more implied criticism. Didn't Andy see a version of the people-pleaser too as she appeased and cajoled him? She still seemed slightly wary of me but gamely tried to engage in the exercise. Andy would see that as care and empathy she thought. He often commented on how caring and kind she was. Was there a part of her that was indeed caring and empathic? Yes, of course, she agreed, and duly selected a button.

I explored how she felt about that part of her: did she like that part? How, if at all, was it related to the people-pleaser? Robyn was beginning to appreciate the complexity of this now. As the exercise progressed, we gradually recovered some equilibrium after my outburst and she now appeared genuinely interested in the exploration.

"Yes, I do like the caring, empathic part, of course I do. I would hate to lose that bit of me."

"And yet when you described empathising with Andy's insecurity in the café the other day, you called yourself 'pathetic'."

"Yes, but… I guess the empathic side and the people-pleaser banded together and shut out something else… another important bit."

"How would you describe that bit?"

Robyn slowed right down, really reflecting on the question. "That bit is… *me*… deep inside. The me that I am underneath the fear… the me that is strong, intelligent, capable. The secret core me."

The atmosphere was suddenly charged. This was a pivotal moment and I was aware that I held my breath. Robyn was owning something important about herself, and not just in a theoretical way; she was really experiencing that part of herself in the moment.

"You look like you're really in touch with that part of yourself right now."

"I am." The mood shifted slightly and she looked at me with a nervous half-grin. "It doesn't happen often. Normally this part is a niggle in the background, overwhelmed by the others, too quiet to be noticed."

"What does this part need?" I deliberately didn't smile back; I was going to take this part of her seriously even if she wasn't ready to yet.

She caught my tone and joined in. "Respect. To be acknowledged. To be seen and respected instead of being dismissed by everyone."

I made a mental note to explore who exactly dismissed this part of her; the mythical 'everyone' who exist only in our heads. For now though, it was important that she cemented her own acknowledgement of this part.

"Which button represents this bit, and what shall we call it?"

Robyn selected a small pearl-like button to represent how precious, but also how currently small this bit of her was. She christened it 'the wise whisperer'. I beamed inwardly!

We now had four parts on the table: the people-pleaser, the empathic caring one, the free spirit and the wise whisperer.

I wasn't finished dissecting the people-pleaser. "I know it's your least favourite part," I teased, "but can we go back to the people-pleaser Robyn? Tell me more about how the people-pleaser appears around your parents. What would they see?"

"They would see a sensible, rule following, *nice* girl. Just like they want me to be."

"And that isn't you?"

"No... maybe. I don't know. I do like to follow *some* of the rules. I really don't like this part though."

"Which rules do you like following?"

"The social rules I guess, be nice to people, be kind, considerate, that kind of stuff."

"That sounds like the empathic, caring part of you."

"Yes, it's the bit that follows the 'be sensible' rules that I don't like. Rules like make sure you save for a rainy day, don't run or, God forbid, skip in public."

"So, the people-pleaser follows the 'be sensible' rules. What does that part of you *need*?"

She looked towards the window even though the drawn curtains blocked the view of the garden outside, and swallowed hard. "That part needs Dad to actually like me."

This was new. "You don't think he likes you?"

She'd talked about her dad wanting to protect her and him being furious with Andy, but never hinted at not feeling loved, or even liked by him.

"He's ex-army and is used to unquestioning obedience. I try, but let's just say he has high standards and I never quite seem to live up to them."

Ex-army? You too? I felt a jolt of resemblance and silently cursed that we wouldn't have time to explore her relationship with her father today. I kicked myself for not asking about her past earlier, it was clearly relevant.

"It sounds like your dad could be important for us to come back to Robyn. We're nearly out of time today, but it sounds like we're really talking about a need to not be rejected?"

"That people-pleaser part of me is terrified of rejection or abandonment! And it really gets in the way of the free spirit. It's like they're complete opposites. I wish I could get rid of the people-pleaser all together."

"And yet the need to be liked and the fear of rejection sound like reasonable needs and fears to me. Fairly primitive, biological fears actually."

Robyn cocked her head to one side, a non-verbal question mark.

"We're pack animals. We were designed to live in groups because in the past we were safer that way. We *all* fear rejection because at one time our very survival depended on not being rejected. It's a basic survival instinct."

"But not everyone is driven by it like me. I must fear rejection more than most people."

"I think that you *expect* it more than most people so it's always there for you, at the forefront."

"Why would I expect it more than most people?"

"Well, possibly it has something to do with your father, I don't know yet. But ultimately what it comes down to is that you expect it more than some people because deep down you reject yourself and so you anticipate that others will too."

Robyn's neck blotched, the rising emotion also making it to her eyes this time as they suddenly glistened. I guessed that she really recognised an important truth in the idea that she rejected herself. Maybe she had also finally understood why her relationship with herself mattered so much. Sometimes it was just a matter of finding the right words, words that meant something to the client.

We only had a couple of minutes left and whilst, ideally we would have stayed with what she was currently feeling a bit longer, I needed to wrap up and reinforce what she had learnt. I summarised the parts we had identified so far and then we both sat and contemplated the collection of buttons. I encouraged Robyn to continue to reflect on the idea of the different parts of herself and their individual needs outside of the session. I wanted her to see what other parts she could identify.

Robyn left and I made a cup of tea, feeling very smug. That had been a good session with lots of insights and experiential learning, once I'd got off my overly directive high-horse, that is. I looked forward to telling John about it. There would be no need to mention the bit where I lost my way for a while; I could just bask in his approval of our insightful exploration of the different parts of Robyn.

I took my tea back into the counselling room and sat for a while, cradling the mug and contemplating the collection of buttons Robyn had left on the table until my familiar self-doubt crept back in. Whose therapy was this actually? Apart from the coincidence of both having ex-army fathers with high standards, there were so many other things that felt weirdly like me, the parts we'd identified for one. I didn't think I'd steered her inappropriately during the exercise. I'd challenged her judgement of various parts and I'd tried to re-frame them as valid human needs for sure, but I hadn't come up with them, she had. And yet they perfectly described me too. I could relate to each of the parts she'd come up with and to the way they interacted with each other. My empathic side and people-pleaser also combine and overwhelm a core part of me, a wise, knowing part.

I thought back to the moment when she reminded me how I used to lose myself by empathising too strongly with Andre and privileging his feelings over my own. I felt a subtle shift, like something loosening, when I thought about our relationship ending.

What had happened to my free spirit? I could still feel it. The box that Robyn had opened was still there, just beneath the surface, a yearning for adventure and life and experience and passion, a desire to live a life full of meaning and connection. It was, in part, the reason why I became a counsellor. So why was there no discernible expression of that part in my life beyond counselling anymore? And what did that cost me?

Of course, at Robyn's age I did have another part that she hadn't identified in herself: my secret yearning for a child was so strong back then. I had kept it well hidden, embarrassed to be so broody when all my peers were focussed on fun, or saving the planet, or how to be the most successful person ever in their chosen field. My broodiness felt homely and boring in comparison, and that part was definitely in conflict with how I saw the free spirit being manifested. But the yearning was a very real part of me, a part that I was well acquainted with, that accompanied me on solitary walks and wrapped me up on lonely nights like a comforting dream.

Eventually I had shared the dream with Mathew and he had been surprised (I was playing the role of ambitious career woman at the time) but delighted. At Robyn's age however, I never told a soul. I smiled as I remembered my youthful naivety when wanting a child counted as a terrible, embarrassing secret.

As I tidied the buttons away, I absent-mindedly wondered which of those in the jar I would choose to represent my maternal side. A little yellow button in the shape of a teddy bear seemed to jump out at me and instantly I pictured the tiny knitted cardigan to which it once belonged. Disjointed memories flooded my mind: a squeal, sunlight on fine blond hair, a toothy grin, a tinkling giggle. My mind threatened to fast-forward a few years, and another darker memory suddenly hovered on the edge of my awareness. I felt the familiar cold shadow start to descend, the heavy ache creeping around my edges, threatening me with crushing pain; my devious mind yet again artfully skipping through memories, link by innocent link, nudging my conscious brain back to the exact time and place it had been trying to avoid.

However I was now highly skilled in distraction and avoidance. At first, I'd had to live with reality dawning anew every single morning, this exact knot of sinking sensations immediately preceding the excruciating agony of remembering all over again. For months, I had relived the horror day after day, as my disloyal brain flouted all attempts to cling on to the blissful oblivion of sleep. Every single morning it had treacherously regained consciousness and remembered. And so, I learnt. And I became an expert in avoidance.

Studiously ignoring the teddy bear button, I picked up the small pearl from Robyn's collection, turning it round in my fingers, examining it from all angles before depositing it back in the jar. What would my wise whisperer say about this session? It had been a good session; I knew it had.

Chapter 6

It was exactly two weeks later that I had my first session with Stephen and really learnt about the impact and complexity of human memory. Stephen was the most captivating, thought-provoking and emotionally challenging client I had met so far. If I could have been objective about him, I would have said he was a fascinating case. But I couldn't be objective about Stephen. Right from that first session, Stephen was one of those clients who tugged at my heart strings and took root in my being for much, much longer than the hour a week we actually spent together. He *was* a fascinating case but he was also a deeply traumatised human being. Some of his story could happen to anyone, could happen to me, could happen to Sam. Some of his story was so bizarre it was difficult to imagine it at all. And despite my deep empathy and connection to him, by the end of the first session, Stephen also terrified me!

He had no memory of anything at all prior to waking up in Fenwick Royal Infirmary three years earlier when he was told that he'd had an accident at work and that he'd been in a coma for three weeks. His family, who were all there when he woke fully for the first time, were complete strangers to him. He had a mother, a father, a brother and a girlfriend – none of whom he recognised at all. He described that time in the hospital with chilling clarity. The terror of not knowing who or where he was. Craving the security of a familiar face and then the dawning realisation that he couldn't bring to mind the image of a familiar face at all. There was no such thing as a familiar face for him. Or a familiar place. Or a familiar anything. He was completely and utterly alone; alone as if his entire family had died in that accident; alone as if he had been deposited in a foreign country where he knew absolutely no one.

In that first session Stephen described that time in the hospital chronologically, as though it were happening in real time. He described waking up, groggy, his head pounding and his mouth dry. He described a doctor calmly explaining where he was and what had happened. He gradually became aware of other people in the room and of the fact that they were crying, but they seemed both happy and sad at the same time. He described his confusion and then the doctor's questions: did he know what year it was, did he know his name, and then, finally, did he recognise these people. His dawning realisation that he should do was truly horrifying to imagine. Hearing the story in the same time order as it happened for him, I shared the experience of emerging understanding. He hadn't come into the counselling room that first time and said 'I have amnesia'. I gradually realised this just as he had done three years previously. It was as though I went through it myself.

In Stephen's case I also felt his family's grief. This used to happen a lot back then, especially when the mother in me somehow got evoked. I felt very maternal towards him and I felt deeply for his family. Three weeks earlier they had had a son, a brother, a boyfriend and now, although he hadn't died, he didn't know them. He didn't know himself. Who would he be now? In a way the person he had been before the accident had died. All five of them hoped beyond hope that his memory would return. It never did.

"So why now Stephen? What made you turn to counselling at this point?" I tentatively asked him. It was a question I often asked when clients came in with problems that started a while ago.

"I've got used to a lot of it," he began. "I have a patter I use to explain if I meet someone who I haven't seen since the accident, someone who obviously recognises me but I don't know them. I have a job now and I'm learning new skills – there's nothing wrong with my ability to form new memories luckily. I'm lucky I guess." He looked at his hands.

"You don't *look* like you feel lucky." And why should he? I wasn't suggesting he should feel lucky; I was inviting him to tell me the rest and stop putting on a positive front when that clearly wasn't how he was feeling.

"The hardest bit is not knowing who I am. I don't mean that I don't know my name or my family or what town I was born in, what school I went to and all that. I've got used to all that stuff. It's irritating, but that's all. I mean, I don't know what *kind* of person I am. At all. I don't have memories of being for example, kind or nasty. I don't have memories of being a bully or a victim, of being in the cool crowd or excluded, of being clever or stupid or being a geek or… how can I possibly know anything about who I actually am? I mean, who am I? Who the hell am I? Really? I could be anyone… or anything."

He seemed agitated and his voice raised gradually a few decibels as he spoke. The agitation seemed out of place three years on and I didn't quite understand it. I guessed there was something I didn't yet know. I noticed a small frisson of fear in me too, and was suddenly very aware of his physical presence – big, strong and young. He could've easily overpowered me. I didn't have time to analyse my reaction in the moment but made a mental note to do so later.

"Go on," I encouraged. It was a cop-out but I had no idea what else to say. I was flustered, and although I tried to imagine how he felt, it was impossible. It was such an alien concept to me.

"I rely on other people to tell me what I'm like and then I feel I have to be the person they describe, but it doesn't feel like me. I'm not saying they're lying, why would they? But maybe they don't know the whole me."

"I think I understand. There's a side we show parents and bosses, and another side friends and peers see, and neither is the whole you?"

"Sort of. And what if there's a bit that nobody sees? I don't know if there were things that no one knew about." He looked down. "I have no way of knowing what my own secrets were."

There it was again: that frisson of fear. This time I didn't know if I felt it first or picked up on something he was feeling. I also felt suddenly transparent, as if the dark secrets of my own past were instantly visible, not the content just the fact that they existed, the fact that I had secrets. Unexpectedly self-conscious, I briefly imagined what it would be like to forget. To forget, even for just a minute, would be indescribably wonderful: light, easy, normal. I would do anything to forget.

Of course, I said none of this to Stephen. His suffering was of a different order; I could barely begin to imagine how it would be to actually forget and then be haunted by the possibility that I had secrets I didn't know about.

On a whim, I decided to come clean. "Stephen, it's really difficult to imagine what this must be like for you. I've never even considered anything like this, let alone come across it before, but I really do want to understand. Can you try to explain it in a way that helps me get what this feels like?"

He stopped and stared at me searchingly, as if he were trying to see through my eyes, into my very being and thereby judge my intentions. I struggled to hold his eye but instinctively knew it was crucial to do so. For a moment it seemed my impulsive honesty had been a huge mistake and I cursed myself silently. People need to feel understood and accepted in therapy and I'd just told him that I didn't understand. *Shit! Think before you speak Maggie!*

"Thank you," he eventually said. "No one has ever admitted that before." He took a deep breath in and out, as though finally really deciding to do this counselling stuff.

"I really do want to understand…" I started to say, still anxious that I'd left him feeling isolated.

"It's OK, I know. But the thing is, most people just jolly me along… jolly themselves along really, pretending that this is OK, normal, when it's anything but. No one gets it. How can they? But no one admits that. They act like I'm a child who needs to be protected, humoured you know. No one ever asks what it's actually like… so… thank you." He smiled for the first time and held my eye with an intensity that surprised me. There was a quiet intelligence in his dark brown eyes that I hadn't noticed until now.

I smiled back and any residual fear and confusion I felt melted away. I hadn't left him isolated at all, just the opposite. He felt isolated by people not acknowledging the strangeness of this. Someone willing to be real and honest and grapple with that with him, someone who would just genuinely try to understand, was a step forward.

"I don't really know how to explain it to be honest with you," he started. "If you think about how you know who you are, what kind of person you are, it's like an accumulation of stories, anecdotes, stuff that has happened, stuff people say about you. It all adds together and there are themes, patterns, stuff that repeats, so you can say, 'trust me to blah, blah, blah' or 'I'm always clumsy… or… shy or… putting my foot in it' or whatever constitutes your patterns. And memories of experiences and whether you enjoyed them or not combine and you can say 'I don't like parties, I'm more of a loner' or 'I like hill-walking, I'm an outdoorsy type of guy'. If you have no memories, you can't say any of those things. You have no images or beliefs about yourself. There are stories others tell you but it's like they're talking about someone else; you can't relate to them. There are no stories you can tell yourself about your past. You don't know the typical things you do that make you who you are. You don't know what you like or don't like. I mean it's like, who are you without your stories? You have no identity. And if you have no identity, you don't know how to relate to people so you're separate… always separate… like you can't connect with anyone because you don't know who is doing the connecting. Does that make any sense at all?"

"Intellectually yes, it does, but I am struggling to imagine what it actually *feels* like to be honest. 'Who are you without your stories'? It's almost impossible to imagine what having no stories, no history, no identity as you say, is actually like. You said you felt separate?"

"Yes... it's like I'm an observer, just watching rather than participating... separate... like I can't join in because I don't know how to be. If I don't know who I am, I can't really relate to people as me, as myself. And sometimes people relate to me like I'm someone else, someone that doesn't feel like me at all. There's one group of people who I've kind of stopped seeing now, but seem to have been a big part of my life before the accident. They treated me like a real jack-the-lad character, and I don't recognise that in me at all. It doesn't fit me somehow. But it makes me wonder if I was actually like that and the accident changed my personality or if it was an act to cover up – I don't know – low self-esteem or something. That's some of the inner secret stuff I can never know because no one but me would ever have known. What was real and what was my mask?"

I gradually started to feel my way into what that might be like, but I was under no illusion that I could really ever fully appreciate what Stephen experienced. For a start, when I tried to imagine losing my memory there was a sense of relief, of liberation almost, that wasn't just about losing painful memories. I could get excited about the idea of starting again with just the core me, unadulterated by my experiences, the proverbial blank sheet. Who would the core me be? How had my experiences, my upbringing, my dad, shaped me? Who would I have become with a different set of stories? Who was I at my core when you stripped my history away?

It was exciting for me to consider it but I knew that wasn't at all how Stephen felt. Thinking about feeling separate and like an observer helped me to appreciate something of how he actually felt. I imagined a profound isolation and confusion.

I was also acutely aware of an unfathomable sense of connection with Stephen, a unique experience for me in a first session. The pull to rescue him from his isolation was compelling, but it was also an irresistible pull to *him*, to his intensity, to his intelligence, to the fact that all he had was his core being which meant that we seemed to connect at depth from the start. It wasn't sexual – there was nothing physically attractive about him for me – but there was something that had passed between us in that first moment of eye contact, when he thanked me for my honesty, something that drew me to him. Maybe in that moment I was rescued from something too.

As we wrapped up, completed the contact forms and made another appointment, I was aware that he hadn't really answered my question about why turn to counselling now? What had tipped the scales towards that decision three years later? He put on his coat and moved towards the door but stopped and turned. I waited pensively. 'Doorknob disclosures' are always significant.

"I've been having flashbacks," he said. "At least, I think they're flashbacks…"

The pause seemed to go on forever and I realised I was holding my breath.

"I'm standing over someone… he's lying on the floor covered in blood… he's not moving… and I'm just standing over him. I don't know who he is or what it means… I think I may have hurt someone… or worse."

My heart sped up before my brain fully computed the implications of what he had just said.

"So that's why now?" I asked, trying to appear calm and professional, totally unfazed by what he had just said.

"Sorry?"

"That's why you've come for counselling now."

"Yes."

"Well, we're out of time for today unfortunately, but that does sound very frightening. An important thing for us to discuss next time?"

"OK… 'bye then." Stephen held my eye just fractionally longer than would normally be comfortable. Checking my reaction? Pleading with me to help him, to not run a mile, to not reject him? He looked terrified and my fear thawed fractionally as I met his eye and determinedly held it, drawn again to something inexplicable about him.

*

I made my customary post-client cup of tea in a daze. What just happened? My heart was still thumping and my head screamed 'danger!'. And yet there was a huge part of me that wasn't afraid. The pull of him was as beguiling as the fear was alarming and I simultaneously wanted to help him and to run as far from him as possible.

As I scribbled some quick notes, inevitably the fear triumphed. Without his concrete presence, my intuitive sense of Stephen faded and the content of what he had actually said overshadowed everything. What had he done? He had practically told me that he had attacked someone. How badly? Was the man he attacked OK? Disabled? Dead? Was he a murderer? Maybe Stephen was a psychopath. That would explain the unnerving pull I could remember feeling towards him but couldn't conjure up in his absence. Violent tendencies masked by charm: wasn't that a good description of a psychopath? Was the pull my reaction to this superficial charm? I remembered the frisson of fear I'd felt earlier in the session before I'd known about the attack. Maybe that was a clue, my subconscious picking up something dangerous about him that I couldn't consciously explain.

I didn't want to work with him, but I was very scared to have that conversation with him. I had always found it difficult to formulate a reason for referring clients on to someone else that wasn't damaging to them. 'Sorry, I can't work with you, you're far too screwed up for someone as inexperienced as me' always seemed to be the clear message no matter how I imagined wrapping it up. Ethically I had a duty to work within my capability, but there were many ways I could harm a client, and perceived rejection would do just that.

With Stephen, the inability to think about *how* to explain why I needed to refer him on was compounded by my new certainty that he was dangerous. How might he react if I upset him? Would I be in physical danger from him? There was also something else that got in the way too: I was haunted by those pleading eyes as he left.

I was still shaken and not at all grounded and calm when Robyn arrived, her session scheduled immediately after Stephen's, with just the usual twenty-minute break in between. She shook the rain off her coat, hung it by the door and made some comment about the foul weather that I automatically acknowledged and agreed with but barely registered.

We hadn't talked about the buttons exercise since the day we did it. I had been immensely disappointed when she hadn't referred to it at all in the following session, preferring instead to focus on some argument with her parents that had occurred that week. I interpreted it as a sign that the exercise hadn't been useful after all, any sense of it being insightful being more about my ego than the facts.

Robyn sat down and suddenly looked a little pensive, although not tense as she had the day she told me about Andy getting angry again.

"Do you think we could get the buttons out again?" she asked.

I leapt at the suggestion, probably the best thing she could have said to recapture my full attention after the session with Stephen. I reached for the jar, curious and in eager anticipation that my self-worth as a therapist might just be rescued. Maybe it had been a useful session after all.

Robyn got out the buttons she had selected before: one for the free spirit, another for the people-pleaser, the empathic-caring one and finally the small pearl that represented the wise whisperer. She stared at them in what appeared to be fond silence for a long while, her head on one side, a half smile playing on her lips.

"It's really made me think about how little I express the wise whisperer," she finally said. "And yet it is quite a strong part of me. It is always there. Even when the people-pleaser is holding forth, grovelling and kowtowing, there is always another voice inside saying something else."

"Something that you never say out loud?"

"No never... actually, there are two voices that never get spoken out loud." She looked in the jar for another button, finally selecting a large black one. "There is also a very nasty voice, a mean, judgemental, attacking voice that says horrible things about people. I think that's sometimes why the wise voice doesn't get expressed when I disagree with someone. They're kind of on the same side, both disagreeing with the other person, but the mean voice is louder and I'm scared that's the one that will come out if I actually speak."

Wow, you're way ahead of me Robyn! Me too!

"And if that voice did come out?"

"It would be awful! Really damaging!"

Although I had completely forgotten when I had contemplated Robyn's buttons two weeks ago, I now remembered talking about my own nasty side during my training and then exploring it further in my own therapy, my 'shadow side'. My nasty side would also be incredibly destructive if it were ever unleashed.

We explored some more, teasing out the similarities and differences between the two hidden parts of her. They may have been on the same side but the 'nasty' one was defensive and protected her by being absolutely vile to whoever it perceived as threatening to her autonomy, self-esteem or intellect. It was fortunate that this part never spoke out loud as its irrational attacks would have been hard to live with afterwards and Robyn anticipated, probably accurately, that she would feel deep shame if it ever did.

We explored how the nasty voice was simply trying to protect her though, postulating that its intentions were altruistic, at least towards her, but that its methods were unhelpful. If Robyn could learn to listen even to this part, she might begin to see the needs it was associated with and get those met too. As it was, she pushed this nasty side away, rightly scared of the consequences of expressing it, but that meant that those needs sat there, unmet and festering, causing pain and fear. I didn't make any suggestions about what she should do with any of this, trusting that awareness would change something without the need for anything directive.

Ten minutes before the end of the session, Robyn fell quiet again, looking at the buttons, deep in thought.

"There's another part that I don't talk about," she eventually volunteered. "It's embarrassing rather than shameful like the nasty part, but I keep it just as hidden."

Robyn reached forward and plucked the yellow teddy button out of the jar. I held my breath, goose pimples prickling up the back of my neck and down the backs of my arms, watching her move in apparent slow motion.

I didn't fully register the exact sequence of words that followed, although I got the gist; Robyn shared the broodiness I had felt so keenly at her age. Dimly, through my uncomprehending astonishment, I heard words like 'longing' and 'yearning' and something about a need to keep it hidden in case her peers laughed and judged her as boring. She said something about not knowing how to reconcile that part with the free spirit and I mumbled something about us maybe exploring that next time. She also said that Andy must never ever know, that he would run a mile and not appreciate the fact that, certain though she was that she wanted a child, even she knew it was too early and that there were things she wanted to do first.

Somehow, I held onto enough awareness to offer a weak challenge to that. How did she know Andy would run a mile? And if it was an important part of her, what did keeping it from him mean for their relationship?

Robyn cocked her head to one side and suddenly looked quizzically at me. "Are you OK, Maggie? You look… I don't know… you don't look right."

I shook myself out of the surreal haze and responded that I was fine, just suddenly a little hot. Maybe I was coming down with something, I laughed nervously.

"Anyway," I said, "we're out of time for today, but there's obviously a lot to talk about next week."

Robyn glanced at the clock. We actually had three minutes left and I habitually overran slightly, never ever finishing early. Robyn looked confused and concerned but dutifully reached for her coat anyway. I barely registered the usual goodbye rituals, the see-you-next-weeks and so on.

When she left, I flopped dumbfounded into the chair and sat unblinking, unmoving, my mind numb with shock. I stared unseeing at a spot on the armrest of the chair Robyn had just left. My eyes gradually re-focussed and were reluctantly drawn to the yellow teddy bear button still lying innocently on the coffee table.

Fragments of the last ten minutes of the session played around in my head but I couldn't make any sense of them. Stephen jumped into my mind and his words danced around with the rest of the jumbled thoughts. *Who are you without your story? And what do you do when someone steals yours?*

Chapter 7

"And then Emma actually kicked him. I know it's wrong and everything but he soooo deserved it! Everybody laughed and Mrs P went mental!"

"Umm hmm."

How could Robyn possibly be so like me? As though we are the same person?

"She made the whole class miss golden time! I hate her! It was soooo unfair! It was Henry's fault and he got away with it completely!"

"Umm hmm."

The coincidences are remarkable. What are the chances of there being so many overlaps? Maybe it was some kind of trick. Maybe someone is playing an elaborate joke on me. Don't be ridiculous Maggie! How would that work? And why would they?

I realised Sam had suddenly stopped chattering away in the car beside me.

"Sam?"

He stared studiously out of his passenger seat window. "I hate it when you say 'umm hmm'. It means you're not listening."

Shit, shit, shit! Spot on kiddo! What a crap parent!

"Sorry Sam, I was distracted by something that happened at work. I'm all ears now sweetheart, I promise. Carry on."

"It doesn't matter." He continued to glare out of his window.

Damn! If we don't listen when children are talking about little things, how can we expect them to talk about the big stuff? Well I've really blown it. He wasn't even talking about something trivial. It certainly wasn't trivial to him, anyway.

"I'm really sorry Sam. You're quite right to be angry with me, it was very rude of me not to listen properly. I am interested, honestly."

"It's OK." His body language said exactly the opposite.

"Henry does seem to be getting into a lot of scrapes lately."

Sam shrugged and said nothing, still staring out of the window. He was still hurt and angry so I would have to take his punishment, perfectly designed to hurt me right back. The silent treatment was the worst thing anyone could do to me, but especially Sam, the most important person in my life! I deserved it. Poor Sam.

At dinner that night, Sam was still politely withdrawn, crucifying me with what felt like his rejection. Mathew was chattering on about some problem at work whilst I nodded and tried to pay attention, surreptitiously glancing at Sam every minute, trying to catch his eye.

Suddenly, in a lull in Mathew's chatter, Sam seemed to come alive: "Hey Dad, did you hear about Johnson? He's going to be out all season with that hamstring injury from Saturday!"

Mathew, who'd seemed oblivious to Sam's mood up until then, responded instantly to him.

"Yeah, I saw that. It's a disaster! I think we'll be relegated without him!"

"Yeah me too, although Bartlett's quite good."

"Not good enough, unfortunately."

Sam loved these 'grown up' conversations with Mathew about sport, and usually I loved observing their relationship. Tonight though I was feeling too guilty about messing up with Sam to enjoy it and I just felt excluded. Excluded and even more useless as I watched Mathew immediately drop his own preoccupations with work and give Sam the attention he needed and deserved. What was wrong with me? My job was to listen, I was trained in listening for God's sake, and I couldn't even listen to my own child!

The shame I felt about letting Sam down lent a new perspective to the session with Robyn too. How ridiculous to let coincidental similarities between us become such a preoccupation. That's all it was, I now realised: coincidental similarities, nothing more. I was obviously still shaken by the previous session with Stephen and then by the yellow button, and I overreacted. Damn, had I managed the session badly as well as Sam? *You're so stupid Maggie!*

Later, as I was saying goodnight to Sam, he sat on his bed fiddling with a scab on his knee and said, "Henry is getting into a lot of scrapes lately, I suppose." He didn't look at me but it was an olive branch.

"Do you know why? Don't pick it!"

He looked up and grinned at me. It was a family joke that I was squeamish about many things, including scab picking, and he loved to wind me up.

"No idea," he said, still grinning and watching my reaction as he deliberately picked the scab.

I grinned back and slapped the offending hand away from the scab. "Stop it!"

He giggled, pulled the duvet over his legs and slithered down. "I wish he'd stop though, it's really annoying."

"I bet. I really am sorry about not listening earlier."

"I know."

"Night Sam." I leant over to kiss his forehead.

"Night Mum." And he giggled and wriggled away under the duvet so that I couldn't kiss him – another family joke. I was forgiven.

*

Mathew was just shutting down his computer when I came back into the kitchen and he came over to wrap his arms around me. "Is he OK? He seemed a bit quiet tonight."

So he did notice then.

"Hmmm. He was trying to tell me something in the car and I was preoccupied with a client. He was a bit cross with me I think. He seems fine now, we made up." I pulled away from his embrace and filled the kettle.

"What was he trying to tell you?"

"Oh something about a row at school between Emma and Henry, and everyone having to miss golden time for laughing."

"Golden time? They earn that time for good behaviour all week. It doesn't sound very fair for them to lose all of it for laughing. Do we need to get involved?"

A flash of irritation. Or was it guilt? It was a bit unfair. Should I have thought that Sam might need our intervention? Or was Mathew being over protective?

"No. Why would we need to get involved?"

"OK, I was just checking!"

Obviously my tone had betrayed my irritation.

"He has to learn to deal with things that are a little bit unfair. I don't think we should get involved in every little thing that doesn't go right for him."

"I wasn't suggesting that we did. But Sam loves golden time and works hard all week to make sure he gets it."

He's probably right, but I can't think about this tonight, I don't want to feel guilty all over again.

"Can we talk about it tomorrow Mathew? I'm really

tired."

"Fine."

It clearly wasn't.

"What?"

"Well, it just seems you're always too tired for us these days. We need to book an appointment and be one of your clients to get any attention round here."

"Mathew, please, not tonight."

"Fine!" He stomped off into the lounge, flopped down and put the TV on.

I stood, hand still on the kettle, with my back to the space he'd just left. This kind of conflict had always been unbearable for me! My heart raced irrationally fast and my mind reeled.

Oh for God's sake, grow up Mathew! You're so fucking demanding. I'm allowed to be tired... aren't I?

And then it changed. It always changed.

Maybe I am a crap wife. I'm certainly a crap mother and counsellor, or at least I am today! Maybe I am selfish and self-centred. You always give me plenty of attention and reassurance. What do I give you back?

Don't sulk, please, I hate it! It's torture! Mathew, please come back to me!

Usually at that point I would need to follow him into the lounge to apologise, to hug him and beg forgiveness, hoping he wouldn't put this incident in the mental filing cabinet full of reasons to leave me that I imagined he kept in his head somewhere.

I didn't follow him though. I stayed absolutely still,

hand still on the kettle as the swirling voices in my head began to coalesce and take on newly identifiable forms. Slowly I recognised the different parts Robyn and I had defined and, more importantly, I began to see the needs they represented. *My* multifaceted needs; the part of me that needed to be loved (that was right now terrified of being alone) was pretty evident. I felt very alone, standing in the kitchen while Mathew channel flicked moodily in the lounge. It wasn't the physical distance – I could go and sit next to him on the settee right now, he wouldn't push me away – but I would still feel a million miles from him. No matter how close we had been immediately before, the row separated us in this moment as surely as a continent. My need to be loved, to not be alone, threatened to overwhelm everything else. Usually it did overwhelm everything else, but in that moment, I also recognised my terror as irrational.

Knowing that it was irrational didn't cure it, but it did soothe it ever so slightly, enough for me to see other parts of me.

I recognised the voice of my nasty side, my own equivalent of the black button in Robyn's collection, attacking Mathew because something felt threatened. Mathew was so needy, such a bloody child! His sulking was so deliberately manipulative! He needed to grow up! My integrity as a wife and mother had been questioned: 'always too tired for us' he'd said. That was so bloody unfair and completely untrue! I put so much into both of those roles, they were my absolute priority, and he knew it. That comment seemed deliberately designed to hurt me. He was such a bastard for using my deepest values against me!

I consciously wondered where my inner wisdom had gone in all of this. I hadn't noticed that part in the mental chaos so far. The wise part, as usual, had been quiet. Now a space was clearing it began to contribute. Maybe Mathew had a point. Maybe I had been preoccupied to an unhealthy degree. Maybe I do need to be more giving. Maybe I should've thought about the implications of missing golden time for Sam more than I had. In fact, now I recognised that even after he pointed it out, I still hadn't really listened to him; I had just sought to repair the relationship to satisfy my need to feel close to him. I hadn't really thought about what he might need. That wasn't a great thought, but from a place of wisdom, I could recognise it as a mistake and something I could rectify. I wasn't drowning in shame and self-loathing.

My wise part pointed out that I had also had a valid point though. I was exhausted, emotionally and mentally drained by a challenging day, and now wasn't the right time to discuss it, or even for me to think about Mathew's accusation really. Mathew hadn't attempted to understand what had gone on for me to make me so tired, so actually he wasn't giving me any attention either. His accusation of me *always* being too tired was very unfair and I suspected his sulking was indeed manipulative. It was certainly unhelpful.

And most importantly, it was his sulk. It was his anger and it was his responsibility to soothe it or express it, to talk when we were both calm about what he needed to change for him. If I rushed into old patterns of wheedling and cajoling to feel close to him again, that would never happen. We'd both push it under the rug, and if there was something we did need to address – properly address – it would get lost as I sought to feel better in the short term.

I went into the lounge, heart pounding irrationally, and hovered by the hall door. "I'm really sorry if you feel that I don't ever have time for you Mathew. If that's true, then I would like us to talk about it and I do want to do something about it. But tonight is genuinely not the right time. I think I'm usually pretty good at listening and responding whenever we have a problem so you're just going to have to trust me when I say I can't tonight. I'm going to have a bath."

I said it and left immediately before he could respond, terrified that if I gave him a chance to answer it would turn into an argument. I don't know what exactly terrified me, he wasn't remotely an aggressive man. I suppose I was terrified that any row could lead to him leaving me, to abandonment.

As I soaked in the bath, I could hear Mathew moving around downstairs. Did his movements sound angry? My heart was still racing nonsensically and I thought how ridiculous it was that I was scared to have said something so innocuous. I hadn't criticised Mathew, called him names, accused him of anything or done any of the things that 'normal' people do in rows. How did they do it? All I had done was express a different opinion to Mathew, and that was really only a different opinion regarding when the best time was to discuss something. What was wrong with me?

*

I'm six years old. I've been naughty and Dad is very angry, although I can't for the life of me remember what I did. He's screaming at me, his face inches from mine. I can see the spittle in his mouth and the veins bulging in his forehead. I'm disgusted as a bit of spit lands on my face. I flinch and screw my face up, but the feeling of disgust is quickly swapped for more fear. I don't know exactly what I'm scared of or what I think he's going to do, but my flinching seems to have made it worse. I try desperately to stand still, to be a statue. If I don't move at all maybe he'll calm down.

Mum is suddenly there, soothing him, leading him away from me, whispering in his ear, saying something I can't quite hear. I stand still. I am a statue. I can hear their voices in the kitchen now, Mum's soothing tone, Dad's still angry but a bit quieter now.

"Needs to learn!"

"... bloody heedless!"

The voices move to the hall. The door opens and then slams. I carry on being a stone statue. After what seems like forever, Mum comes into the living room. She doesn't notice I'm a statue and bustles me off to bed. She says nothing but her eyes are red and watery. Dad is not in the house. I don't know where he's gone. I stay awake for a long time listening for him coming home. Please come back Dad, I promise I'll be good. What If Mum goes too, to wherever he has gone, to be with him because she's sad he's left? Who will look after me?

It's morning. I can hear Dad downstairs. He sounds happy. I can hear him laughing with Mum. I tiptoe down and peep round the corner of the kitchen door. He looks at me sternly, tells me to hurry up and get my breakfast or I'll be late for school. Nothing else is said.

*

It was a memory I knew very well. I had revisited that flashback several times in therapy. The adult me understood that my father probably went out in order to calm down, but it doesn't change the fact that ever since then, anger had always triggered an intense fear of abandonment in me. Understanding that this experience probably caused that anger-abandonment link didn't extinguish the fear, but it did diminish it slightly. If understanding always equalled cure, the job of a therapist would be so much easier.

I stayed in the bath till it was cold, avoiding Mathew and any potential scene. I still felt unbearably anxious, my heart would not calm down, but simultaneously there was a flicker of something else: I was pleased with myself – I knew it was the right thing to do. I could hear him still watching television downstairs and had been silently pleading with him to come upstairs and make up with me, to be the first to apologise so that I could too and we could be OK again. Eventually I was forced by the cold water to move. Climbing into bed alone felt terrible. We always went to bed at the same time, never separately and I hated it. It felt weird and wrong, an uncanny symbol of the aloneness that I simultaneously feared and expected. It took all my willpower not to go downstairs and make it up. The anxiety was horrible but I was still just angry enough with him to stay put. It was important for us, and especially for my own self-respect, for us to face this properly. I would prevent that by a disingenuous apology now, designed to end rather than deal with any problem.

Surprisingly I must have dozed off because I woke suddenly at the sound of the bedroom door being quietly opened and then closed as Mathew eventually came to bed. I didn't move or open my eyes, but held my breath as he slid smoothly under the duvet, clearly trying not to wake me. My heart sank as he turned his back to me and curled up. I blinked back tears. He was lying right next to me and yet felt so far away. His breathing gradually slowed to the deep, even, unmistakeable rhythm of sleep. How unfair that he could sleep while I was in torment! He obviously didn't care at all about what was happening between us!

Looking at his back turned towards me was unbearable and so after a few minutes I turned away too. Jesus! How did we end up here? We never slept without holding each other or touching each other somehow. I lay awake wondering what had happened, doubting myself, being angry with him, being scared, feeling ashamed, feeling small and not having a clue how to fix any of this. This was such unchartered territory for me, and it was over nothing! Such an insignificant conversation led us here and now I didn't know what to do.

Eventually I must have fallen into a light sleep again because I woke suddenly as I felt Mathew turn over. I held my breath again as he wriggled closer and moulded his body around my back. He hooked an arm around my waist and sought out my hand with his. I could breathe again!

Sleep was now out of the question as I was overcome with relief and gratitude. He had made the first move and I loved him for it. A few excruciating hours of being separate and alone and now I needed to be as close as possible to him again. I wriggled free and turned to face him, putting my hands on either side of his face as I kissed him passionately on the lips. He returned the kiss equally passionately and then started to plant tiny delicate kisses all over my face. Abruptly, he pulled away, startled as a salty taste gave away the presence of tears. He looked at me confused and concerned and we locked eyes for a moment. Then he pulled me towards him and wrapped me in a bear hug that said, *we're OK, we're going to be fine*.

When we made love in the dark it wasn't with the desperate passion I had felt when I turned and kissed him, but silently and tenderly, a mutual communication of care and profound love. Afterwards we slept deeply, wrapped tightly around each other until daybreak.

Only in the morning did I notice that for the first time in seven years I hadn't felt guilty making love. Then I instantly felt guilty about not feeling guilty!

As the early morning sun filtered through the blinds, we lay in bed and talked – properly talked – about how we both felt. Mathew was indeed struggling with my preoccupation with my work. He had been used to him and Sam having more of me, having all of me in fact. I was able to explain how anxious I sometimes was about my inexperience and what felt like the huge responsibility of my work. Mathew listened and tried to reassure me that I was good at my job although, as I explained, the isolated nature of the role meant that actually nobody, not even John, could possibly know that for sure. Only myself and my clients could really determine whether I made a difference or not.

All therapists ultimately have to live with the fact that since neither they nor the client really has any objective measure of what constitutes 'getting better' they can never really know to what extent they're helping or whether simply time, the process of unburdening or taking an active role in their own treatment or some other by-product is actually what makes the difference.

I also managed to tell Mathew how hurtful it was for him to say that I was *always* too tired for them and he agreed that wasn't true. He did think that the balance was wrong though, especially for Sam, and that stung. I didn't want it to be true and deep inside I wasn't sure that it was, but in the spirit of truly hearing each other, I tried to be open to the possibility.

By the time we got up I felt closer to him than ever and marvelled on the irony that it took a row, a difference and a separateness to achieve that. I still felt a bit shaky; the conversation hadn't been easy and I hadn't liked everything I heard, especially the bit about Sam needing more undivided attention and thought from me. But we had really listened to each other and each tried to understand the other and, importantly, I had also managed to say that I thought Mathew had been unfair, which felt new.

Later that morning, I drove to supervision distractedly ruminating on our conversation. I suddenly understood that I didn't have to agree with everything Mathew said. We could have different opinions and still be OK. It felt so obvious a thought that I felt ridiculous to think it now, as though it was a new revelation. I'd theoretically known that before of course, the stuff I'd studied about couples needing to be separate in order to be truly close had resonated so strongly because I rationally believed it. I'd even said to John that Robyn needed to know that she could be different and yet still fully connected to others, and that difference doesn't sound a death knell in relationships, but I don't think *all* of me really believed it until just then. Before then I'd only known it cognitively. Now I felt it and that was a very different thing. I felt light, and somehow more whole.

Chapter 8

"I've got a new client and I need to refer him on," I blurted out instantly to John

"OK, tell me more." John's reply was as irritatingly measured and non-committal as ever, considering that what I'd just said was pretty dramatic by any standards.

"I think he may be violent and dangerous and…" I rushed the words, wanting to get Stephen out of my life now as quickly as possible.

"You *think*?" John interrupted.

"Yes, well, it's a bit complicated." I took a deep breath, deliberately slowed myself down and proceeded to tell John about Stephen's accident, about his amnesia, and finally his flashbacks.

"Hmmmm, very interesting." John was sitting with his hands touching at their fingertips, held up to his mouth in a parody of wise concentration. "And you think he's dangerous because of this possible flashback?"

"Well, yes." (*Err, obviously!*).

"What were your instincts about him before he told

you about that?"

"Are they really relevant, given the flashback? Instincts can be wrong."

"Possible flashback," he corrected.

Why is he being so pedantic?

"Humour me, what did you think and feel about him?"

"Well, I..." I wasn't expecting this and hadn't prepared. I had imagined we would discuss the practicalities of referring Stephen on; practicalities like who to, and how to do it without him feeling rejected by me. I hadn't at all expected to be examining any other feelings I had towards him apart from fear.

"Take your time, think your way back into the session before he told you about the image of the bleeding man."

"I found him... compelling I guess."

"Compelling?"

"Yes, I was drawn to him somehow. He talked about not having an identity because he didn't have any memories about who he was. I'd never thought about identity like that before and somehow it made him... very present. He wasn't reacting and engaging from a script or habit, he was reacting to what was happening in the moment. Funny now I think about that, because he said he actually felt separate from people and yet I felt a deep connection with him."

"So you were drawn to him and felt a deep connection. Your instincts weren't about danger?"

"No, but psychopaths charm people don't they? People aren't scared of them, they're taken in by them."

"You think he's a psychopath? I think it would take a lot more evidence than this to use that label." John had an adverse reaction to labels, which he believed to be limiting, pigeon holing and generally unhelpful.

"Well… I don't know. I did have a moment of fear earlier in the session that I didn't quite understand. That could've been me instinctively picking up on something."

"Go on," he encouraged.

"He was telling me about not having any memories about the sort of person he was, basically whether he was good or bad, a party animal or a more wholesome sort, that kind of thing, and he started to get quite animated and distressed. He raised his voice a bit and I noticed I felt a bit scared."

"And that tells you he's dangerous?"

"Well… no, not exactly…" It suddenly sounded ridiculous, even to me.

"That's emotional reasoning: 'I'm scared, ergo it must be dangerous'. It's a so-called thinking trap in some therapy models. By that logic, agoraphobics are right that the outside world is dangerous and the rest of us are mad for ever going outside! We know why you get scared when people shout, we've talked about this before. Stephen was probably triggering your own memories of being repeatedly shouted at by your father."

"Pooosssssibly." I strung the word out warily, not committing to any particular stance.

John's logic floored me. I couldn't argue with him and yet I didn't agree. I felt confused, wrong-footed and stupid. Again! Recognising that, I felt an instant flash of self-protective anger; putting me in that unsure and deskilled place was unhelpful and unnecessary.

"But aren't we getting away from the main issue here – Stephen's flashback?" I felt absurdly pleased with myself for standing up to what felt like an onslaught, and holding on to my own thoughts and opinions.

"Possible flashback," John corrected again, maddeningly.

"You keep saying that. Why 'possible' flashback?"

"I'm so glad you asked," John grinned. "Have you followed anything of the recovered memory versus false memory debate going on in the States over the last couple of years?"

"No."

"Ever heard of Elisabeth Loftus?"

"Yes, of course. We covered her work on eyewitness testimony in my training."

"Good. That work validates a lot of our focus as therapists. If memories can be so easily distorted then who we think we are based on our childhood memories is subject to distortion too."

"Stuff like kids being called stupid and growing up believing it and then only remembering the times and experiences that support that belief?" I was trying to show that I'd got this, that he didn't need to go into the lecture mode he seemed to love so much.

"Exactly. But now she's gone further. She's now challenging everything we ever thought we knew about memory, and her latest work is going to have enormous implications for our field. Or at least it should do. It's already resulting in therapists across the pond being sued for implanting false memories."

John must've caught the look on my face; my fear of doing something 'wrong' was always near the surface and easily triggered by stories of other therapists being sued.

"It's OK, those therapists used what appear to be quite dubious techniques including things like hypnosis and drugs from what I can gather. But it's important that we take note of the stuff that's coming out about memory because it turns out that memory is even more fallible than we could ever have imagined. The ease with which memories become distorted or confused was always quite shocking in itself, but the ease with which entirely false memories can be planted and totally believed is truly incredible! So, first of all tell me what you know about the Loftus studies." John settled himself, clearly now in teacher mode despite my efforts.

I really didn't like this one-up, one-down dynamic he seemed to keep creating between us. I eye-rolled inwardly.

"Loftus's studies looked at how eyewitness testimony could be manipulated and their memories distorted just by the way questions were asked." I'd found her work fascinating and knew it well but mostly I just really wanted to show John that I knew it and meet him as an equal on this. "There had apparently been several notorious miscarriages of justice when the conviction had relied solely on eyewitness testimony," I continued, "and Loftus had become fascinated by that and studied one in particular: the Titus case."

"Go on."

God, John was patronising sometimes. This felt like a school test now. Well I was going to ace this one!

"In 1980, Steve Titus was convicted of rape when the victim stated in court that she was absolutely positive that he was the man who attacked her. However, when she'd first been shown a picture of Titus in a photo line-up, she'd said he was the most *similar* to her attacker. Steve Titus's conviction ended up being overturned relatively quickly compared to other cases when the real rapist was identified. However, Titus had already lost everything: his fiancée, his job, his savings. He was understandably angry and bitter. He died of a heart attack aged thirty-five, just two days before a court case to claim damages for his suffering."

I still remembered how appalled I'd been when I first heard that story.

"Anyway, Loftus got involved with the case and wanted to know how a witness could go from 'he's the most similar' to 'I'm absolutely positive it was him'. And so she conducted several studies to show how leading questions could distort memories. The most famous one was when she showed that if people were shown a film of a car crash and were later asked to recall how fast the cars were going when they *smashed* into each other, they 'remembered' faster speeds than people who were simply asked how fast they were going when the cars *hit* each other."

John was smiling and nodding but didn't say anything so I carried on talking, showing him just how much I knew about this.

"There have been all sorts of similar studies by Loftus and others that show the many different ways that eyewitness memories of events are spectacularly unreliable and shouldn't be relied upon as the sole evidence in a court case. She became an expert witness in many court cases, and pretty unpopular as a result."

"Not with people like Steve Titus though," John piped up.

"No, probably not. I guess to those falsely accused she must be quite a hero." This was more like it. A discussion between equals.

"Yes absolutely. But for people whose memories were effectively being challenged she became a figure of hate. It turns out that people get very upset when someone tries to say that something they think they remember very clearly might not have happened that way." He grinned, getting ready for his punchline. "It got worse when she showed that it might not have happened *at all*!"

"At all?" *What? Did he really just say that?*

"At all!" John beamed, clearly enjoying his trump card. "Just last year, she published another experiment that has rocked the basis of many child abuse cases involving apparently repressed, and then recovered, memories. She and her team devised an experiment that involved planting a false memory of being lost in a shopping mall. They interviewed the families of volunteers to establish some genuine childhood events. The subjects were then questioned, ostensibly to glean how much they remembered about four key events from their childhoods. What they didn't know was that only three of the four events had actually happened and came from the interviews with their families. The fourth was entirely fabricated, a story about them being lost in a shopping mall for a period of time before being found and returned to their parents. Not surprisingly, since it never actually happened, they didn't initially remember ever being lost in a shopping mall. However, when they returned a couple of weeks later, a significant number of them not only now apparently 'remembered' this entirely fictitious event, they had even 'remembered' extra details about it that no one had ever mentioned: it was an old lady who had found them, they remembered how scared they'd been, etc. They had confabulated around an event that never even happened and, most importantly, they were absolutely convinced that this was a genuine, albeit newly remembered, event from their past. They believed this new 'memory' totally!

Can you see the implications?"

"Erm... wow... I'm not sure, that's a bit mind-boggling."

John beamed and nodded encouragingly whilst I tried to put together what this meant.

"Soooo... if false memories can be planted so easily, we can't completely trust our own memories? Things we think are true memories might not have even happened?"

"Exactly! They might have been things we have been told about, or imagined or even dreamed. Even if they did happen, we might remember key aspects of events so differently that it changes their meaning and impact. When you add in the fact that so much counselling theory ultimately boils down to how childhood events might have affected someone and might be influencing their behaviour now, if memories of childhood are so fallible, the whole edifice is built on sand."

I sat dumbfounded, struggling to take in all the implications. Stephen's amnesia mingled with thoughts of my own memories that minutes ago had been indisputable facts and now seemed, at least in theory, to be anything but!

John, undeterred by the fact that I was a bit baffled by the whole concept, continued unabated.

"Think about it; if each of us is the accumulation of our experiences, then who we are is, at least in part, the sum total of what has happened to us."

Just like Stephen was describing. I get this bit.

"If those memories, the record if you like, of everything that has happened to us are so easily distorted, confused or even fabricated, it's like *we* are fabricated! The very essence of who we are might be built on misinformation."

"Blimey!" Despite the obvious validity of the research, I still felt defiantly dubious. I heard the words and intellectually could understand and even accept them. However, a core part of me steadfastly refused to believe that my own memories weren't the same as facts. "It's really hard to get my head around this. Are you saying that we're not who we think we are, and things that we think shaped us might never have happened? That's like something from a science fiction film!"

"Not really. In practice, the truth is that for most of us, the things that we remember, or *think* we remember, can be corroborated. Other people were there, so some stories from the past become family folklore, and are told again and again so we know that, broadly speaking at least, they did happen. But it's the 'broadly speaking' bit that causes the problems. We remember the *essence* of an experience only, and we actually create the detail if, and when, we ever need to recall that particular memory. Memory is not a recording that we play back at will, it's an impression combined with creative construction at the point of recall. That explains why family members sometimes remember a thing slightly differently, doesn't it? And it's those differences that are sometimes key to the emotional tone of a particular memory, don't you think?"

"Yes, absolutely." This concept I understood and was familiar with from the distorted memory studies. "The other part of that of course is that events don't happen in a vacuum anyway. Everything that happens is interpreted through the lens of past experiences and opinions we have formed of the world as a result."

"Yes, exactly. We put our own spin on everything that happens to us so that we see the world not as it *actually* is but how it is when we look through our own unique filter. We discount anything that doesn't fit with a world view that we *already* hold."

"Cognitive bias." I nodded. *I know John, I know! Stop lecturing.*

"So, even the essence of an experience isn't stored factually as it actually occurred; the essence is distorted by the filters through which we experienced it and the meaning we made of it at the time. These experiences are then recalled through today's filters, which may have changed a bit in the intervening years. The creative construction of a memory, from the already distorted essence, will be done in a way that serves our current biases. It's a minefield!" John clearly loved this subject but even he had finally run out of steam.

"And the recovered memory versus false memory debate?" I tried to appear intelligent and involved in the discussion by prompting John back to his starting point.

"Ah yes. As well as proving that memory could be inadvertently fabricated and therefore false, Loftus has upset a lot of people by challenging whether wholesale repression and then recovery of trauma memories is even possible. Freud's original concept of repression was that it was a more or less conscious avoidance of unpleasant memories. The idea in several high profile child abuse cases seems to have been that an *unconscious* decision was taken for an entire trauma memory to be stored, intact and whole, somewhere the conscious brain couldn't access it at all. According to this version, it remains there for years, hidden totally until some clever therapist comes along with just the right techniques to unlock it."

"You're obviously sceptical."

"I am indeed! And there have been cases that back up my scepticism. There was one case where the victim apparently 'remembered' being raped several times by her father and even got pregnant by him and was forced to self-abort in barbaric fashion. She was utterly convinced she remembered these events in multicolour detail, refusing to waiver from that belief even after a medical examination showed she was a virgin!"

"Blimey!"

"Exactly! And the point is, she wasn't lying, or mad or anything like that. Memory is just that fallible and suggestible! Add in dubious therapist techniques like hypnosis during which clients are dangerously impressionable and you have a recipe for inadvertent but unsafe errors in so-called recovered memory."

"So there's no such thing as recovered memories?"

"I wouldn't say that yet – I think the jury is still out. The debate is certainly heated on both sides. All I think we can say for sure is that the issues are complex and that there is a lot more to memory than we previously thought or understood. And as therapists we have to tread very, very carefully when there are suggestions of repressed or otherwise unavailable memories in clients."

There was an awkward pause. I was still stuck in a battle between two different bits of my brain. Intellectually I understood the theory but my experiential mind had always rebelled against the concept of my own memories being imperfect anyway and now he was saying they could be completely false.

"So, what do you now think about Stephen's situation?"

"Well I understand why you keep saying 'possible' flashback now."

"Good! Especially given his otherwise complete amnesia, it could actually be anything couldn't it: a dream, a suggestion, something he saw in a film, anything at all? And even if it is a flashback and at some point he was actually standing over a bleeding man, you don't know – and he doesn't either from what he's saying – what that means. He's scared it means he injured the man, and your fear is possibly projective identification."

I felt myself bristle at the long words and psychodynamic labels, the irritation covering the familiar flush of embarrassment that these words weren't second nature to me, that I still had to concentrate hard to understand what John was saying. Why couldn't he just use normal, everyday language?

"The danger is that like the latest Loftus study, he'll make assumptions about the flashback, and his fear, and fabricate details around it about him doing something that never happened."

"So, what do I do?"

"The same as you should always do: remain open to *all* the possibilities and encourage him to do the same until if, or when, he knows for definite. We should always hear our clients' stories as just that – as stories. Not as lies but as stories that are true for them for sure but are not *absolute* truths. We have to hold the idea that there are no absolute truths. Absolute truth doesn't exist and we can never come even close to knowing what the objective truth of any given situation would be. This is even more the case when talking about the past. Think about 'the past as it is currently construed' by the client as opposed to 'the past as it actually happened' and you won't go far wrong. Now, think of Stephen in the light of all this research and theory and tell me how you feel."

I took a deep breath and leant back in my chair, gazing at a spot where the ceiling and wall joined just above John's head. I tried to look inside myself to answer John's questions, momentarily distracted by the spider's web my eyes had landed on.

"I feel relief," I finally answered, surprised and cautious.

"Go on."

"I liked him before I thought he was violent. I'm glad he's not... glad he *might* not be."

"OK. Now, think very carefully before you answer this: do you feel safe working with him?"

I thought, or rather I *felt* my way in answering him. "I do... yes, I do actually."

"Safety is not an exact science of course; we can't know if any new client is dangerous or not. Therapists being attacked by their clients is thankfully a very rare event but tell me, how do you generally safeguard yourself with clients anyway?"

"I always sit in the chair closest to the door so that my exit isn't blocked if anything happens, and actually I have a hidden personal alarm behind my cushion too. They covered the sitting-in-the-chair-closest-to-the-door thing on my course and the personal alarm was Mathew's idea – he really wasn't happy about the concept of random strangers coming into the house to see me when he was out at work."

"Good, that all sounds good. And at this point, Stephen doesn't intuitively feel any more dangerous than any other random stranger?"

"No, no he doesn't now." I was strangely moved by John's tenacious questioning on the point of how safe I felt. I felt cared for and I liked it.

"OK." He smiled at me. "Is that enough on Stephen for today then? Obviously I expect we'll keep coming back to him. He sounds absolutely fascinating!"

We both glanced at the clock. Ten minutes to fill. Awkward.

"Is there anything else you'd like to talk about for the last ten minutes?"

With hindsight I don't know why I said what I said next. Perhaps it was that I was feeling cared for and safe and so dived in without thinking. Perhaps my brain was addled and still not thinking straight after trying to comprehend the implications of the fallibility of memories. Probably I was just searching for something to fill the time so that I didn't have to face the awkwardness of a silence.

"Well, there's something weird going on with me and Robyn."

"Weird how?"

"I did this exercise with her to get her thinking about the different parts of her identity and what they needed."

I proceeded to tell John about the buttons exercise and the different parts we identified. I really wanted to impress him with how we were working on Robyn's relationship with herself and the integration of all aspects of her identity. His body language and expression were encouraging and he did actually seem to be impressed. Maybe that was why I let my guard down even further and rashly continued.

"The thing is, it's like she's me."

"Like she's you?" John was genuinely confused.

"Well yes... like there's some sort of connection between us. All the parts she identified describe me perfectly too. All of them! Every time she tells me something about herself I think 'me too!'. It's not just our values and beliefs, it's practical stuff too, like we both had ex-military fathers. And when she picked out the yellow teddy bear button I was astounded. It's the one I would have chosen, and it was like she was talking about me not her. I can't get my head around it. I don't understand what it means."

"What it means?"

John's face might have continued to appear impassive and neutral to most people, but my skills were more honed than most. I'd been reading and interpreting miniscule changes in expressions since I was three years old, acutely aware of the danger those changes could signal. John's face had contorted quickly through several different arrangements. And I had seen the subtle flash of disbelief, followed by a pretty well-hidden disappointment and finally something approaching scorn.

I deflated instantly. "Well... I... errr... I can't explain it. It feels like there's... I don't know," I stuttered, trying to find a way to explain myself and drawing a blank. I felt my ears burn with shame!

"You don't think that many people, possibly most people, would come up with those same parts? And were there many buttons in the jar that were so obviously associated with babies?"

John tried to make his voice gentle but my people reading skills were too good for him. I saw his concern and confusion that I could be suggesting something so preposterous and, quite frankly, odd.

I had flinched briefly at the generalisation of 'babies' but quickly recovered from that aspect of John's challenge. The actual substance of his challenge was a different matter though and not so easy to bat away. He was right of course, and I'd even come to that conclusion myself after my preoccupation with the coincidences had got in the way of listening to Sam. Why on earth had I now returned to the idea? And why on earth did I think it was a good idea to share such a ridiculous notion with John of all people? I didn't even know what exactly that ridiculous notion was. What precisely was I trying to say? That Robyn was a long-lost twin? That we were psychically linked in some way? I didn't believe in that kind of rubbish! *Ground, swallow me up!*

*

I drove home alternating between ranting at myself for being so stupid and ranting at John for always managing to make me feel like this. What had I been thinking? Why couldn't I let go of the ridiculous notion that there was something weird going on? The idea had caused me problems twice now, both times with people who were important to me, albeit in very different ways. Enough was enough. I was going to pull myself together and drop it.

My thoughts turned to Stephen and the memory stuff John had told me about. If it was true that memory was so unreliable, so prone to suggestion and interpretation, and if it was also true that who we are is based on what has happened to us, then the whole identity thing is muddled. Nothing can be relied upon. Identity becomes who we *think* we are based on what we *think* happened to us!

I thought back to my training and Carl Rogers' idea of people being 'in process'. He said that none of us were fixed, that we were all flowing from one experience to the next. He said there is no such thing as a fixed identity, no permanent answer to the question 'who am I?'. We are whatever we feel in that moment. And since what we feel, and even how we interpret our experience changes, who we are changes too. I'd loved that concept from the start. It was liberating to think that we could flow and change and just be whoever we are right now. We just have to be open and aware of our experience in the moment. All any of us have is the present.

When I combined it with the idea of memories being fallible, it all made sense in theory, and indeed when I applied the theory to Stephen. When I tried to think of it in terms of my own memories though, I floundered.

Disjointed memories flashed into my head: Dad shouting, Mum weeping silently as she sat staring out of the window, Andre's hand out of the corner of my eye, me curled up on the bed in the early morning light. Those things happened. They all happened just like that. They made me who I am. Those memories are facts. I can't believe they didn't happen exactly as I remember them. They're so clear, there's no way they can have been distorted.

But then I thought of Robyn again, of the memories I had locked away about me and Andre, memories that were being unlocked through hearing about her and Andy; how I would always appease Andre, always seek to repair any ruptures and misunderstandings. I remembered how often it didn't feel like my fault but, just like Robyn, I apologised anyway, and how I was always a bit scared of his moods even before. The time he hit me might have been the only time he was physically violent, but it didn't really happen out of the blue. That's just what I had chosen to believe. Maybe this was what memories being fallible actually meant: small distortions and omissions that change the meaning of the memory, protecting me from what I don't want to know, protecting me in this case from having to consider that maybe Andre was bad news, or our relationship was, even before he hit me.

Maybe other stuff wasn't quite as I remembered it. Maybe it didn't happen the way it appears now. My mind reeled. I couldn't look straight at *that* memory, my heart raced just at the idea of it and I pulled back instantly. I shivered. That was close; my sadistic, self-destructive mind had nearly achieved its goal. I had almost been tricked into going back there. *Be more careful. Keep your guard up Maggie. That memory will destroy you.* The cruel voice wouldn't let go without a fight though and continued to wheedle away at that part of me that knew better; how could I ever examine it, explore it, know the truth of it if I couldn't bring myself to remember it? *I don't care! I can't face it, even obliquely! It happened, and the details don't matter. It happened, and the pain is beyond words. It happened and nothing will ever be the same.*

Chapter 9

June and the colour scheme in the room had become duck-egg blue, a refreshing, cooling colour to offset the heat. And it was hot. Later in the day, the sun directly on the glazed patio doors would mean that the heat in the room would become oppressive and soporific. By late morning I would be opening the doors between each client to try to cool it down, letting the floaty, translucent curtains billow in the breeze. For the first client of the day though, straight after the school run, it was still cool, the sun having not yet arced its way round the corner of the house to shine on the wall of glass. By the end of this first session I would be squinting as it cleared the roofline and always aimed directly for my eye, no matter how I angled my chair. The client would be fine; it was possible to position the client chair so that the sun was behind them throughout the day.

Robyn looked different. I couldn't say what it was but as she arrived she looked different somehow, not upset or excited or pleased with herself exactly, there was just a calmness and a strength about her that I hadn't seen before. And a sadness. There was definitely a sadness.

"So much has happened," she said as she sat down. "I don't know where to start."

I smiled encouragingly and waited. She and Andy had gradually drifted back into a sort of relationship over the weeks, but she still hadn't made a definitive decision and that had bothered her. Andy felt on probation, which he was, and that inevitably caused problems too.

"He got angry again, but this time I didn't apologise… I didn't make it OK." She looked calm and resolute.

"And you're pleased about that?" I certainly was! *Maggie, keep your own agenda out of this.*

"Sort of. I'm scared too. I haven't heard from him for three days. I'm guessing it's over… actually, scared isn't quite right…" She sat back, reflecting for a moment, trying to find the exact words to express her complex feelings. "I am kind of scared, but I'm also resigned. And sad. And sure. All at the same time."

"What happened?" It was a terrible intervention that came more from the nosey, curious human than the clever therapist, but sometimes I needed to know the facts of an experience to be able to keep up and help the client to unpick it and to reflect. I was sure some counsellors could just follow the emotional trail and understand but I never could.

"It was a perceived slight on his part again, the same

as last time. Actually, you know, I think he needs therapy himself on that and if I got a chance I would probably tell him that now... basically, a group of us met up and Andy thought that I was paying too much attention to this other guy, Pete. I like Pete and actually I've known him much longer than I've known Andy. We go back ages. We've been friends since primary school, our mums are friends, we ended up at the same uni and we are really close. He's like a brother to me and Andy has always known about that. Anyway, I was talking to Pete. His girlfriend has just dumped him and he's gutted about it. I could see Andy glancing over at us out of the corner of my eye and I could see he wasn't happy. I kept thinking I should wrap it up with Pete and go and give Andy some attention, but then another part of me thought 'why should I? Pete's a mate. He has been for years. He needs a shoulder to cry on right now. Why should I short-change Pete because Andy isn't happy?'. It's perfectly reasonable to want to listen to a friend when they're upset. Isn't it?"

Robyn looked at me for approval and I was so wrapped up in the story I automatically nodded encouragingly. *Damn, it doesn't help her trust her own opinions if I reassure her whenever she expresses a little bit of doubt.*

"Well, when I'd finished talking to Pete I went over to Andy and he was sulking and I felt so angry. In the past I would've been scared but I wasn't, I was just really pissed off with him. I couldn't say anything of course, the scared bit still gets in the way of that, but I consciously decided that I wasn't going to pander to the sulk, to make it all OK. So I just laughed and joked with the group, and him, and pretended he wasn't sulking at all. His face just got darker and darker, stonier and stonier. And by then I was a bit scared, but I'd made my bed and I knew that if I backed down I'd be selling out on something important in me. Actually I was very scared and a big part of me wanted to rush in and soothe it and make it OK again, but I was also still angry. And embarrassed. It was really awkward for everyone who was there because it was so obvious he was fuming by now. I think part of me wanted to calm it all down to make it OK for everyone else, to stop it being awkward. I felt responsible for the awkwardness but at the same time I knew I wasn't responsible, Andy was. And I also knew he was being unreasonable."

She paused and glanced at me again, automatically checking my reaction. This time I remembered not to nod even though I was inwardly delighted at her apparent new understanding.

"Eventually the group drifted away and it was just me and Andy. He didn't say anything at all, just sat there sulking, so eventually I said, 'So are you going to tell me what's wrong then?'. He said 'as if I didn't know' and then started with this tirade about how I obviously don't want to spend time with him, I obviously prefer Pete, we might as well call it quits. And something just snapped! I was very calm, but I said that it was perfectly reasonable to spend time talking to Pete and that if Pete needed a friend I would always be there for him. I said that I didn't want to call it quits but that if we were going to have any sort of future together, he was going to have accept that Pete was a close friend and that I would spend time with him. He looked at me with a look I'll never forget, it was pure hurt and shock. He didn't say anything at all, he just got up and walked out. And that was it. That was three days ago and I haven't heard from him since."

"Three days? How does that feel?" I was thinking about how just those few hours slightly apart from Mathew had felt so awful.

"Terrible! I couldn't eat at first, I couldn't sleep. At one point I thought I'd been totally wrong. I started seeing it through his eyes again. All this time I've kept him dangling, not really committing, of course he would be jealous of Pete. And yet, I also knew I couldn't keep being the one to apologise every time. It stopped being about who was right or wrong this particular time and became about that dynamic, that pattern between us. We probably both play a part in our problems most of the time and yet I always apologise. Always. And I can't keep doing that. The wise part won't let me keep doing that anymore. I guess I decided that if we couldn't discuss issues and conflicts like two reasonable adults then we probably didn't have a future."

"It sounds like it felt very clear to you."

"It was. It is. And it breaks my heart! It literally

breaks my heart. I know I can't live like that, but at first I thought I couldn't live without him either. It hurt so much, literally physically. And I cried like I've never cried before, for two days solid. I woke in the early hours of the morning on the third day… yesterday – God, was it only yesterday – and couldn't face my life. I didn't want to go to lectures or see anyone or go home or anything. I couldn't think of anywhere I wanted to be. I thought of 'phoning you and asking for an extra session but I didn't want that either. I felt dead inside. I couldn't engage with the thought of anything left in my life. I didn't know how to be."

I held my breath. Where was Robyn going with this?

"I got up and just drove. I had no idea where I was going, I don't think I really cared. I ended up in the Lake District. There was a truckers' café in a layby and I stopped to get a cup of tea and then I drove again and suddenly I was at this lake."

Robyn was staring into the distance, like she was back by the lake again. I stayed very quiet, focusing intently on her, totally absorbed and a bit apprehensive about what was coming next.

"The sun was just coming up and I sat by this lake cradling the polystyrene cup in my hands, wrapped in a blanket from the car. It was so quiet. The sun was casting this pinky-orange light over the sky and it was reflected in the lake. It was probably the most beautiful sunrise I'd ever seen and I suddenly had this overwhelming sense of peace. There were no thoughts with it, no blinding revelations, just this sense that it would be OK, that I would be OK. Even without Andy. No matter what, I was OK. Sad. Bruised. Hurting. But still fundamentally OK."

I felt tears prick my own eyes.

"When the sunrise display was over I stripped off and swam. It was freezing at first but then after a while it just felt really... sensual. My skin was tingling and I could feel the water moving over my arms and legs, like my skin was suddenly hypersensitive or I was hyper-aware. The light was still that early morning variety and the lake was still dappled. There was something about being there in that light, being naked, being alone, being the only one to see this, to experience this. Something about the idea that this stuff happens every day, we just don't usually turn up to experience it, it happens without us."

I held my breath, intuitively aware that some kind of momentous shift had occurred for her.

"I suddenly realised, this was what it meant to be truly alive. That in this moment *all* of me was living, the wise part that *knew* what I was doing with Andy was right, the bit that needed to be loved was still *really* hurting, the sensual part that needed to feel this lake on my skin and see that light, even the free spirit that had perhaps brought me here without me consciously deciding to come. All of those bits of me felt very real and important in different ways. I still felt unbearably sad, it was still so painful, but there was something about being naked, vulnerable and exposed whilst also being emotionally wide open. I felt vulnerable, yes, but very alive. I could live, I could be all of me, with or without Andy."

The tears I had felt pricking my eyes welled until they were on the point of spilling. Robyn suddenly looked directly at me for the first time and, recognising my emotion, her own eyes, moist to start with, instantly mirrored mine. I wiped away an escaping tear and smiled. Robyn returned my smile and knew that I understood. Perfectly! No words needed. No words appropriate.

*

That evening I sat in the garden with a glass of wine after a tiring day of five clients. Sam was in bed, although not yet asleep due to the heat in his bedroom. Mathew was due back late. I lay back on the cushioned swing seat, eyes closed, and idly wondered how other counsellors managed with more than five clients in a day. I was restricted by school runs and a refusal to work in the evenings when Sam and Mathew were home, but even if that weren't the case, five clients left me exhausted, mentally and often emotionally. Just the level of concentration required to focus and listen in such an intense and holistic way was draining, without factoring in the impact of empathising with all those distressing feelings too.

Then there were the notes. Not just a record of the session, but for me a chance to process everything that happened during it; to record things that I noticed but didn't say, things I wondered about, things they didn't say but might have been expected to, reactions in me that might say something about the feelings they engendered in other people. The notes were onerous and mentally challenging too. Five client hours and five sets of notes came to eight to ten hours of intense focus, and I always still had notes to finish once Sam was in bed.

Back then I wasn't really conscious of the intensity of it, just the exhaustion. I actually believed that I only worked part-time. After all, there were only five hours booked in my diary when you looked at it, and so I was bewildered by my tiredness. I couldn't imagine ever doing more and felt inadequate next to therapists whose books I read and who talked of ten plus clients in a day. I instantly pictured John's face and imagined him rolling his eyes at my self-criticism rearing its head yet again. We'd had a couple of sessions since the disastrous one where I talked about Robyn and I being connected somehow. I still cringed at the memory but we'd had constructive sessions since and I knew deep down that John rated me as a therapist and had my best interests at heart.

I smiled as I thought about telling him about today's session with Robyn. I guessed she would be ending her counselling soon: it felt like we'd achieved both of our goals. She had made a decision she could live with – her goal – even though she still hadn't decided directly whether to leave or stay with Andy. She had decided what behaviour was and wasn't OK for her, which in the end had amounted to the same thing. Her improved relationship with herself – my goal – was what had enabled that. She hadn't ended it with Andy but she had made it clear that his behaviour wasn't acceptable and she wouldn't be putting up with it in future, and it looked as though Andy had then made the decision for her that they were finished. Effectively she had reached a crunch point, as many relationships do, where a person is faced with a choice between their own integrity or the relationship. Robyn had chosen herself.

I realised Robyn's decision had been made by the wise part of her, not the people-pleaser as had been the case with me. Although the outcome was the same, I knew that would make all the difference for her going forward. She wouldn't live with regret as I had had to do.

As I lay there savouring the wine and the feel of the cool breeze on my face, I wondered if I'd actually been wrong about that. Maybe the wise part of me had made the decision too. Certainly I had been stuck in the same dynamic as Robyn, always apologising, always soothing, always trying to predict and avoid anything that might upset Andre. Was I aware then that it wasn't healthy? Had I subconsciously realised that that night was just an extension of a pattern that was already abusive long before it was violent?

Why then had I convinced myself that I had left because I was worried what everyone else might think? I had beaten myself up about that for years, castigated myself for not being strong enough to stand by my own beliefs about Andre. Maybe I had actually acted according to what I believed about him, what I *knew* about him, deep down. Maybe I just wasn't ready to admit that. In fact, maybe I hadn't been ready to admit that until just now: I had been in a relationship with an abusive man and I'd put up with it. I felt the shame of that hit me as soon as I thought it, and this shame was what I'd avoided all these years. I hadn't been weak to leave, I'd been weak to stay – weak to pander to him, weak to grovel and soothe and apologise. I'd been telling myself the wrong story about that relationship and why it ended for years.

As I catapulted back through the years, my thoughts turned again to Robyn. I would hate Robyn to feel ashamed of having stayed with Andy until now. She needed love and was guilty only of empathising too much so that she lost sight of herself and colluded in Andy's bad behaviour. They'd co-created an unhealthy dynamic. She had nothing to be ashamed of and maybe then neither did I. Robyn and I were so similar, as were Andy and Andre. Andy had been guilty of manipulating Robyn's empathic, caring, see-the-good-in-everyone nature and maybe so had Andre. The wine was having an effect and all four of us – me, Robyn, Andre and

Andy – swirled and mingled together in my mind until I could no longer distinguish between us.

I got up and lit a fire in the chimenea. As I wrapped a blanket from the house around myself and pulled it tight, John's memory lecture drifted into my mind. I'd remembered and interpreted a key event in my life a certain way for years and now I was questioning that memory and interpretation. If I'd been wise and strong to make the decision to leave Andre, as Robyn was undoubtedly being with Andy, then did that change who I was? Did it change how I saw myself? Was I not the weak people-pleaser who'd sold her soul after all? My head swam, the heavy thoughts, the wine – I couldn't think about it anymore.

Sam suddenly appeared.

"I can't sleep Mum, it's too hot in my room," he moaned sleepily.

I opened the blanket and signalled him to get in with me and we lay curled up together in the dusk, watching the fire and the night insects that were buzzing chaotically round it. I heard his breathing slowly change as he started to drift into sleep and although I couldn't quite see his eyes I could imagine them, heavy like mine, closing against his will.

Sometime later, Mathew came home and found us like that. He smiled at me, touched by the scene, and I smiled back, suddenly aware of how much I loved him and how loved he made me feel. He carried Sam up to bed, poured himself a glass of wine and we sat together on the swing seat chatting about his day. There would always be that one terrible dark cloud that could never be erased, but I felt more at peace than I had for years.

Chapter 10

I simultaneously both dreaded and looked forward to sessions with Stephen. It wasn't that I was afraid of him and who he might have been in the past – I no longer thought about that much – but the sessions were intense and I felt totally transparent and exposed with him. Stephen could read the slightest change in my expression and equally I could read his expression as he registered that change. Because he was trying to figure out who he was, he was highly attuned to how others responded to him; the reflection of himself in others was all he had to know himself by. If I was distracted for example, I could see instantly that he spotted it and I would have to explain where my head had gone. It had invariably gone somewhere in the service of helping him – I was never thinking about what to have for dinner or something not connected to Stephen – but Stephen could easily misinterpret my distraction. If someone looks distracted the obvious explanation is that they're bored, and that was never ever the case in our sessions. Far from it; usually I was trying to marry some theory with what Stephen was saying, or thinking hard about how to respond to something profound and insightful that he had just said. Once, when he seemed particularly distressed, I was trying to work out if I could fit in an extra session with him that week.

And it wasn't just distraction that Stephen spotted. If I was confused, sceptical, apprehensive, unsure of myself, in awe of him, or any of the other myriad of reactions I might feel in that hour, I watched Stephen's face register it. It was an unnerving and totally honest way of relating, both deeply satisfying and totally exhausting!

I had drip fed John's memory theories into our sessions. I hadn't bombarded him with it all in one go as John had done with me, but I had challenged how he could know that the bleeding man image was definitely a flashback, and then explained some of the Elisabeth Loftus stuff about the suggestibility and fallibility of memory. He had been fascinated, relieved and confused in equal measure. If it wasn't a flashback, where did it come from? If it was an image from a dream, or TV or someone else, why had it implanted itself in his brain so tenaciously?

I also encouraged him to consider that, even if it was a flashback, then just like a photograph, it had only captured one moment in time. He had no way of knowing what happened immediately before it. His fear could lead him to fabricate other events around that one moment, to suggest explanations that would then morph into 'memories' that may or may not be totally false. It wouldn't necessarily tell him the truth.

We became archaeologists, excavating around the image, both of us now keeping an open mind, carefully not jumping to conclusions about what it might mean. We were truth seekers, but truth seekers who knew and accepted – at least in theory – that we could never actually know the truth.

That meant we had also talked a lot about the wider issues of not knowing who he was, about what it meant that he might never know the truth of his own story. Stephen found the idea discombobulating and depressing. I helped him to articulate his fears and concerns which mainly centred on his inability to relate to others if he didn't know how to be.

Although I listened and tried hard to empathise, I found I couldn't fully appreciate Stephen's concerns. I think because of my own experience of relating to him deeply, not in spite of but *because* of his memory loss, I found it hard to afford his fear any significance. He was so totally present, so grounded *in* the present precisely because he had nowhere else to be. It was a unique and extraordinary experience to spend time with someone like that. Our connection was profound and so I held a much less bleak picture of his future relationships.

I hadn't challenged his view yet, or pointed out explicitly that our own relating seemed to refute his fears. Despite our connection, it felt too early in our relationship somehow – I'd only seen him four times and we'd delved into very weighty areas already. I didn't want to challenge everything and leave him feeling isolated again. It was important to try to *understand* how he felt, not change it all at once. Tempting though that often was, it wouldn't work – the paradoxical theory of change: that to change we must first accept things as they are. In college, we'd been taught not to rush to vanquish every unpleasant emotion; our job was meant to be to understand, to help the client articulate and to support them to do whatever they needed to do to move forward. It was so hard though, my pervasive need to fix was forever getting in the way, especially with Stephen somehow, and I fought to push it away.

That said, I reasoned that I was a real human being in this relationship too. His concern was about relating and here we were, relating. I could use my experience of him to help him gain insight into how others might experience him, couldn't I? I could be the mirror he was seeking in order to see himself more clearly. It was all about timing and balance I decided – exploring, respecting and valuing his experience and, when the time was right, congruently sharing mine.

Usually very thoughtful and measured, Stephen burst through the door that day looking rushed, dishevelled and excited. He started speaking while he was still closing the door. He was barely in the room, let alone in the chair.

"It's not all a blank!" he blurted out.

I was taken aback and took a moment to catch up. I had been about to offer him a glass of water as usual but didn't want to cut across what he was saying. I gestured with the jug and an empty glass while trying to grasp what he was saying.

"Really?"

He nodded yes to the water and flopped into the chair.

"Yes, it never has been, I just didn't realise. I'd been looking for the wrong things!"

"It never has been?" Now I was really confused. I poured water for us both and sat down, already fully engaged and with my mind whirling. Had his memory come back? Had it never been away?

"No, it never has been. There's a trace, there's always been a trace!" He grinned at me.

I imagined he wanted me to share his elation but I was still struggling to know what on earth he was talking about. "I don't understand Stephen. You'll have to explain more."

"OK, OK…" He took a deep breath and sat back. "So I was at a friend's house, Barry's, I think I've talked about him."

I nodded. Barry was a new friend Stephen had met in hospital, someone he felt no pressure to be a particular way with.

"And this guy arrived, a friend of his apparently, called Joe, and he obviously recognised me. I didn't recognise him of course but I felt an instant aversion to him. It was really strong, but I had no idea what it was about. He went white when he recognised me and started behaving really oddly. He kept looking at me as if he'd better not let me out of his sight or I might actually kill him. He looked really scared of me and I just felt this… aversion. I can't describe it any other way, but I had no idea who he was or how I knew him. I just knew he was bad news!"

I thought of the flashback and wondered if there was a connection. Yet again I felt momentarily apprehensive as I remembered that I was sitting alone in a room with a man neither of us really knew anything about. Stephen didn't look scared though, not like he had been about the bleeding man vision. He looked excited so I anticipated that this story probably had a safe ending. Any fear I had felt must have been fleeting because for once Stephen didn't seem to pick up on it. I had never seen him so animated.

"Barry thought it was all very weird. He hadn't known him long but he'd never seen him behave like that apparently. Anyway, the guy left pretty quickly and I went home soon after thinking how weird it was to have such a strong reaction to someone I didn't know. I mean it's been three years since the accident and I'd never met him and no one had ever mentioned someone called Joe so I couldn't see how he could possibly have been part of my life. So, I arrived home still a bit distracted trying to work it all out and Tom was there."

Tom was Stephen's younger brother.

"And he said, 'Penny for 'em' so I told him and then he started acting strange too. Then I knew there really was something going on, so I said 'what?', and he said 'nothing' and looked guilty and secretive and concerned all at once. Anyway, to cut a long story short he eventually said to ask Sally."

Sally was Stephen's girlfriend before the accident. Seemingly they'd been going out for about a year when he fell off the scaffolding, and they'd apparently been happy. When he woke from the coma and didn't recognise anyone it was hard for them all, but his family were his family whether he knew them or not. To continue a relationship with someone who was now a stranger to him relied on him falling for Sally a second time. It didn't happen. Gradually they had mutually agreed that it wasn't going to work but they had stayed in touch, not friends exactly, but more than acquaintances, bound by a history that he could no longer remember.

"So, I called Sally and told her what had happened and she went quiet and said to come round, she didn't want to tell me on the phone. So I went round and she told me all about this scumbag! It turns out he'd been her boyfriend before me and he'd been violent and abusive. When she'd eventually had enough and plucked up the courage to leave, he raped her and beat her so badly she'd been hospitalised! We met soon after that and we were together when it finally went to court eighteen months later. This was about six months before the accident apparently. During the attack she'd somehow managed to dial 999 and, although she couldn't speak, the line had been kept open and so there was a recording of him beating her and her screaming and pleading with him until the police arrived. They played it in court. I imagine it was horrendous for everyone to listen to that, especially Sally. My God, what a brave woman!"

He suddenly stopped, obviously emotional and needing to compose himself before he could speak again.

"She said I was a rock."

His moist eyes locked directly on to mine – that connection again – and I knew what that meant to him; more evidence that he was one of the good guys. I felt emotion tingle along my thighs and up the back of my neck.

He took a deep breath to steady his voice. "All through the build up to the trial, before we were together even, I was a rock, apparently. She said she wouldn't have gone through it if I hadn't been there for her. In the court room that day, she had been prepared by the prosecution lawyers that the tape would be played and everyone expected and understood that she might not be able to stay and listen to it, but she said I held her so tightly, wrapped her up in my arms and she felt safe, protected. I was between her and him for the whole trial, but as they played the tape I wrapped her in my arms and just glared at him she said, daring him to so much as look at her. Sally and I talked about it for hours. She was obviously emotional remembering it and I was emotional imagining it. I don't love Sally in a romantic way anymore but I do have a kind of love for her. And even if I didn't I would feel for anyone going through that. It's just horrendous! We both cried a bit."

It wasn't the moment to point out that that thought, right there, that reaction to Sally, said something about who he was, what kind of person he was. His reactions in the present, to the present, were relevant too. He spent so long looking for clues about who he was. He studied reactions in others and asked questions about the past yet he discounted his own feelings and responses in the now. I saw him register something in my face as I thought how much I really admired him and he looked momentarily puzzled. He obviously also decided that now wasn't the moment and carried on.

"After the accident, when I first woke up, they were all told to keep things as calm and stable as possible for me. No stress, the doctors said. So they all decided not to tell me about what had happened to Sally straight away and then later on, when I was well enough, the moment had past and it just never happened. Even when they all heard he was being released from prison, they decided it was so unlikely that I would meet him, and even if I did I wouldn't remember anyway. They decided there was no point in telling me and upsetting me."

His relief that a fragment of his memory had finally

returned was evidently greater than his frustration with his family for not telling him about this.

"Later, at home, I was trying to process everything I'd just heard and I went back to the aversion I felt when I met him and suddenly realised that although I didn't know him, in some way I kind of did! I had no memory of anything Sally told me – no memory of the story – but my response to him was spot on! A bit muted perhaps, rage and hatred might have been more appropriate, but I knew something! Don't you see? It's not a total blank!"

This time I did get it. I didn't understand how, but I did clearly appreciate that his memory wasn't totally lost. I felt both his excitement and my own for him.

"Yes, absolutely! I get it, I really do… but how…?"

"I have absolutely no idea, and right now I don't care." He literally beamed. "It's not a blank!"

"So, although you don't remember the facts, the events themselves, the story if you like, you have a sort of… emotional memory?"

I learnt a long time later about the theory of implicit and explicit memory and the fact that the way we store events in our brains is complex and not limited to one brain region. We have an explicit or 'declarative' memory, a story we can tell about something that happened, and separate implicit, process and muscle memories. One famous study involved a woman with no short-term memory who greeted her psychologist every morning as though she'd never met him before.

One morning he hid a pin in his hand as he went to shake hers. The next day, despite the fact that she still didn't remember ever having met him before, she wouldn't shake his hand! She had retained a 'memory' that shaking his hand wasn't a good idea even though she had no idea why. Stephen had lost his declarative memory but only his declarative memory, not the rest.

Back then though, neither Stephen nor I had any explanation for what he had experienced. We were both delighted, bewildered and astonished that he could have had an appropriate emotional reaction to someone he couldn't remember.

We talked for a while about what this meant to him and then, tentatively, I braved the question that had been niggling away at the back of my mind since he told me about first meeting Joe.

"Stephen, what do you make of Joe's reaction to you?"

"Of the fact that he looked scared of me, you mean?"

"You said he looked like he thought you might kill him."

Stephen's deep brown eyes locked onto mine again and I imagined I actually saw them physically darken. His expression was indecipherable. *Shit, shit, shit!* I often struggled to distinguish what was mine and what was a client's so I didn't know whether I was empathising accurately with his fear that he had done something to the bleeding man or whether it was my own fear I was feeling. Before I said it, it had felt important to bring up the elephant in the room. *'If something is being avoided, nothing else gets worked on'. Who said that? Yalom, I think.* But now, as he stared at me with those eyes, I wondered if I had just inadvertently disclosed some repressed uncertainty about whether or not he was actually a violent monster.

"You know me really well, don't you?"

He didn't break eye contact and I saw a glimmer of hope that I hadn't just completely screwed up. I still didn't let out the breath I had become aware I was holding though, not yet.

"What do you mean?"

"Joe's reaction really, really worried me. I'm guessing you knew that though, that's why you brought it up."

I finally allowed myself to breathe but still, neither of us broke eye contact. I was goosepimply again. The connection was intense.

"I thought you might be feeling something like that, yes."

Stephen continued to stare, holding me with his eyes, locking me in.

"The thing is…" He finally looked away and broke the spell. "The thing is, how can you know me when I don't know myself? I didn't think that was possible, yet you do it all the time."

His eyes weren't focussed on anything at all now, he was looking inside himself, trying to puzzle it out.

"How do you do it?"

Suddenly the eyes were back, boring into mine. I was mesmerised.

I eventually realised that it was a question and that it was my turn to speak. I mentally shook myself out of whatever it was that was holding me so that I could attend to the basics of normal everyday relating.

How do I do it? "It's not actually that hard Stephen. It's not hard to know you. You seem to imagine that it is." I didn't really think about what I was saying, I just honestly shared my experience of him.

Now it was his turn to be flustered. "I do imagine that it's hard. I don't understand why it isn't."

"It isn't because you communicate all the time how you're feeling, how you're reacting to something. Sometimes you tell me in words, but often it's just written all over your face. Like when you first told me about the bleeding man image. It was obvious that you were really scared that you'd hurt him, and that fear actually says something about the kind of person you are. I guess somehow I add all of those different reactions and responses together and piece together a kind of picture of you. Isn't that what we all do with everyone we meet? We observe them in the present and form conclusions about them. We don't need to know their history necessarily."

"I guess." Stephen was wary.

"Like earlier, when you were telling me about the conversation with Sally, you were suddenly moved when you told me about her saying that you were a rock during the court case. I instantly knew why because of all the things we'd talked about before, about not knowing what kind of person you were. I knew that her saying that was evidence that you were one of the good guys. I knew what that meant to you because I already know what's important to you *now*. I can also make assumptions about your character precisely *because* it's so important to you to be one of the good guys, because it matters to you to be a decent bloke. And I can believe my assumptions are correct because I saw the emotion, the relief, in your response when you told me about that. It all forms the picture. So yes, I believe I do know you well. I believe that I know everything I need to about you."

We both stopped as we simultaneously realised the full implications of what I'd just said. The words weren't explicit but somehow we both knew what I meant. I hadn't even realised myself that that was how I felt before it came out of my mouth; I hadn't realised that I really did feel safe now with Stephen, that I wasn't frightened anymore by what he might have done. I trusted him as he was now and his past was irrelevant to that.

Stephen spoke slowly, checking out what he thought he'd heard. "I thought we were keeping an open mind about the bleeding man. Are you saying that you don't think that I hurt him now?"

"Honestly... I still don't know Stephen."

His face fell slightly and he looked down at his

hands, which were entwined together on his lap. I felt a twinge of guilt as I knew how he had really wanted me to answer that question, but this was a time for honesty not platitudes. This was important.

"I don't know who you *were*. I can only know who you *are*. I'll admit, I was scared at first…"

I was acutely aware how delicate this was, how hard this might be to hear, but I really believed if he could hear me out, my message wasn't a painful one.

"I think anyone would've been. I didn't know you at all and you described a violent scene that neither of us understood. I didn't know what kind of man you were. But the more time I've spent with you, the more that fear has diminished. As I said, I can never know who you *were*, but I have a hard time imagining that the Stephen I've met would hurt anyone or anything. And I have met you Stephen. We have really *met*, haven't we?"

"Yes… yes we have." He looked at me briefly and I knew that he understood the way I was using the word.

"So, I do know you then don't I? You as you are now?" I pushed him to acknowledge it, like the proverbial dog with a bone.

"Yes… I guess you do."

"And I think that you also know yourself as you are now. You know that you're not a violent man." I wouldn't let it drop and failed to register Stephen's discomfort and unusual lack of eye contact.

"No… no, I don't think that I am… not now at least."

"Isn't now all that matters?" I was so pleased with

my brilliant rhetoric, and fully expected an appropriate eureka reaction from him.

"Maybe... but what if there's a small part of me that's different? A part I haven't met since the accident, a switch that can be flipped by something I haven't come across yet, that triggers some sort of violent rage?"

As he challenged me, I finally noticed the distance between us. I failed to register that we'd actually reached an important insight, uncovered another layer. Instead, my heart sank. I'd wanted Stephen to like himself so much that I'd practically tried to force him to feel the way I wanted him to and ignored all the rules and theory of therapy. *Damn!*

I berated myself. Rules and processes were there for a reason. I'd been so genuine, so honest and direct, and I thought that I had been so clever, but I'd stopped following the client. *It's supposed to be 'client-led' Maggie, you idiot!* I'd stopped following Stephen and tried to impose my own perspective instead. I'd had such a strong agenda for Stephen to feel at peace with himself that I'd stopped listening to him. It was lucky Stephen had felt able to say what he had and we had uncovered another layer to his fear, despite his lousy therapist. I wondered if I did this with other clients too, and whether some of them just stayed quiet rather than disagree with me. *Shit, I'm never going to get this stuff right!*

I weakly continued in the same vein, whilst looking for a way out.

"Don't we all live with that possibility to some degree? I mean, some people argue that every single one of us is capable of murder in the right, or rather in the wrong, circumstances."

"I never thought about it like that." He didn't look hugely impressed with the idea; it didn't appear to reassure him.

"It sounds like you imagine that your trigger, your switch, is more sensitive than most though and therefore more easily triggered. Like you think it would be triggered by less extreme circumstances than the hypothetical average person, and that would give you more of a tendency to violence?" Now I was getting back on track, exploring his experience rather than sharing mine. *That's better, Maggie.*

"Yes, absolutely. That's exactly how I feel!" He looked a bit surprised, like he hadn't realised until that moment that this was the belief he carried round.

I waited while he thought about that. I thought I'd better stay out of his way this time and anyway, we were taught that sometimes empathy – really identifying what's going on for someone – is actually more challenging than a more obvious direct challenge.

"I don't actually know why I think that…" He was clearly deep in thought. I waited. "There's no evidence for that really, is there?" He was challenging himself.

"Is there any evidence to the contrary?"

"… I don't know."

I assumed this was because his head was spinning

rather than because he really didn't know, so I waded in to give him the benefit of my wisdom again! I really couldn't let this drop. John would be horrified!

"It seems to me that you have three years that you can remember, and presumably you've had the same triggers for anger in those three years as the rest of us. You haven't been in some sort of protected anger-free bubble. You've been exposed to lots of triggers and yet you haven't been overwhelmed with violent rage."

"I suppose." Stephen looked thoughtful, and sad if anything. If I had been hoping to see a eureka moment again, then yet again I was going to be disappointed. I didn't have the experience not to expect that kind of breakthrough. I knew the theory though, and the theory said that if Stephen was ever going to accept this, he was going to need time to think about it, to play around with it for himself and to come to his own conclusions. I really did need to back off.

*

After the session, I pottered about making my ritual between sessions cup of tea and contemplated what would have happened if I hadn't pushed it. What if I had let him continue to muse on the fact that there was no real evidence to back up his belief that his trigger for violence was more sensitive and prone to go off than most people's? Maybe he would have got there himself if I hadn't interrupted his thoughts.

As it was he seemed entrenched in his fear that he was somehow bad, and I finally started to ask why he was so attached to this belief. What if I was missing something else entirely? What if the belief was nothing to do with the bleeding man image? Thinking about it, what if it was actually a schema, a core belief about his very identity that he formed a long time ago, way before his accident? It was certainly behaving like a schema in that it seemed resistant to rational argument, even my brilliant rational arguments! It was likely, from our many conversations about it, that even Stephen no longer truly believed that he had done something unilaterally malicious to the bleeding man, assuming it was actually a memory anyway.

So, if 'I'm bad' was somehow a core belief Stephen formed in childhood, could it be true that he would continue to hold onto that belief even with amnesia? What if core beliefs work like the emotional trace memory he had when he met Joe? Would it work like that? I had no idea. I wished I knew more about the brain and memory and schemas, and actually just more about everything. Once again, I felt incompetent and nowhere near up to the job. A better therapist would have at least considered that much earlier on and could have helped Stephen so much more by now as a result.

I was suddenly very tired. At least I could hold onto the fact that I had got something right with Robyn. I smiled at the memory of her strength and self-sufficiency. Yes, that was exactly what I'd hoped for Robyn. I couldn't be that bad a therapist. Could I?

Chapter 11

When Robyn walked through the door for our next session she was glowing! The strength and self-assurance from last time were still visible in her body language somehow, but there was something else too. I waited, curious and eager to build on the huge gains of our last session.

"Well, he contacted me," she began. "The day after our last session, he called and asked if he could come round."

I waited, staying out of her way, dying to know what had happened and how the newly self-appreciating Robyn had handled it.

"I wasn't sure what he was going to say, but I could tell from his tone that he was remorseful and I knew that would weaken my resolve so I said we could meet but not at my place. I wanted to be able to leave when I'd had enough, not have to wait for him to go or, worse still, try to make him leave if he didn't. Just me deciding where we would and wouldn't meet seemed to shift the dynamic between us again. I felt empowered, and I guess he felt that change in me too somehow."

I smiled professionally and encouragingly but inside I was beaming and fist punching the air. *Go girl!*

"We went to the park. I thought we could go to that little coffee shop or if that felt awkward we could go for a walk, and there are lots of people around to minimise the chances of a scene. He started as I expected, apologising for being a prat about Pete and saying he knew that Pete was just a friend really, but that he missed me so much and was so desperate for us to be together again, that seeing Pete and me obviously so emotionally close made him see red.

"It was a kind of plea, I guess, for me to understand him again, forgive him again. He didn't quite say he couldn't help it but that felt like the subtext. I felt myself starting to empathise with his perspective, I could easily understand why he would feel the way he felt and so I said exactly that, and I saw him relax, but then I added, 'But what about me?'. He looked confused so I said, 'Do you know how your anger and sulks make me feel?'."

She had come so far since our first meeting; the Robyn I had met all those weeks ago would never have advocated for herself like that.

"That's how we started," she continued. "We talked for ages. I said stuff that I never dreamed I'd ever say to him, but I think it was because I had nothing to lose. I couldn't carry on the old way and I knew that, so I said it all: how scared I was of his anger, not physically but emotionally, how terrified I was of abandonment. I even told him about the Lake District and how I realised that I could be truly alive without him, that I knew now that I didn't *need* him even though I still *wanted* him. I even said that I believed he was truly remorseful about hitting me and actually I believed that it wouldn't happen again, but I also said that his anger generally was a big issue, one that I couldn't ignore anymore.

"I told him that I couldn't carry on apologising and soothing and making up for things whenever he sulked or got angry. I told him that he behaved like a spoilt brat at times and that I wasn't going to continue to be a foil for that; I wasn't going to continue to pretend that it was my fault when usually it was him behaving like a prick. And I told him how much the fact that he let me be that foil hurt. It meant that somehow he actually believed that it was my fault that he was angry every time it happened, and so in his eyes it was my responsibility to make it right again. I said that I couldn't be with someone who saw me as being that wrong all the time."

I felt so proud of her that I didn't even think about maintaining a neutral expression.

"I didn't realise that I was actually going to say those words until they came out of my mouth, but suddenly it was that clear: I couldn't stay with him. He looked really taken aback. He hadn't expected it at all either, I could tell... and I felt really sorry for him. I mean, this wasn't just a specific act we were talking about anymore, a one-off behaviour that I couldn't forgive.

This was a character trait. I was saying that who he was, some of the time, was so bad that the wonderful human being that he was the rest of the time didn't compensate for it and that it wasn't OK.

"He looked completely crestfallen and I knew that meant he'd truly understood what I was saying, but it also meant that I did too, for the first time. I'd thought about what it would mean to me to lose him from my life but I hadn't really thought about him… I thought I had, but I hadn't really. And I definitely hadn't prepared myself for what it would feel like to hurt someone so much. In that moment I wanted to take it all back and put my arms around him and tell him we were OK. Suddenly I couldn't look at him. I just wanted to cry."

I wanted to cry too at this point. This was everything she'd been struggling with, everything she'd talked about in our sessions, concentrated in one single moment. The choice between her integrity and her relationship; between her self-respect and her need to love and be loved. She had touched all those contradictory needs in that one moment. We both knew she'd done the right thing, that she couldn't un-see what had now become so clear to her, but I also knew – because I felt it almost physically – just how hard that had been for her.

"We sat there in silence for several moments, both of us fighting back the tears, and then he left. He stood up and looked me in the eye and said that I would never know how sorry he was. He said that I should always know that I was the best thing that ever happened to him and that he would never forgive himself for screwing it up. And then he left. I sat there numb for God knows how long, arguing with myself, trying to find a reason to undo everything I'd just done. I have never felt so wretched."

The thing with empathy, as I later learnt, is that it is embodied. I genuinely felt everything she was feeling at that point because my body and brain were mirroring hers. Back then though, I understood nothing about the science of empathy, only that I too felt wretched; I too felt the sadness, the loss, the senselessness, the waste, the certainty, the doubt, and above all of that, the calm that comes from knowing it was absolutely the right thing to do.

"And then he came back."

Suddenly, reality ripped like a bad advert. I almost heard the upward rasp of the tear. Whatever imaginary sad tune had been playing in my head stopped abruptly. Robyn was grinning from ear to ear and I knew, without her saying anything more. *Oh no! Please no!*

"Oh Maggie, he was wonderful. He accepted everything I'd said totally and knew it was true. He said he recognised everything happened exactly like I saw it. He didn't know why he behaved like that but he saw that he did. But he said that he couldn't just give up on us though, that I really was the best thing that ever happened to him and so he couldn't just walk away. He said that he was going to do everything it took to understand and change his behaviour, not just empty promises, he was going to start by getting therapy to sort out why he did it and how to change."

Her words were tumbling over each other, she was so excited and relieved I guess, to find the reason she'd been looking for to undo what she'd just done. Suddenly she looked so very young. My heart sank.

"He told me about Nietzsche's concept of eternal return. Have you heard about that?"

I shook my head dully. I wasn't really interested anymore. *Oh Robyn.*

"Nietzsche said that if the universe is truly infinite, then everything in it is repeated infinitely. Which means that each of our lives must be repeated infinitely and so we should live in a way that we would be happy to have repeated forever. We should live *this* life in a way that will be OK when we return, repeatedly and infinitely, to it. No regrets. Isn't that brilliant?"

I didn't know what to say but what I was thinking was, *smooth bastard!*

"You don't approve do you?" Robyn had seen my expression, which admittedly I hadn't thought to put much effort into hiding, I'd been too shocked by her about-turn. "You know what I'm going to say and you don't approve."

"I don't know Robyn. I have to trust your instincts on this. I don't know Andy like you do." It was weak and implausible but it was the best I could do. "Tell me why you took him back. Help me to see this as you do."

Robyn looked dubious; she was far too astute to be anything else. "If you'd been truly listening to me over the past five and a half months then you'd already see it like I do," she said, almost under her breath.

I felt like I'd been winded. If she believed what she'd just said then our whole relationship, and therefore the whole of her therapy, was suddenly in jeopardy. All I could do to save it would be to be totally congruent, transparently honest and hope that protected enough mutual respect. I certainly couldn't pretend that I did approve, it was already too late for that, and she was far too perceptive, even if I was inclined towards that kind of deception, which I wasn't.

Robyn sighed. "I took him back because he accepted everything I said. He didn't argue or try to wheedle out of it, he accepted totally that his sulks were a problem, that his anger was a problem and that they were both his problems to resolve. And he took steps to resolve them straightaway. He's already booked his first therapy appointment."

"And you think he really can change?"

"I think anyone can change and so do you, otherwise why would you do this job?"

Touché

"Look, I didn't just leap back into his arms if that's what you're thinking. I didn't agree straightaway. We talked for a long, long time and he's clear that I'm not going back to how we were. We even agreed a code-word for when I'm feeling scared of him leaving me emotionally, for if and when he sulks again and it gets to me. We agreed that when I use that word we'll both take time out to sort out what's going on for each of us before we talk about it. That way I don't have to challenge him directly in the moment, which I know I can't do, not yet anyway. But maybe this way, I'll actually get there one day.

"Because it's not really just his problem, is it? It's a dynamic that we both play a part in. He gets unreasonably angry and that's his problem but I collude in that by soothing and cajoling and pretending that it's my fault. That's what we've been working on here isn't it, my part in that dynamic. Well, I have changed so why can't he? I won't accept responsibility for stuff that isn't my fault anymore, although it still won't be easy in the moment. It'll take practice and I've got bad habits to change, just as he has. But we've agreed to help each other and started that process by having a code-word to signal that we're doing it again."

It sounded credible and in fact, years later, the idea that relationship problems are always co-created became a cornerstone of my couple-counselling work. However, at the time I couldn't see past my dismay that he'd won. He'd persuaded her to go back, and it felt like everything we'd achieved would now unravel. I couldn't see how she could hold onto her fledgling self-belief with him around. It would work for a while probably – he'd be on his best behaviour – but eventually he'd revert to type and then so would she.

"I thought you'd be different." Robyn's eyes, disappointed a moment earlier, hardened. "I thought you'd be all for giving people a chance, a chance to change. I expected this kind of doubt from my parents but I really thought you'd be different."

"You're angry with me." I fell back on the ever-valuable process intervention. Observing that the client is angry with you serves two purposes: the official line is that it helps the client to articulate that anger, but it also depersonalises it somehow for the therapist. Suddenly, there's a professional distance: *here we are discussing all your feelings. They're nothing to do with me, not really.*

"Damn right I'm angry with you!"

"Can you put that anger into words?" Sickly sweet, dripping sincerity. *I don't mind what you say, do your worst, I can take it, I'm here for you. Shit Maggie, really?*

"I really thought that at least you would understand, that you'd actually be pleased for me." And suddenly she was a little girl wanting approval, wanting me to say, 'Well done Robyn, good for you!'.

"And because I don't seem pleased for you, you feel... what?"

"Like it's me and Andy against the world!" She stuck her chin out like a five-year-old, belligerent, defiant.

"Umm-hmm." *Shit, Sam would go mad!*

Robyn does too although she doesn't comment on it

directly. "The thing is, how can you possibly do this job? How do you justify being in the business of people changing, if you don't believe it? It's a bit hypocritical isn't it?"

"I do believe people can change." *I think I do anyway, just not maybe people like Andre and Andy.* "I don't know Andy, I know you. If Andy was sitting in front of me instead of you, who knows what I would think. But he's not, you are, and so everything I do and say is done and said with the intention of being in your best interests."

"So you don't think it's in my best interests to go back to Andy?"

"Honestly? I don't know." There it was, said out loud.

"Well, thank you for being honest at least." There was a long silence. "Is it him you don't trust or me?"

"I don't understand."

"Either you don't trust him to change…"

"I don't know him." I interrupted.

She ignored me and spoke over my words. "Or you don't trust me to keep up the changes I've made." Her eyes were challenging now.

Damn, this girl was sharp! There was no going back now, all I had was honesty.

"I guess I'm concerned that it's too soon. The changes you've made are still new, they haven't had a chance to bed in… in easier circumstances."

"Easier than Andy, you mean." The challenging,

petulant tone was still very much apparent.

"Well, as you said, you *both* have to change and in your case at least, I know you're talking about changing the habits of a whole lifetime. It's only been a few short weeks out of that whole lifetime that you have actually started listening to yourself and trusting yourself. And, as you also said, actually *speaking* your own truth is still very hard, understandably so. It's going to take practice and hard work."

Robyn stopped looking pointedly down and peered sideways and upwards at me through her fringe. Her lips were still pursed but I had her attention. *Please let this work!*

"Andy has his own work to do and I'm glad he's making a start."

Robyn snorted her disbelief and looked away again.

I continued regardless. "But you and he are undoubtedly going to get in each other's way. His way of being is going to be difficult for you to stand up to, and your way of being makes it easy for him not to change. As you said, you collude in his issues."

"We're going to help each other. The code-word thing will work. We'll be able to work through our shit together!"

"I'm not saying that you won't, only that I believe that it'll be harder for each of you if you're together."

Am I really saying that? Have I strayed from my plan to be totally congruent? Actually the honest answer was that I really didn't think that they could work through their shit together, or at least I didn't think that Robyn could with Andy in the picture. I knew how hard I found it, still found it, to speak from my own wisdom. Even with Mathew – kind, gentle Mathew who had proven time and again that he would stick by me come what may, whatever horrific, tragic mistakes I made – I still feared abandonment too much to really speak my mind most of the time. It would never in a million years have been possible with Andre. And at her age? I had nearly two decades on her. I could never have done it at her age.

"I've had enough of this!" Robyn stood up and moved towards the door.

I glanced quickly at the clock, we still had ten minutes left. With her hand on the door handle she turned and looked at me sadly.

"The wise whisperer made this decision Maggie. One day you'll see that. I'm not going to change my mind."

And then she was gone, leaving me staring at the back of the door, wondering what the hell I'd just done.

*

"You didn't do anything."

Mathew was trying to reassure me. Now I was not only struggling with how badly I'd handled the session with Robyn, I would also have to live with the fact that I'd talked to Mathew about a client. I'd done it anonymously of course and told him the absolute bare minimum – just that I had a young client struggling with whether to stay with her aggressive boyfriend and that she'd decided to go back to him and had seen my disapproval – but it was still a breach of confidentiality.

"How could you approve? She's making a big mistake."

"It's my job to stay neutral, to help the client find their own answers, not decide for them. I don't even know the guy."

"But you know his type, and they don't change."

"As she said, everyone can change, it's my job to help people who want to change. I'm a counsellor for Christ's sake, I should have been able to keep an open mind rather than pigeonholing someone I've never even met."

"Yes, but you're a human being too and if you care about this girl – which you clearly do – and you can see it's a mistake, then it's bound to show, isn't it?"

I appreciated Mathew for trying but this wasn't helping. I felt a sick feeling in the pit of my stomach every time I thought about Robyn, about the session, and now for talking to Mathew about it too.

I hadn't intended to tell him anything but he couldn't avoid seeing that there was something wrong, and when I tried to say it was just work, I sensed he was offended and I feared another sulk. I really couldn't face that tonight so I tried to tell him just enough that he wouldn't feel shut out. Then I ended up saying more as he tried to help me to feel better. I realised with bitter irony that Robyn, despite her youth, was already dealing with her fear of emotional abandonment better than I was. I'd put Mathew's feelings and my fear of the consequences above professional ethics! *Shit Maggie!*

What a mess! I realised that all the times I'd been insecure about my practice in the past was just that, insecurity. The complexity of human nature meant that any relationship, including professional ones, would never be straightforward and I would never do everything perfectly right, but this, here with Robyn, this was what a real fuck-up looked like!

I wondered what she was doing now. Was she talking to Andy about our session? Were they bitching about how the world doesn't understand them? Had I turned them into star-crossed lovers? Had I thrown them even closer together?

I tried to imagine what I could've done differently, what I should've done, but I couldn't come up with anything. The problem was, I realised, that I did actually have an agenda. I wasn't as neutral as I'd thought. I had really wanted her to leave him. Maybe not at the beginning, when I was reminded of what it was like to be young and in love, but certainly lately, when she was finding herself and liking what she found. Everything she said about him from then on had rang alarm bells in my head and I was sure he was no good for her. I could've tried to hide my feelings from her when she'd told me she'd taken him back but that would've been totally incongruent. Congruence – counsellors being genuine, authentic and transparent – is one of the three essential conditions for therapy to succeed (according to Rogers) so what was I supposed to do?

*

"But what about empathy?" John challenged me two days later. "Yes, you were congruent and yes, you could possibly argue that you had unconditional positive regard for her, but all three conditions are required. You lost the empathy for the part of her that loves him."

"I definitely have unconditional positive regard for Robyn." I felt bad enough without criticism that was unfounded, and I wasn't so humiliated and desolate that I couldn't defend myself.

"You think?"

"I think that Robyn is a wonderful, wonderful person and I have never judged her."

"But you don't trust her judgement. You don't trust her to know what's best for herself."

"Unconditional positive regard doesn't mean that I have to agree with everything she does or that I don't think that she will ever make mistakes does it? It just means that I respect her *intent* to make the best decisions for herself based on the information and experience she has. That I respect her as a human being doing her best."

"OK, but what about the empathy?"

Bloody hell! Did I just win an argument with John? Was that just him backing down?

"I don't know. At first I definitely had empathy for the part of her that loves him. I even thought that I had too much empathy for that part."

"Too much empathy?"

"Well, I identified I guess, and didn't want her to lose that." I remembered how much that had been true at the beginning, how Robyn had woken a passion in me that I had buried long ago. Maybe because I hadn't really been neutral then either, I had somehow subconsciously steered her to this point. So I had started this work wanting her to stay, to have what I thought I'd lost when I left Andre, and ended it wanting her to leave because she had found her voice in a way that I was still unable to achieve. Was neutrality a myth then, unattainable in practice? Or just apparently impossible for me?

"Maybe Robyn has done the work you still need to do for yourself." John read my mind. "Maybe she's ahead of you."

"Thanks!" I responded sarcastically in a weak attempt at humour.

"Sometimes it's easier to help a client to do something than to do it ourselves. The clients do our own growth work for us."

*

On the drive home I thought about all my clients one by

one. Was I really helping any of them? How could I help someone with terminal cancer anyway? What difference could I possibly make? And the suicidal teenager? Yes, he wasn't discussing suicidal thoughts anymore, but maybe that would've happened anyway. Maybe time was the healer, not therapy. And my gentleman with depression? Well a lot of people recover naturally from depression after a few months without any interventions.

Sure, there's plenty of research evidence that talking therapies are at least as effective as pills, but what about *my* talking therapy? How would I know whether or not *my* talking therapy is making any difference? Clients tell me that they feel better, but there's no way of knowing whether that's anything to do with me or not. It could be time, the simple catharsis of talking about it, or the fact that talking about it makes them face up to their problems and make the necessary changes, have the necessary conversations. It could be any one of a number of things and nothing whatsoever to do with anything I have said or done.

All the theory says that it's about *being,* not me *doing* anything anyway, that it's 'the relationship that heals'. I was supposed to let go of any agenda to *fix* something and 'enter their world'. It was so bloody hard to do though. If I had a real relationship with them, then I started to care and then it was really hard not to want them to feel better sooner rather than later, to 'trust the process' to achieve that without me aiming directly for it. Sometimes I felt that the process was just too damned slow!

John was right: the problem with Robyn was that I'd stopped empathising with the part of her that passionately loved Andy. I had such a strong agenda for her to have a better relationship with herself that when she started to achieve it I didn't want her to risk it for anything or anyone.

And Stephen? It was the same with Stephen. I had a strong agenda for him to like himself and it got in the way of my empathy for the part of him that's really afraid that he's bad. How can I empathise with him anyway? How can I possibly imagine what it's like to not know what kind of person you are?

I felt miserably useless and, in that moment, ready to give up counselling totally. It was only because I would feel guilty about having spent so much money on the training that made me feel that I had to continue. I would just have to focus on learning as much as I could and trying harder to get this right.

Chapter 12

It was hot again and Stephen's session was midday so I had the patio doors open to get some cool air circulating before he arrived. Except there was no cool air, no breeze at all. The tulle curtains hung straight down, limp in the heat. It was stifling and oppressive.

As I sat waiting for Stephen to arrive I contemplated how to *be* in today's session, how to be *better*, how to actually have a therapeutic conversation rather than just share my opinion. If last time I rushed off on my own crusade towards the holy grail of Stephen letting go of the fear that he's bad, this time I would follow him, go back to basics, use reflective listening skills and simply focus on the core conditions: empathy, congruence and unconditional positive regard.

And therein lay the problem. It was anything but simple to be both congruent and empathic at the same time. That's what had gone wrong with both Robyn and Stephen. In trying to be congruent I lost the empathy for at least a part of each of them. I knew the core conditions were supposed to be an aim and not necessarily perfectly attainable but, even so, I was nowhere near sometimes.

Just hold the session Maggie, follow his lead.

Stephen arrived and I strained to read his expression, but it was indecipherable. He looked contemplative, which told me nothing. I had to close the doors to protect his confidentiality and that meant he had to wait for me to get out of the way before he could sit down. He knew the drill, he'd been here on hot days before, but it was still awkward. I poured us both a glass of water as he sat down and then I waited.

Stephen didn't look at me at first, he seemed strangely distant. "It's hot isn't it?" he began.

My heart sank fractionally. Had it come to that now? Had I been so far away from his experience last time that we were going to be reduced to small talk?

"This heat is getting me down. It's so tiring."

I waited. Stephen sighed and in doing so visibly abandoned the idea of small talk and evidently decided to get real.

"Erm so, I thought about what you said... actually, I thought about little else." He half smiled nervously. He was behaving very oddly, as though he had just remembered what it was he had planned to talk about but his real thoughts were still elsewhere. His words had my full attention regardless.

"Which bit in particular?"

"All of it. About how you really do know me as I am now, about you being confident that I'm not a violent person, at least not now. About there being no evidence that my trigger for anger is any more sensitive than anyone else's."

I waited, holding my breath. *Maybe, just maybe…*

"I decided that you're right."

I breathed out.

"There is no evidence that I'm any more prone to angry outbursts or violent rages than anyone else, and the thing is… I don't actually *feel* like a violent person, I just don't. I feel quite laid back and un-rattled by most things. If anything I'm probably less rattled than people around me, so me having indiscriminate violent rages just doesn't make sense…"

He broke off and suddenly seemed lost in thought. His usually intense gaze shifted to a spot on the floor and defocused. He seemed to disappear inside himself and I got the impression yet again that he was actually thinking about something else entirely. It was curious, as though he really wanted to talk about this but was distracted by something else. Eventually he shook himself out of his reverie and smiled at me, as if he suddenly remembered where he was. He continued where he had left off, leaving me thoroughly confused about what had just happened.

"I think you saw it before I did because you knew me… kind of before I actually knew myself. But when I thought about it, I do feel known by you. I feel really known by you and somehow that helped me to see myself more clearly. I think I've been so scared of who

I might be, that it somehow got in the way of me seeing something of who I actually am. Does that make any sense at all?"

I nodded. There was a bit of a lump in my throat. We would come back to his momentary absence later if it was relevant. This was important stuff.

"I think that I needed you to see it first. And it really helped that you were honest about being scared at first, because quite frankly I'd have worried about your sanity if you weren't."

It lifted a bit of the intensity and we both smiled weakly.

He looked down for a moment and then locked those intense eyes onto mine again. "Seriously though, I don't think that I would have believed you when you talked about you knowing that I wasn't violent if you hadn't been wary of me at first, before you got to know me. That made it all so much more believable. I could really buy that when you did get to know me, you felt safe. It really made me think. If you could trust me, if you could see that I wasn't violent, then why couldn't I trust myself? What was holding me back?"

Is this what they mean by 'it's the relationship that heals'? Was it actually me being so completely real that had got him here? Although I wasn't totally clear yet about what *here* looked like for him, it was sounding hopeful. Maybe I hadn't completely screwed up after all.

"Obviously it was that image. It was only that image

that was getting in the way. So I decided to find out about it. I finally decided to stop faffing about and ask about it."

Whoa!

"You see, I wasn't scared anymore of what I might find out or what I might inadvertently confess to… well, I was a bit scared – I could've got into a fight and accidently hurt him more than I intended – but I knew for sure… well, almost knew for sure… that I didn't just attack him. I reasoned that there must have been some extreme provocation for me to even get into a fight… I mean it would have to have been someone like Joe, something that extreme. So I asked some people."

His tone was more subdued than the content warranted. I grew wary about what was coming. Something was wrong.

"Tom had no idea what I was talking about. He hadn't heard about anything that might explain it. That bothered me. Tom and I apparently did everything together before the accident. I'd been sure he would know…"

He did it again: abruptly he wasn't in the room with me, he was somewhere else. This time he was gone for ages. A fly buzzed loudly around his head but he didn't appear to notice. The air was heavy and seemed to grow even hotter. Stephen was apparently oblivious despite the fact that his forehead was shining with sweat and dark patches were beginning to spread under his arms. My own head drifted off momentarily and I randomly started thinking about what changes I could make to the room to keep it cooler. This heat wasn't conducive to the work. The ticking of the clock, apparently silent a moment ago, suddenly seemed to fill the room, demanding to be noticed, as if deliberately pointing out the extent of time passing. I pulled my thoughts back to Stephen but couldn't begin to guess what was going on so I decided I would have to interrupt his thoughts.

"Stephen?"

"Hmmm? Oh." He suddenly realised where he was, like he'd just woken up. He looked immensely sad.

"Long story short, I went to see Mum... on the way over here, actually. She was my last resort and I didn't actually expect her to know anything... how wrong can you be..."

The last sentence was said very quietly, almost to himself, and then he disappeared, looking lost and distracted again. Abruptly he looked up and directly at me. His eyes were brimming with tears.

"It was my dad. The bleeding man was my *real* dad." His eyes locked onto mine and I held his gaze, desperately trying to hold him metaphorically as he struggled to absorb this new information. "I didn't even know that my dad, Terry, isn't my real dad."

I was shocked. "Did you... have you ever known? Did she say?"

"Yes, apparently, Tom and I always knew. It was another complication, something else that had seemed too problematic and pointless once I was well enough to hear difficult stuff… actually, I can't say I blame her for this one." He fell silent once more, but not for long this time. "I was seven… she said I was seven years old when he was killed."

A solitary tear spilled. I was intensely aware that he'd only just heard this. He wasn't just reporting a historical event, he was trying to absorb and process it at the same time.

"Stephen I'm so sorry." I almost whispered it.

He brushed angrily at the fugitive tear. "I found him Maggie. Seven years old and I found him! He'd been stabbed fourteen times and I bloody found him! Fuck!" He folded his arms across his stomach and bent double, like the pain was physical as well as emotional. Tears began streaming unchecked down his cheeks. "Fuck! Fuck! Fuck!" He buried his head in his hands and sobbed.

I watched him, not knowing whether to go over and hold him or not, aware of the 'rules', of how physical contact can be misconstrued, and yet also aware of an intense human pull to help him, to soothe him, to rock him. Christ, to just be there for him! My eyes filled too until ultimately I had to look away and surreptitiously wipe my own cheek.

Eventually the sobbing subsided and he reached for the tissues.

"Sorry," he mumbled nasally.

"Don't." It didn't need anything more.

"I don't know why I'm upset though. I mean I don't

remember him at all and I don't remember what happened other than the image, and that's not new. And it means that I didn't hurt anyone. I should be relieved."

"There are no 'shoulds' when it comes to feelings. We feel what we feel, and why is irrelevant. It could be shock, it could be grief, it really doesn't matter. And we'll never know anyway," I said gently.

He looked up at me and smiled a wan, grateful smile.

Gradually, Stephen relayed in fits and starts what he had been told about that day. How his dad, who worked nights, had stayed at home to sleep whilst he, Tom and his mum went out for the day. On the way back Tom, then aged four, had fallen asleep in the car so his mum had opened the front door to let Stephen in and then gone back to lift Tom out of the car. Stephen had gone straight into the living room and his mum had carried Tom upstairs and put him to bed, struggling to manhandle the clothes off the comatose boy.

"She reckoned it was at least five minutes before she went back downstairs... she walked in and I was just standing there, rigid, with my back to the door... she didn't know what was going on until she took another step into the room. Dad's body was hidden by the settee until then... there was blood everywhere." He looked up at me. "I know that bit; in the image there's so much blood." And then he gazed into the distance again "So much blood... my dad's blood, not some random bloke's." His eyes filled once more.

"Oh, Stephen."

"When she tried to pull me away I couldn't move and started shaking violently. I wouldn't sleep on my own and didn't say a single word for months apparently."

"Did you get any help?"

"I dunno… I think so… I think she did say something about therapy, but I was struggling to take everything in by then to be honest. I think she said that I did. I know she said that I was in such a state that they never told Tom how he died, just that he had gone, but never how. That's why the bleeding man image meant nothing to him. Mum is devastated that I remember it. She said that for her it was the one silver lining of the amnesia: that I didn't have to live with that memory anymore."

"Did you tell her about your fear that you'd hurt someone?"

He nodded. "She was gobsmacked! She said the man who killed my dad was a nutter, a maniac, who was well-known to the police for violent rages, for losing it big time. Drugs were involved, and the day he killed my dad he'd broken in to steal stuff to fund another fix. He'd apparently gone mental – well obviously, fourteen stab wounds – when my dad disturbed him. Mum said that as a result when I became a teenager I was passionately anti-violence. I'd go on every peace demo there was. I went out of my way to stop fights, to reason with people, to talk them down. I'd get thumped for my trouble sometimes but still would never retaliate. I'd just keep talking instead of fighting." He locked his eyes onto mine as they were quickly overwhelmed by tears again. "She said the idea that I had ever hurt anyone was laughable!"

My own eyes mirrored his and I nodded, pursing my lips together tightly in an effort to contain the emotion that was threatening to overpower me. When I could eventually speak, I simply said, "So, now you know."

"So now I know," he echoed, nodding in time with me.

And we sat there, each trying to compose ourselves, each trying to absorb the dual enormity of what his mother had told him; he had never ever been a violent man *but* his father, his real father who he didn't know existed, had been murdered in gruesome fashion and he had found the body. The myriad of emotions running amok in me were bewildering enough, I couldn't imagine what it was like for him.

He seemed to retreat inside himself again for several minutes, trying to work it out, make sense of it, trying to understand this new world order.

After a while, when I felt my own head begin to clear slightly, I tried to engage him again, to pull him back to me. There was no point in asking what he was feeling or thinking, those questions were simultaneously too big and too trite. I simply asked very gently, "How are you doing?"

"I don't know really... I can't get my head around it."

"No."

We sat in silence a bit more, but it was a

companionable, together silence this time.

"The thing is the angle's all wrong."

"The angle?"

"Yeah. If it's a memory of seven-year-old me looking at my dad, the angle's wrong. In the image I'm too tall. It's the image of a bleeding man seen through the eyes of another adult, not a child. It doesn't make sense."

"Well, we know memories can be distorted. I guess in this case that distortion made all the difference in terms of the conclusions you came to though."

Stephen looked at me quizzically.

"Well, if the image had been of a bleeding man seen through the eyes of a seven-year-old, if the angle had been right, I'm guessing you wouldn't have assumed that the seven-year-old caused those injuries."

"Yeah, I guess not... if it had been an accurate memory of the scene I actually saw, as I saw it, then I wouldn't have had all this angst."

"Can you see his face? In the image?"

"Clear as anything." His expression added 'why?'.

"So, possibly you know what your dad looked like."

His mouth literally fell open. "I never thought of that... wow... blimey." He looked genuinely blown away by the thought. "I mean, all the faces I woke up not recognising... and I remember the face of my dad."

"Possibly," I cautioned. "Given the other distortions, we can't know for sure that it's accurate. I suppose you could check if it's the same face?"

"Mum must have a picture I guess." He looked dumbstruck by the idea that there might be someone from before the accident that he actually remembered. "I will check, I'll ask her... wow, that would be phenomenal!"

We spent the rest of the session talking about memory and what a strange and unfathomable beast it was. How could it have been that he remembered no one from his recent life yet the one face he apparently remembered was someone he hadn't seen for twenty-five years? How could he have an emotional memory of Joe but no declarative memory to account for why he hated him? And why did that emotional trace live on but not the emotional trace of his love for Sally?

(Later he would confirm that the face in the image was similar, but only slightly so, to the face of the man in the photos his mother had kept of his father. He was disappointed but not completely surprised that this memory had been distorted too, it fitted with everything we had learnt already.)

*

Hunched over my notes later that afternoon I realised that whilst the revelations about Stephen's father were astounding and shocking, the therapeutic leaps that enabled him to make that discovery were equally significant. It was easy to overlook them because the content was so dramatic, but the therapy actually had been equally noteworthy.

Apparently Stephen had needed to be pretty certain that he wasn't violent before he could face the answer to his question about who the bleeding man actually was. He had been very clear in his reflections that *my* belief in his nature was what enabled his own at first and then, when he looked inside himself, he didn't *feel* violent, it didn't *fit*.

I thought again about who we are without our stories, the narratives of our pasts that we believe shape who we are. Although Stephen didn't remember his story, he had built a narrative around that image anyway, despite our rationalising about the theory of memory or lack of evidence. This hypothetical story got in his way of seeing who he might really be, in the same way that the stories others tell us growing up about who we are get in the way of us seeing who we actually are. The child who is told she's bad believes it so thoroughly that she can't see her own goodness; the child who is told he is stupid, stops being able to see his own intelligence. And just one person who can see past the wrong stories we tell ourselves can make all the difference.

In Stephen's case there were many people in his life who could've told him that he was one of the good guys but he didn't dare tell them of his darkest fears so they had no opportunity to reassure him. It had to be a counsellor – not necessarily me, I wasn't that egotistical – but someone independent, not part of his life, someone bound by confidentiality, someone he would never have to see again if it all went wrong.

By being real, and by genuinely believing in him, I had given Stephen the courage to face up to what he might have done. I didn't feel pleased with myself, or suddenly supremely skilled as a counsellor, as I might've expected. I just felt a kind of wonder at our connection, the warm spark of our relationship that got us to this point. It hadn't been about me doing something to Stephen to get him here; we genuinely got there together. My familiar self-doubt was nowhere to be seen but it wasn't replaced with any kind of pride, just a kind of sureness, a sense of calm appropriateness. And there was also a clichéd, but nevertheless, present feeling of having been honoured to have been part of it all.

The phone rang, interrupting my musing.

"Maggie, it's Robyn."

"Oh, hello," I said breezily.

Clients never phone between sessions. I actively discourage it except for practical arrangements such as making or changing appointments. I was thrown off guard and temporarily lost in my very enjoyable contemplation of the session with Stephen. I had momentarily forgotten that Robyn had been upset with me the last time we spoke but a fraction of a second after I spoke, it came rapidly back to me and my heart immediately sped up as apprehension flooded through me.

"I'm calling to say that I won't be coming to our next

session."

Shit!

"Oh?"

"I think I need to call it a day actually, so I'm going to make last week my last session." She sounded very cold, hard even.

Shit! Shit! Shit!

"Well, it's your choice obviously." *Remember the ethics – client autonomy is sacrosanct.* "But it's usually good practice to have an ending session, to wrap up the work and review." I sounded like a text book!

"I don't think that's a good idea."

Shit! Come on Maggie, be real and stop stepping round the elephant!

"Robyn, I know you're upset with me and that's perfectly understandable, you have every right to be. I've been doing a lot of thinking since our session and I would really like us to talk about this. Could we not have one last session? I promise I won't try to persuade you to stay on longer if that's not what you want, but it wouldn't be good to end on this note."

"Not good for you maybe. It actually feels fine for me to end on exactly this note."

Ouch!

Robyn sighed and with the sigh she softened slightly. "Look Maggie, I am grateful for everything you've done for me, genuinely! I have found my voice, I'm listening to my inner wisdom and I'm learning to stand up for myself. I wouldn't have even noticed the wise whisperer if it hadn't been for you, let alone trusted that part of me. But the truth is that I trust that part of me more than you do. You don't actually trust my inner wisdom."

"I never said that."

"You didn't need to. Be honest Maggie, you tell me to trust my instincts, but when it comes to Andy at least, you think they're flawed. You don't believe in my wisdom as much as you pretend to and that's why I have to leave." She suddenly stopped before continuing softly, almost apologetically. "If I stay I'll stop believing too."

I heard an intake of breath as she stole herself to follow this through.

"You got me to this point, but from here on in you'll hold me back. Even if I'm making a terrible mistake, I have to trust myself to be able to make it and deal with the consequences... and I believe I can. But the truth is that you don't."

There was no answer to any of that. She was right. I couldn't deny any of it. What could I say?

"I don't know that it's true anymore that I *don't*." Was it true now? I really didn't know. "But it's true that I *didn't* and for that I'm really sorry. If you feel that I'll hold you back, then you're right not to come back. I fully support that – no one should hang around someone who they feel holds them back."

Once I started to speak, the words just seemed to flow. I was speaking the truth as I genuinely felt it in that moment. I had nothing else to offer her.

"I still wish that we could have this conversation face-to-face, but I respect your decision. I mean, I really respect it, that's not just a set of words. Irrespective of what has happened between us recently, I really admire you Robyn. Ironically I even admire this, you having the courage to walk away from this! It makes me sad and very sorry that I have caused a rupture that we don't seem to be able to recover from, but always know how much I truly admire you."

"Bizarrely, I have always felt that, that's what made it so good, that's what got me here."

"Good luck Robyn, with everything."

"'Bye Maggie." Her voice cracked slightly

"'Bye."

Shit! Over the next few days and weeks, I went over and over what went wrong, what I could have done differently. How could I have avoided the rupture when I did actually think she was making a mistake? I might have been less sure about that now, especially given the way she conducted herself and the things she said when she ended the counselling, but I did believe at the time that she was making a mistake. Should I have hidden that belief? Could I have done? Would she have seen through the incongruence? Could I have parked it temporarily while I explored some more? Would that even have been possible?

Surprisingly John didn't share my view that it had been a complete disaster. He encouraged me to stand back and see the bigger picture. With his help, I started to take Robyn's words in that final phone call at face value, to believe that I had actually facilitated a positive change for her. I began to see that without our work together, Robyn would never have been able to make that call, to stand up for her own opinion against someone else's, especially someone she seemed to value. I came to realise that if we'd reached the end point that I wanted for her, she would have been able to stand up to me and still continue to have a relationship with me. As it was she had reached a point where she would privilege her own beliefs over mine but didn't trust herself to be able to hang on to them if I was still around implicitly undermining them. We hadn't reached my end point, but we had moved forward.

I often wondered how she was doing, hoping she'd been able to hang on to those gains, hoping Andy wasn't undermining them as she feared I would do. What a crazy circle of mistrust. I didn't trust Andy not to undermine her, and that very thing was what meant that she didn't trust me not to undermine her by not believing she was strong enough to resist him! Maybe she was actually stronger than both of us. How could I ever have thought that the similarities between us were uncanny? We were not at all alike! I would never have been as strong as Robyn at her age. I still wasn't, seventeen years on!

*

Stephen came for a few more sessions. There were still aspects of himself he didn't understand, such as was the party animal version an act for his friends, evidence of an underlying insecurity or something else? We theorised a little about the nature of memory and its link to identity. We wondered if you had to remember the stuff that happened to you for it still to have an effect, or whether the event itself changed you forever whether you remember it or not.

He spent a long time with his mum talking about his real dad and he cried with me for the father he couldn't remember, and the things he missed out on irrespective of his memory loss. Gradually he grew settled and accepting of his amnesia. He learnt to live in the present and become who he was now rather than worrying who he had been in the past. I envied him that. We would never know what events, if any, from his past affected the way he was wired, but at least he had no conscious self-limiting beliefs to undermine him.

Sometimes I felt I was much too aware of my own history and self-beliefs, that they were ever present in my thoughts, never leaving me alone, tying me in knots as I tried to fathom who I really was. What had happened to the adventurous part of myself that Robyn had so reminded me of? Had it ever been real or was it just a little bit of Andre rubbing off? Deep down, was I really just the timid people-pleaser I had believed myself to be? Did I simply borrow courage from him for a while?

I could never accept the people-pleaser as I had steered Robyn to do. I hated the people-pleaser, the damned people-pleaser who had interfered at the most pivotal moment in my life and led to such desolation. The weak, loathsome people-pleaser who couldn't even stand by her inner knowing when— *Stop! Don't go there!* Self-awareness – an important trait for a counsellor – came at a price sometimes. Amnesia, even just for a day, would be a relief.

Six months after we met, Stephen's sessions came to a natural end. He came back for five more about two years later and I got an email from him a year after that telling me that he was getting married.

I didn't hear from Robyn again for ten years but when I did, it changed everything.

PART TWO
2006

Chapter 13

Julian didn't much like the real story of his childhood so he made up a different one. Bounced repeatedly from foster home to care home and back again, he was horrendously neglected and bullied by the adults who were supposed to look after him. He was also repeatedly physically and sexually abused. By the time he was kicked out and abandoned by the so-called 'care' system aged sixteen, he was already a seasoned petty criminal, a drug user and was heading towards a life of crime.

Then he met a girl. It was love at first sight, he said, when he first saw her across the counter in a shop where he was intending to steal trainers. He'd planned to pretend to try them on and then simply walk out wearing them. She was clearly out of his league and he knew from the way she held herself that there was no way she'd be interested in a low-life like him. He made an instant decision. He put the trainers back and there and then walked out of his old life. He was determined to change and win the girl.

It took him six months and just one more theft – a suit and tie for an interview – to get a job and get through the probationary period before he dared approach her. At first she turned him down but he went back every week and wore her down with his wit and persistence until she agreed to one date 'just to shut him up'. That was over forty years ago and the girl, Chloe, had become his wife.

Julian devoted his life to taking care of Chloe, to providing for her and their two girls, to making sure they wanted for nothing and that they were nurtured and loved in a way he'd never known. Children like Julian, who had never experienced a mother's love, usually have a hard time loving themselves or believing that others love them and so often struggle to form lasting, affectionate relationships. Julian couldn't accept love, but he could give it. He asked his family for nothing whilst showering them with kindness and care. I actually had no reason to believe, from what Julian told me, that they didn't love him just as much as he loved them but this fact simply never occurred to Julian. It never even entered his head that anyone could love him, especially not someone like Chloe whom he still kept on a metaphorical pedestal. Chloe had grown up in a loving family, the antithesis of his childhood, and to him she was perfect. She was loved because she was lovable, unlike him. For him, it was as simple as that.

The trouble with our childhood stories is that we try to make sense of them long before we have the tools for the task. When our pre-frontal cortex is barely formed and when we are still egocentric, we make crucial, barely conscious decisions about ourselves and the world. Anything and everything that happens does so because of us. If we are neglected, it's not because the adults are incapable of giving us what we need, it's because we don't deserve care. If we are not loved, it's not because the adults can't love, it's because we are unlovable. If we are beaten and abused, it's not because the adults are bad, it's because we are. The shame is ours.

Julian never told anyone the truth about his childhood because the misplaced shame drove him to hide it. Chloe knew he'd been in care and foster homes but nothing about the neglect, the beatings, and especially not about the sexual abuse. Julian pretended it hadn't happened and he pretended he was someone other than the 'bad' person who caused all of those things to happen. Julian pretended for so long that he became someone else.

Then one day the police knocked on the door as part of an enquiry into historic abuse at the children's home. His history collided with his carefully constructed present and Julian finally had to face his past. The police were paying for his therapy with me.

I adored Julian and admired him hugely. The path that his childhood had started him on is not an easy one to get off; not many turn their lives around after such a beginning. I had begun to recognise over the years that my counselling practice was often about helping people to re-write their stories and helping them to re-interpret their childhoods using a now fully formed adult brain. Julian had already re-written his story in a different way. He hadn't re-interpreted it; he had simply told others, and thereby himself, a different version, and had pretended to be the kind of person who might have actually had that childhood. He became a kind, compassionate, wise man, no longer the 'bad lad' he thought he really was. Eventually, he forgot that he had ever been anything different.

Now fifty-one, he was like everyone's favourite uncle. Despite being generally confident as a counsellor now, I noticed that I often felt very young and childlike with Julian. I made a mental note to take that to supervision as feeling young around him would be unhelpful to our work. Awareness of the feelings he evoked however, was informative and I postulated that Julian had also taken on the role of protecting me, just as he protected his family. I knew that none of the adults in Julian's childhood had ever protected him and I wondered if I could create a reparative relationship for him in adulthood, where he could feel protected by someone for the first time. It wouldn't be difficult as I did genuinely want to protect Julian. Imagining anyone hurting him, especially as a child, enraged me.

Although I hadn't seen him for years, I often thought back to Stephen during my sessions with Julian: Stephen couldn't remember, Julian had chosen to forget.

Now forcibly reminded of the truth, Julian also grappled with who he really was. He felt fraudulently 'normal' but no longer truly 'bad' either.

Not only that, he now also had to face going to court and telling others the truth. Julian was the key witness in a case against his worst abuser. The police were desperate for him to testify but Julian was unsure. He still hadn't told his family any of it, and he was in the process of untangling the conclusions he had come to in childhood from the facts as he could now see them.

"I was thinking the other day about how to actually describe it in court," he said, "what I would actually have to say… you know… what actual words I would have to use."

I waited. The court case was scheduled for two weeks' time and Julian was running out of time to decide if he would go. It would be tough for him I knew. If he decided to go through with it, then they would need to hear graphic details. Although I knew plenty about what had happened to him, Julian had never even spelled out the graphic details to me; he'd said just enough for me to understand what had happened (it was an example of how he protected me). What I did know though tore at my heart strings. I often imagined I could see the vulnerable child in his eyes as Julian related stories of being locked in cupboards for days, of beatings and torture and being bent over bannisters. Despite him clearly holding back a lot, it was tough stuff to hear, but obviously not nearly as tough as it had been to endure.

"And I suddenly realised... 'rape' is the right word isn't it?"

He'd never used that word before although he had alluded to what had happened and it was quite clear to me. I held my breath.

"It was actually rape."

"Yes, it was," I said, mirroring his quiet, almost whispered delivery.

"I'd never actually thought about it like that before... I was raped, and he was a paedophile."

"Yes he was."

"I was the victim of a paedophile."

He sounded incredulous, like he really hadn't known this previously. I'd seen this before with abuse. He'd always known what happened, but because he'd ascribed the meaning to the events whilst still a child, probably before he even knew the words 'rape' and 'paedophile', he'd never thought about it as a crime before. Even with the police involved and the court case looming, re-interpreting is not instant; it had taken time for this new understanding to land but, if he could absorb it, it would make all the difference to him. This was crucial.

"And how does that feel? To know you were the victim of a paedophile?"

Early on, stereotypically of his age and gender, Julian had struggled to articulate his feelings. He was getting better at it though, now we'd been working together for a few months.

"Dirty," he said quickly. "I feel dirty... and angry!"

"Tell me about angry."

Anger is a self-protective emotion. It was good that he felt angry, it was a sign that he was starting to recognise, on an emotional level, that this wasn't his fault and shouldn't have happened. I wanted him to focus on the anger, to make it bigger if possible. I wanted the adult Julian to be able to stand up for the child he had been.

"I don't know... I just feel angry... like I actually want to punch someone... and upset, like I could cry... but more angry than upset... actually, both. I want to punch *him*, the bastard!"

He looked down, slightly embarrassed at his outburst. It was out of character, Julian was never angry and never used such language. It was good to hear it finally and I needed to encourage it, let him know that it was OK to speak like that in front of me.

"He *was* a bastard. You were a child. He had all the power."

"It was a punishment... I can't even remember what I did."

"Rape isn't a punishment. That's what he said so that you believed it was *your* fault. It ensured your silence and meant *you* carried the shame that was rightfully his." I needed to re-frame it, to undo the long held but ultimately erroneous childhood beliefs. I was desperate for Julian to see it through adult eyes, and although he was just starting to feel anger, I had been furious for a long time now with the bastard who had done this to a little boy.

"I think it was apple scrumping."

He'd stopped listening to me.

"It doesn't matter what you did."

"I was always up to something I shouldn't have been."

He was falling back into old belief patterns.

"You were a child."

It was futile; I needed to up the ante.

"Always getting a hiding for something I'd done."

"And did you beat your kids when they did something wrong?"

He looked up, shocked. "No, of course not!"

"Why not?"

"I would never hurt them. They would never deserve that!"

"They never went apple scrumping then?"

"No, but—"

"And if they had? Would you have beaten them then?" I interrupted deliberately.

"No!" he said emphatically before adding more softly, "No. I'd have made them take the apples back, made them apologise, explained stealing was wrong."

He was thoughtful as he spoke and I could see the links forming.

"Why wouldn't you beat them?" I asked softly.

He didn't answer.

"Why wouldn't you beat them Julian?"

"Because they're children," he whispered. His skin blotched with emotion that didn't quite make his eyes fill.

I waited for a few moments before I spoke. "You were a child too. And you were raped. And he was a bastard." I blinked so that my eyes might stay dry too. I would have to feel more anger on his behalf than he felt himself for a little while longer, but we were getting there.

*

Sam's friend, Jordan, was lounging on the settee again when I emerged from the counselling room. I loved the fact that Sam's friends felt at home in our house. More would turn up later before they all went out and I would wake to find several had crashed at ours overnight.

"Where's Sam?" I asked Jordan.

"He's gone to collect Sean from the bus stop. Should be back any minute."

"OK. Dinner's at six."

"No? Really?" he said sarcastically, and then grinned at me cheekily.

It was a standing joke that dinner was always at exactly six o'clock at Sam's house. Counsellors live by the clock, starting and finishing at consistent, predictable times. Maybe I'd got a little bit OCD about things happening reliably at the same time, or maybe I just remembered it as being that way when I was growing up. Whatever the reason it seemed to work, especially now Sam was eighteen. Everyone knew where they stood and what time they had to be in (or needed to let me know if they wouldn't be).

"Yeah, I thought just for a change…" I joined in the joke.

I grabbed a cup of tea and went back into the counselling room to make a few notes before starting on dinner. The two together – making notes and then pottering in the kitchen – constituted my ritual transition from work to home. Not driving to and from a workplace meant there was a danger that the two would merge into one. It was one reason I was very boundaried and encouraged no contact between sessions. I prided myself on being extremely present when I was with clients, but I had to protect my own life and thereby my energy levels, in order to do that. I couldn't be infinitely available or I would burn out. It didn't stop me thinking about clients between sessions though. I did genuinely care about them, well, most of them, and thought about them often, just as I would friends.

I chopped vegetables while listening to the radio. Slowly my thoughts turned from Julian and the others I'd seen that day to Mathew, Sam and his friends.

I enjoyed these evenings the most; evenings when the house would be full of young people. Being around young people changed my energy and lifted my mood. Young people still believe in dreams, and I envied them the opportunity of having their whole lives in front of them with those dreams. They weren't worn down by cynicism and suffering or defeated by disappointment and rejection. They could still laugh in that carefree way that small children do. And, whenever I was around them, I found I laughed too, although laughter was still inevitably followed by guilt, even after all these years. I wondered if that would ever change or if it was too ingrained a habit.

Later at dinner I watched the three boys laughing. As ever, their jokes were crude and outrageously inappropriate. I tried to admonish them sometimes with a shocked, "Sam!" or "Sean!" More often than not though, I ended up spraying a mouthful of something across the room as I collapsed in helpless laughter. They made me laugh so much, and tonight was no exception. Soon, tears rolled down my face and my sides were splitting again. They were shockingly, daringly hilarious, and I loved it. Having teenagers in the house energised me and lifted me out of a gloomy view of the world that counselling could leave me with. I spent my days listening to stories of distress and trauma. Laughter was the antidote. I needed this; it was my tonic.

The boys teased each other all the time, viciously sometimes, and Sam often extended this to me and Mathew. Often his jokes at my expense took on a kind of tongue-in-cheek sexist tone. Tongue-in-cheek or not, I felt I ought to object but it was just so funny. Telling him off whilst clearly trying to stifle laughter just made them all laugh at me more and I knew he was respectful of women; a lot of his friends were girls too. Sean and Jordan laughed at Sam teasing us but held back from initiating a joke at mine or Mathew's expense. That would have crossed some sort of line, I guess. I wondered what it would have been like if Sam had had a brother to bounce his jokes off rather than just his friends.

Stop it Maggie!

Once they'd all helped with clearing the table, Jordan flung some insult or other Sam's way and that was it, a mad stampede up the stairs ensued; all three of them chasing, squealing and piling on top of each other, bizarrely laughing whilst apparently being hurt. They played rugby together at school and their friendship was a very physical one; wrestling and punching each other seemed to be an important part of it. I didn't get that bit at all but it still made me smile, albeit whilst wincing. They were just so irrepressible.

As I loaded the dishwasher and Mathew washed the pans, I thought again of how much I loved this age group. They had so much energy. Work, play, adventure, friendships, love; they throw themselves into everything with such abandon, they really do seize the day. *Carpe diem*. Robyn popped into my head. After all this time, I still thought of her occasionally and wondered what she was doing, whether she'd stayed with Andy and how it had all turned out. In the last few weeks though, for some reason I'd been thinking of her more often.

After the boys left for their night out, I curled up on the settee with Mathew to watch a film. It was quiet. Too quiet. It should have been nice, this time alone together – cosy, romantic even, and it was. But it wasn't funny. My sides weren't splitting and there were no tears rolling down my face. It was just very quiet.

Sam would be gone by this time next year, off on a gap year before university and into his own life. I would be semi-retired from the most important project of my life, bringing him up. I didn't feel ready to retire, semi or otherwise. He'd be back part-time, I knew that, but I wasn't ready to not have him full-time. It was the everydayness I would miss: not knowing what he was up to each day, not being able to read the emotion in his face every day, not laughing with him every day. He would make new friends and I wouldn't know them. Sean, Jordan and the others would be off to launch their own lives and I would lose them too. Nights like this felt too quiet simply because they were a glimpse of things to come.

Raising Sam, nurturing him and guiding him, had given my life meaning for a while. Now on the brink of losing that role, I was forced to re-visit my early questioning of what it was all for. Watching Sam trying to figure out his future, trying to find his own meaningful path, took me right back to my youthful idealism and yearning to do something worthwhile.

Without Sam living here, needing me in the same way he had for years, I wondered whether it was worthwhile. Would counselling be enough? I'd been thinking of that zoomed-out perspective again lately. Yes, I made a difference to individuals sometimes, but what was that in the service of? Did any of it really matter from a whole cosmos standpoint?

Funnily enough those questions didn't even enter my head when it came to raising Sam. They should have – the point was as valid when applied to Sam as to my work – but mothering Sam just *felt* meaningful. I never questioned it.

Everything was genuinely possible for Sam. He was bright and engaging with a winning smile that drew people to him. I was proud, obviously, but I also envied where he was right now, about to leap into a future full of possibilities and adventure. I was excited for him.

And sometimes I was excited for me and Mathew too. We were talking about what it would mean for us when Sam went away. Without the tie of school and Sam's recently redundant taxi service requirements, we planned to travel more. Mathew was even tentatively talking about early retirement, and my job was flexible enough to mean we could then take long weekends in Europe or the odd trip further afield. I started to daydream of train trips to far-flung corners of the world, and for the first time in years thought about the trips I'd taken after Andre and I split up. I wouldn't put myself into some of the positions I had been in back then – I wouldn't be sneaking into countries illegally under a tarpaulin any time soon – but there was something liberating about not having the everyday responsibility of work and family. It meant I could touch that adventurous side of me again. Maybe that was why I had been thinking of Robyn so much lately. If I couldn't find meaning, I could find adventure again.

I snuggled into Mathew. It had been a lovely, crisp October day and we'd lit the log burner for the first time since spring. It smelt of burning dust, and my eyes strayed from the television to the flames dancing in the windows of the burner. Those same windows would be blackened by soot in a few days but for now the flames were visible and they were hypnotic.

Reflecting on my inner world of thoughts and feelings was an occupational hazard. I noticed now what a complex assortment they were: sadness about Sam's imminent departure mingled with pride and excitement on his behalf; eager anticipation of travelling combined with a loss of meaning that I couldn't square with the contentment that I was feeling right now, in this moment, lying in Mathew's arms, watching the fire.

The phone ringing interrupted the moment. Mathew groaned and pressed pause on the DVD.

"Re-fill?" he asked, holding up my wine glass.

As ever my instant reaction was that something had happened to Sam, and as ever I pushed the thought away as I went out to the hallway to answer the incessant ringing. I nodded to Mathew as if to prove to myself that Sam was fine, I wouldn't need to drive to any hospitals tonight.

"Hello?"

"Maggie, I don't know if you remember me? You saw me a long time ago, when I was Robyn Harper."

"Robyn, of course I remember you." I was delighted to hear from her and failed to register the edge in her voice.

"Are you still counselling?"

I tried to think how long it had been since I'd last seen her. "Yes, I am. I—"

"I think I need to come back," she interrupted. This time the tremor was unmistakable.

"OK." I slowed down to match her delivery and waited.

"I didn't know who to turn to… there's no one else I could talk to about this… I need… I need to know how to live again."

"OK, it's OK Robyn, we'll make an appointment and—"

"I need to tell you why now, on the phone… I don't think I can say the words face-to-face." Although she spoke over me, her voice was small, whispering. She sounded broken, and a shiver of apprehension rippled through me.

"OK." My voice betrayed my wariness.

There was a long silence as she stole herself to speak.

"I had two children, two boys." Her voice cracked, she was struggling to contain the emotion. "… five months ago my eldest child got meningitis…"

I didn't hear the rest. My usually impenetrable guard failed me. Robyn's words were the key to a vault deep in the recesses of my mind. Without warning, I was engulfed by the memory.

Chapter 14
1989

It's May Bank Holiday weekend and we've been camping in Wales, but now Harry is not well. He's had a cold for a few days but now he seems worse rather than better. He's a funny colour and very listless and whiney so we decide to leave early and get him home.

"Perhaps a good night's sleep in his own bed will sort it out," I say.

But Calpol doesn't seem to help and he seems to be getting worse in the car. Then suddenly, out of the blue, he has some kind of fit. I glance round at him and his eyes are rolling back in his head and his whole body is shaking violently.

"Stop the car!" I yell, instantly undoing my seat belt and swivelling round in the front seat to be able to reach Harry.

Mathew glances over his shoulder and swerves across the inside lane of traffic, banging on the horn whilst trying to stop quickly without flinging me through the windscreen.

By the time the car has stopped so has the fit. I fling the front door open and lunge round to the back one.

"Harry!"

"Hmmm?" he responded sleepily.

*

The wait in A&E is now taking forever. It is over an hour to be triaged, even in paediatrics, and I know something is seriously wrong with Harry. The triage nurse takes his temperature: it's 38.5 and she gives him some more Calpol even though it hasn't been four hours since the last lot.

*

The doctor is examining Harry now while I jiggle Sam on my hip. Harry has a bit more colour but still looks grey to me. He keeps falling asleep through the examination. He never does that. We joke that he sleeps with one eye open and it's normally impossible to sneak past without disturbing him. The doctor frowns as he listens to Harry's heart and lungs, shines a light in his eyes and puts a thermometer to his ear. He examines every inch of Harry, looking for a rash or something. It's all very thorough. I feel safe now a doctor is here – he'll know what to do.

"And he's had a cold you say?"

"Yes, for three or four days now."

"Harry," he says loudly as Harry's eyes droop again. "Harry, is anywhere hurting?"

Harry closes his eyes and shakes his head. He winces but no one else except me seems to notice.

I hand Sam to Mathew who's standing behind me, keeping out of the doctor's way.

"Harry, does your head hurt?" I ask, putting my arm round his shoulder.

"No," he murmurs sleepily as he snuggles into me, burying his head in my shoulder.

"I think he just needs to sleep this cold off," the doctor is saying.

What? No, no, no, it's not a cold, he's had colds before! It's not that! Check again. You've missed something.

"But he had a fit."

"I think it was probably a febrile convulsion. Some children have them when they have a temperature. I'll give you a leaflet. They're scary to witness, especially the first time, but they are harmless and actually quite common in this age group."

No, it's something else, I know it is! I can't argue with him, I'm not medically trained and what could I say, 'I just know you're wrong'? Another neurotic mother, he'll think. *Listen to the doctor, do as you're told.*

"Take him home and keep up the Calpol every four hours, alternating it with ibuprofen, to keep his temperature down. I'll write out a prescription for both.

Bring him back if he gets any worse." He's already on his way out of the door.

*

We drive home in silence, Harry sleeping, Sam sucking the silky edge of his blanket, and me in the back squashed between the two car seats. I glance at Harry every few seconds. I can't speak; the thoughts in my head are too vague for words. I can't describe the irrational sense of dread I'm feeling. I don't want to make it real by giving it air, and don't want to be told not to be silly. I feel stupid and weak. But I know I'm right. I withdraw into my private anxiety, powerless, and faced with an all-knowing doctor telling me everything is fine. But it's not fine, something is wrong. Something is very wrong. I know it.

*

8.00 p.m. Harry seems a little brighter. He hasn't eaten and is still ashen, but he's woken up fully now and is drawing in bed. He holds up the picture.

"Mummy, look, I've drawn a man with a willy!" He giggles weakly and then coughs before falling back on his pillow.

I've never been so pleased to see Harry being his naughty, cheeky self. I'm slightly reassured. *Maybe the doctor was right. Maybe I am being a neurotic over-protective mother.*

*

9.00 p.m. Harry's asleep in bed and Mathew and I are watching TV. Everything seems normal. There's no reason to be worried now; he's getting better. It was nothing.

I can't settle though, can't concentrate on the programme. *I'll just check in on him.*

"Mathew!" I scream back towards the direction of the open door.

Footsteps come running. I hold Harry in my arms and look up helplessly. Mathew takes one look at the rolling eyes and flailing limbs and grabs Harry from me, rushing to the bathroom. *Why is he doing that?* Then I notice the vomit and shit everywhere. Mathew strips Harry's pyjamas off and wraps him in a towel and we wait for the shaking to stop. *It's just another febrile convulsion, right? Scary to witness but 'harmless and quite common in this age group', right?* The shaking stops but his eyes are still white, rolling back in his head. Then it starts again.

"Should we phone a doctor?" Mathew says, his eyes pleading with me to know what to do.

"I don't know." *It's just a febrile convulsion, right?* "Yes!" *I don't know what to do.* I walk (*walk?*) down the corridor to get the phone

I start dialling.

"Maybe it should be an ambulance," Mathew says.
What?

He looks terrified. Harry is still unconscious. We can't wake him.

I dial 999.

"Emergency. What service do you require?"

"Ambulance please." My voice sounds calm. *There's no need to panic, everything is fine, really.*

The operator askes for my phone number, name and address before she asks anything else. I want to scream at her: *'My child is seriously ill, send someone NOW and stop asking stupid fucking questions!'* But I don't. I stay calm. *Everything is fine. It's not serious.*

I tell her about Harry. "He's unconscious," I say. "I can't wake him up." I tell her about the poo and the wee and the vomit and the eyes and the start-stop shaking.

"Right, the ambulance is on its way. I'm going to stay on the line until they get there. Now, I want you to check a few things for me, OK?"

Why is she staying on the line? They don't normally do that, do they?

"Can you feel a pulse?"

I repeat the operator's question to Mathew.

"I don't know…"

This is silly, of course you can, check properly.

"Yes, yes, there's a pulse."

I breathe.

"Good, now what about his breathing?" the operator

says.

I repeat it for Mathew and he bends over Harry, putting his ear to Harry's mouth and nose.

"He's just checking," I report back.

"Sshhh!" hisses Mathew, "I can't hear anything!"

This isn't happening! No, really, it's not!

"I can't... I don't know..." Mathew holds his hand to Harry's mouth, frantically trying to determine whether our son is breathing or not.

"Put me on to your husband," says the operator. "The ambulance has just arrived outside. I need you to go and let them in."

I do as I'm told.

The paramedic is getting his bag out of the van when I arrive at the front of the house.

"He's this way," I tell him, leading the way into the hall and up the stairs. "He's in a bit of a mess, I'm afraid, there's lots of poo." I'm making conversation, apologising for the inconvenience like it's a normal day.

"Don't worry about that, love." He's walking so slowly behind me, almost sauntering. I'm already several paces ahead of him down the corridor. My voice may be calm but my urgent steps give me away. *Hurry up, damn it!*

"Yes, they're here now... thank you... yes... 'bye." Mathew hangs up the phone and shuffles back on his knees to make room.

The paramedic feels for a pulse and bends his head to put his ear next to Harry's mouth, echoing Mathew's actions moments earlier. Without saying a word, he scoops Harry up, shitty towels and all, and strides down the corridor. I have to jog to keep up. Suddenly he's not sauntering.

He gets to the top of the stairs. Harry looks tiny and fragile, limp in the big man's arms. The second paramedic is at the bottom of the stairs coming the other way.

"Watch me down will you mate, we need to vent."

What? You need to what? Excuse me, I don't understand. What do we need to do?

The big paramedic, cradling my small son in his arms, can't see his feet to walk safely down the stairs. His colleague walks backwards in front of him, touching his elbows, making sure each foot is planted safely on each step, guiding the big man and his precious cargo. I'm touched by the care and efficiency of it.

Once they're at the bottom I run back upstairs and grab the phone from the bathroom floor. Mathew is clearing towels and vomit.

"I'll phone Rachel to look after Sam," I say.

"I'll follow in the car," he says. Or is it the other way round? Does he speak first?

Rachel's phone rings five times and then goes to the answer machine. *Damn!*

I dial another number as I run back down the corridor. Julia answers sleepily as I run down the stairs.

"Hello?" They're farmers; they will already be in bed.

"Julia, I need you now! I have an ambulance here for Harry. I need you to look after Sam."

She's instantly awake. "I'm on my way," she says and hangs up. She doesn't ask questions; she just does what I need. I want to weep with gratitude.

I peer into the back of the ambulance, not wanting to get in the way. Both paramedics are working on Harry. One is trying to get something into the back of his hand while the other is threading some kind of tube down his throat.

Julia seems to arrive instantly and joins me, peering in. "What's happened?" she asks.

"He won't wake up and he's not breathing properly," I say, and notice my voice is shaking. *How strange, why is that?*

Mathew appears too just as I'm climbing into the ambulance.

"Can I see him?" He looks petrified as he strains to catch a glimpse of his son through the big adult bodies that block his view.

"Sorry sir, we need to go." And the door is closed on both him and Julia.

The ambulance pulls away.

"OK Harry, we're going to go very fast mate, so it's going to be a bit bumpy I'm afraid."

He's talking to Harry as though he's awake, maybe I should too.

I lean forward. "It's OK, Harry, Mummy's here too. We're going for a little ride in an ambulance. Isn't that exciting?"

There's a tube coming out of Harry's mouth and the big paramedic is rhythmically squeezing a balloon on the end of it. In… out… in… out…

What's that for?

I can hear the other paramedic talking to someone on a radio whilst driving but I can't hear what he's saying. The blue light on the top of the ambulance illuminates the inside.

I didn't know you could see it inside too, how strange.

There's no need for the siren, the streets are dark and empty.

I gesture to the blue light. "He'll be gutted he slept though this, he loves ambulances and fire engines," I grin.

"You can tell him all about it love," he smiles back. We both pretend everything's fine.

*

We arrive at the hospital and as soon as the door opens I jump down and out of the way quickly. I stand redundant outside the back of the ambulance while they get Harry ready to move. A security guard tells a drunk who's smoking in front of the door to get out of the way. He's too drunk to understand. The instruction is repeated and the drunk staggers towards the guard to hear him better. He's even more in the way now.

Fucking idiot! Move! I want to throw him headfirst out of the way. The guard is quicker; he steers the drunk gently out, away from the door. Running, the paramedics push Harry's trolley through the automatic doors into A&E while I trot behind and naïvely wonder how long the wait will be.

They veer right, away from the waiting area, and crash though another set of double doors. The room is full of people wearing scrubs in various shades of blue. Several of them – five? six? seven? – are standing in a V-shape. As the trolley goes in, the V closes around Harry and everyone grabs an arm or a leg and starts working. I feel an instant flush of more adrenalin and my heart skips a beat.

Blimey, it's like 'Casualty'. Like a TV drama, not real, not happening.

A nurse materialises from nowhere and placing a hand on each shoulder, wheels me round to the left.

"Don't worry, I'm not taking you away from him," she reassures me.

She steers me towards a computer on a desk to the side of where they're working on Harry.

"I need to ask you some questions." There's a checklist open on the computer screen.

I give her his full name.

The phone rings. "Yes?" she answers. "No, sorry, he's trying to tube a five-year-old boy at the moment... no, he's with the paediatric crash team... no... OK, yes, 'bye."

Crash team?

I try to see past the bodies around Harry. Someone at the head of the bed is threading a different tube down Harry's throat. The others are attaching drips and lines into the back of his hands and feet. It's difficult; he keeps fitting and they have to stop and wait for a lull.

"He's three," I correct her when she hangs up. She taps it into the computer.

Someone is holding up a phial of something pink.

"Has he eaten or drunk anything in the last few hours?"

"Ribena. He had some Ribena at about half past seven."

They all breathe, smile and catch each other's eyes. It's just Ribena, ha-ha, silly us, not blood after all then.

When did they pump his stomach? That's going to ache when he wakes up. Was that strictly necessary?

The nurse is speaking. "So, it's called a coma cocktail. Until they figure out exactly what's wrong they'll treat him for everything."

Coma?

The door behind me opens.

"Here you are." Someone shows an ashen faced Mathew into the room.

"How is he?"

"They're giving him a coma cocktail, treating him for everything until they know what's wrong. They've pumped his stomach."

Harry's tiny body starts to shake again.

"Oh God!" Mathew starts to cry.

"Stop it!" I hiss furiously.

Tears are not appropriate! Everything's fine! I cannot – will not – entertain any other thought!

"We need to be strong for Harry," I tell Mathew.

He sniffs and dries his eyes, visibly pulling himself up and together, swallowing the emotion I refuse to let him infect me with.

The activity round the bed is suddenly more frantic.

"No need to worry. What's happening now is…" The nurse's voice is exaggeratedly calm and soothing. Her job is to look after the parents, to explain things, to keep us out of the way. "They've given him something to stop the fitting and that's just slowed his heart a wee bit…"

I glance at the heart monitor. It's almost straight, just a few spaced-out blips on the flat line.

"It happens sometimes, it's all perfectly normal."

Her voice is just slightly too high but I believe her anyway because I'm desperate to. My eyes don't leave the monitor.

"They have to try different things until they get the right balance to stop the fit and maintain his heart rate."

Slowly, the number of blips increase and the monitor looks more normal. Mathew and I simultaneously let out a breath. Then the shaking starts again. *Shit!*

It goes on for hours, or is it minutes? Time seems to both expand and contract. Eventually, they tell us Harry is stable. Most likely meningitis, they say. Very little else makes a child so ill so quickly. They say it casually, matter-of-fact, like it's an everyday thing. *Meningitis!*

There are just two people by the bed now, fiddling with drips and lines, checking charts and monitors.

"You can go and hold his hand if you like," the soothing nurse tells us.

I hold Harry's hand and talk to him but I feel self-conscious. He looks asleep but is now in a medically-induced coma we've been told. There are tubes and lines in every vein and he's attached to a ventilator. I don't know what to say to him; my child and I don't know what to say. *What kind of mother am I?*

I look at the notes next to his bed. I don't understand most of it, names of drugs he's been given and medical terms that make no sense. 'Triage code red', I read. 'Status epilepticus'. I don't want to read any more.

They're going to transfer him to Alder Hey children's hospital. He's too poorly to stay here. He needs paediatric intensive care and they don't have the facilities here. But he's stable and meningitis is obviously normal here, an everyday occurrence. No one seems unduly alarmed. The everyday-ness of it is contagious. But I notice they never leave him alone either. They'll send a second ambulance and a transfer team. Do I need to phone anyone?

It's 1.00 a.m. Julia will need to be home to look after her own children by 5.00 a.m. so her husband can go out to do the milking. I go out to phone my mother to take over looking after Sam.

In a side room I find the paramedics still here, holding plastic cups of tea and looking anxious. *It's been hours, why are they still here? They must see hundreds of sick children.* The soothing nurse is speaking to them now.

"... transfer team... did all you could... go home now... it's OK."

They've been waiting to know Harry is OK. They glance up, awkward when they see me, and I nod my thanks.

I phone my mother. She's a worrier and I can't risk her voicing the things I've been refusing to think, so I say as little as possible. "He had some kind of fit... Yes... No, it's stopped but they don't know what caused it yet so they're moving him to Alder Hey... Mathew's here... Can you...? Sorry... Yes, yes... Thank you." I don't mention meningitis or code red or status epilepticus.

When I go back in, Mathew looks at me grimly before turning back to the activity round the bed. The consultant has been summoned again and a nurse is showing him something on Harry's arm: vivid purple blotches that weren't there before. They literally seem to be spreading as they watch them. I know, without having to try, that they wouldn't blanch if I pressed them with a glass, and I shiver. The consultant peers at them, frowning and then sends the nurse out for something. She returns quickly with another pouch of clear fluid. She deftly hangs it from the drip stand and hooks it up to the intravenous line that feeds into Harry's bloodstream, along with all the others.

*

It's quiet now: 3.00 a.m. and there's a surreal lull. Did all of that drama really just happen? The transfer team has arrived. They're taking Harry off one ventilator and putting him onto another that will go with him in the ambulance. They work without needing to speak because they've done this hundreds of times before. Everyone exudes a calm efficiency that is bizarrely reassuring given the sinister purple rash that is now covering most of Harry's limbs and half his torso.

The soothing nurse is explaining that I can't go with them in the ambulance this time. There will be too many people looking after Harry. There won't be room for me, so I'll have to travel in the car with Mathew. The ambulance will need to go at speed she says, we mustn't try to keep up. We nod numbly. As they wheel Harry outside, she stops us.

"Oh, I just thought: you'll need toiletries. Wait there, I'll get you some."

I know it's a trick to delay us so that we don't follow the ambulance but I collude in the charade anyway. *Be a good girl, don't make a fuss. It's all fine. Everything's fine.*

Minutes tick by. She returns eventually with a toothbrush, comb and flannel. When we get outside, the night is dark and still. There's no sign of the ambulance.

The streets are eerily empty and we cover the miles quickly without needing to speed excessively. Occasionally one of us speaks as some random thought pops into our head:

"He's supposed to be going to Jamie's to play tomorrow. I'll phone his mum in the morning."

"Okay."

Silence.

"I'll cancel my meeting in London on Wednesday."

"Okay."

Silence.

"I hope Mum's OK."

"Once we've seen him and he's settled, I'll go back so she can sleep." Mathew is in denial as much as I am.

Silence.

Suddenly, we see an ambulance stopped by the side of the road. The blue lights are still flashing but it's otherwise completely still. There's nothing else around but we're on a dual carriageway and we're past it before we can think what to do. Anyway, there's nowhere to stop.

"Is that...?"

"I don't know." I try to peer inside to see if I recognise the driver as we pass it but there's no one in the cab.

"We'll just get there... wait for them there."

"Yes." Mathew is taking control and I'm grateful.

Neither of us speak again. Was Harry in the back of

that ambulance? Has my son woken up? What are they doing to him? He'll be frightened. He'll need me. My limbs ache with yearning to be in the back of that ambulance, to hold Harry and reassure him. But I don't tell Mathew to turn around. I don't yank the steering wheel and shout at him to stop driving past. I sit there, and we continue doing what we'd been told to do. We drive to the hospital. In silence.

Finding where we're supposed to park takes a while. Then we can't find the entrance. It's dark and there's nowhere obviously open at this time of night. Eventually, we spot a door where we can see a woman behind a desk in a lit entrance hall. As we get closer we can see another ambulance parked outside an entrance a few metres further down. Another ambulance or the same one?

The woman behind the desk gets up and comes to unlock the door when she sees us. She looks confused and slightly annoyed.

"Can I help you?" she asks. She makes it clear that she shouldn't be having to help anyone at this ridiculous hour of the night.

"Our son's just been transferred from the Countess of Chester." Mathew speaks for both of us.

"Name?" she asks with a sigh, returning to her post behind the desk and tapping the keyboard. We tell her. "Do you know what ward?" She's still irritated and now squinting at a computer screen.

Please don't let this be difficult, I need to get to him

quickly.

"Intensive care," I shoot back at her. *So he's seriously ill, OK? Now stop being fucking obstructive and tell us where to go!*

She taps something else and then points down the corridor. "Take the lift on the right up to the fifth floor. You'll come out right opposite intensive care." This time she speaks with far less of the attitude.

*

The doors to intensive care have a buzzer for admittance. We press it and wait. *Come on, come on!* I can't keep still.

"Yes?" a disembodied voice asks through the intercom after what seems like an age.

"We're Harry Fenton's parents," Mathew says.

"Come through," the voice says kindly. They know his name; he must've arrived safely.

The doors lead into a corridor. At the end there are another set of double doors, through which we can see the intensive care ward. Before we reach them, a nurse hurries out and intercepts us. She looks harried.

"If you could just wait in here." She pushes open a door on the right of the corridor that I hadn't noticed, and gestures inside. "Someone will come and see you in a minute."

What? No! I want to see my son!

I do as I am told.

It's some sort of parents' room, L-shaped with tea making things at one end and school tables with orange plastic chairs at the other. A clock ticks loudly on the wall. I sit on one of the chairs and almost instantly stand up again to pace around the room. I can't settle. *Come on! What's keeping them? I just want to see Harry.*

A woman comes in. Her face looks strained but she gives a small half smile anyway. I wonder what's wrong with her child. It's another world here – a parallel world – paediatric intensive care. A world that has always been here, co-existing beside our world. We choose not to see it, not to think about it. To think about it is too terrifying so we pretend these places don't exist. When we picture children, we see swings and parks and footballs, not intensive care units. Children don't belong here. *My* child doesn't belong here.

I sit again. Mathew hasn't moved from the seat he chose when we came in. He's unnervingly still. I can't stop moving. We don't look at each other, each of us scared of what we might read in the other's eyes. They're taking too long.

I go over to the sink and absently wash one of the cups someone has left there. It's soothing, scouring the inside to remove an old, dried tea stain, reassuringly normal. *It's all fine.*

But deep inside I know.

I already know.

I've known from the beginning.

*

It's starting to get light outside. I can see the silhouette of buildings and a pale glow on the horizon. We've been waiting for a long time now. I don't want them to hurry up anymore; I want them to never come.

The knowing that's deep inside keeps bubbling up to the surface. I try to push it down, to push it away, but it won't stay there.

Footsteps. Not another parent this time. These are heavy, weary steps, delaying steps.

The door opens. *Please no, I need more time!*

I see her face and I disintegrate. Time splits into a before and an after.

"I'm so sorry," says a voice from far away.

Chapter 15
2006

"Maggie?"

Mathew's voice in the distance.

"Maggie."

The voice was closer.

I pulled myself back into the present, to the bottom step I was now sitting on, to a different house in a different part of the country.

"Maggie, what is it?"

Mathew, crouched in front of me, concern etched across his face.

I wiped my face with the back of my hand and was confused to see it come away wet. "It's happened," I answered simply.

"A client who's lost a child?"

I nodded, although I couldn't actually be sure of anything Robyn had said after that first sentence. "I think so."

Mathew and I had talked about this possibility since I started training fourteen years ago.

"Meningitis?"

I nodded again, that bit I had heard. I squeezed my eyes shut to hold back new tears.

"Maggie, you have to refer them on, you can't do this," Mathew said gently.

"I think I have to," I said, avoiding his eye. I glanced at a note on the table by the phone. 'Robyn, Friday, 11.00 a.m.' it read. I couldn't remember writing it.

*

"Well, at least see what Sue thinks."

Mathew wouldn't let it drop even as we lay in bed later that night. He knew the counselling world well enough to know that as my supervisor, Sue would probably tell me not to see Robyn under the circumstances. I promised to make an emergency appointment early the next week.

*

Driving to Sue the following Tuesday, I thought through what I would need to tell her about Robyn. Five years earlier I had reached a point with John where I felt I had outgrown him; like he was holding me back. As my confidence as a counsellor had grown, I started to notice just how often I felt de-skilled after a supervision session with him. As I started to find my own way of working, we also disagreed more and more in terms of theory. There were so many models and theories out there and I had begun to move away from a pure person-centred approach to incorporate other ideas. John didn't like that and he seemed to undermine me every time I strayed from his own model of choice. In the end I felt I believed in myself as a counsellor more than he did, despite his repeated assertions to the contrary.

As I thought back to my sessions with Robyn ten years earlier and the way they had ended, I noticed for the first time the parallels between our ending and my ending with John five years later. Yet another parallel, I thought, albeit a small one by comparison. Or maybe it wasn't a parallel at all, maybe I was looking for them now, seeing them everywhere, imagining them. I shook my head; I was being ridiculous. I wondered what Sue would make of this parallel, the big one, the one that I definitely wasn't imagining.

Ever since Robyn's call I had felt strangely detached from the real world. Whatever had happened to me during that call, it was as if I hadn't quite come back to where I was before, like I was still half in the present and half in the past. I had floated through the weekend, distracted and harbouring a very physical anxiety that left me feeling nauseous and unable to eat. I couldn't shake the hollowed out empty feeling that was an echo of something much stronger from seventeen years earlier. Every so often I had looked up from some faraway place to see Mathew staring at me, worry seeping from every pore.

In the rare moments when I could think logically, I suspected what had happened during the call was some form of disassociation. Although I felt guilty at the thought of hiding it, I knew that I would have to be very careful how I talked to Sue about that. If she suspected I had disassociated she would never let me work with Robyn. And I really wanted to work with Robyn. Yes, I was terrified of the content and didn't know if I would be able to bear it, but I also felt drawn to Robyn and compelled to help her. It was very risky for both of us and therefore ethically dubious to say the least, but I didn't care: I had to work with her.

I told Sue about the similarities between Robyn and me last time, before I mentioned what she was bringing to counselling this time. I focussed on our philosophical ideology, our need for both adventure and security, our penchant for questioning what life should be about. I didn't mention any of the crazier fantasies I had had at the time about our similarities, and I skated over the Andre/Andy stuff. Irrationally, I thought that if I could just convince her of our connection, she would endorse the work despite the obvious risks.

"OK, so it's great that she is coming back after a unilateral ending like that. It validates the connection and work you did last time."

"Yes, I was so pleased."

"Do you know why she's coming back now?" she asked innocently, picking a piece of fluff off her sleeve.

"I think she's lost a child." I tried to sound

innocuous.

She stopped what she was doing instantly and looked at me incredulously. "You *think*?"

"Well it was quite hard to follow what she was saying on the phone, to be honest. I'm not one hundred percent sure." It was sort of the truth.

"Quite hard for anyone to follow, or just you? Given your own history." Sue was no idiot.

"For anyone. She was pretty distressed." *What am I doing?* Now we were in the realm of downright lies.

"There are other counsellors who can help her you know Maggie."

No there aren't. It has to be me. No one will understand like I do. "Yes, I know but I really think that I will understand her better than anyone precisely because of my history – my personal history and my history of working with her."

"You don't have to share a personal history to understand a client, otherwise we all would have had to have gone through everything."

In this case you do. The death of a child is the exception. No one knows what it's like. "Yes, I know but…"

"Maybe you're trying to compensate for feeling like you messed up last time, trying to change the ending between you?"

Possibly. "No, I really don't think so. I processed that with John and reached a point where I was genuinely fine with it."

There really was no point in being there. I clearly wasn't going to listen to Sue even though I felt terrible about that. This was so out of character for me; Sue and I had a good relationship, much more collegiate than it had been with John, and yet here I was, hiding from her. What had got into me?

"And how are you going to feel Maggie? It's bound to bring back a lot of difficult memories for you."

There was such warmth and gentleness in her voice, I couldn't keep lying to quite the same extent.

"That's going to be hard." I looked down to avoid seeing the concern in her eyes. I still had to avoid showing her how vulnerable I was, and if I felt her care and warmth I would be undone.

She waited.

"It was seventeen years ago," I said lamely.

"And does that make it easier?"

Not in the slightest! "Yes and no."

"Tell me about the 'yes'."

"You learn how to function, slowly, like learning to walk again and eventually, after a long, long time, you can appreciate small moments of joy. You allow yourself to laugh occasionally – albeit accompanied by guilt – and the emotion gradually fades. It never goes away, but it does fade... or rather... it changes into something bearable. That's what Robyn has ahead of her. And I can help." This was all true, and articulating precisely why I was so desperate to work with Robyn helped a lot.

"And the 'no'?"

Damn! I don't want to talk about that bit.

"I still can't forgive myself." *And I can't bear to remember.*

"Oh Maggie."

Don't look at me with such tenderness please. I won't be able to keep this up!

"I still wish you'd consider going back into therapy. That's such a burden to carry."

"But that's the whole point; that's why I need to work with Robyn. Therapy only helped me to a point because I couldn't quite get over the feeling that she couldn't possibly understand. I held back, and I probably still would. Robyn would know that I really understand."

"She wouldn't know your history." Sue looked apprehensive, like she didn't quite know where I was going with this.

"She wouldn't need to; it would be obvious that I get it."

"I don't know Maggie. You already identify with her so much. Maybe this is an identification too far. I don't see how your own stuff can't help but get in the way with this one."

"It won't because it's not my story. This is *her* story. But mine will help me to know what she's going through in a way that no one else can."

Sue was quiet, thoughtful. She looked at me for a long time, evidently weighing the risks. I started to feel uncomfortable under her intense gaze but held it and tried to convey a sureness and strength that I was far from feeling.

Eventually she broke away and acquiesced with a sigh. "OK."

I let out the breath I'd been holding.

"OK. I'm not one hundred per cent happy about this but I know you're a good counsellor, boundaried and ethical. I'm going to trust you to know what you're doing, what you can cope with and what's ethically right."

Ouch! Sue could not have made what my responsibilities were any clearer, and how far away from them I was about to stray. I felt excited, scared and deeply ashamed, all at the same time.

*

The rest of the week dragged interminably on. Clients were a welcome distraction from my thoughts and I marvelled at how easily they pulled me into their worlds, despite what was going on in my own. In between clients though it felt weirdly like waiting for Christmas. I was inexplicably desperate to see Robyn again despite the agony I knew she would bring, and so each hour felt like a day, until suddenly it was Friday.

And then it wasn't Christmas; it wasn't Christmas at all. I couldn't understand my thinking. Why had I agreed to see Robyn in the first place? And why had I convinced Sue that I was up to it? It was madness, I was like a moth drawn to a flame. I knew it could only end badly and yet I had been compelled to meet her again, to hear what had happened to her son, to sit there and listen and try to help, knowing that it would probably rip me apart. It was the strangest form of self-harm I had ever come across.

Julian had the appointment immediately before Robyn's and I wondered how on earth I was going to be able to concentrate and focus on him. I was jittery and restless now, aware only of my complete folly in agreeing to see her. The compulsion was gone, replaced by an abject terror of what her hour would hold for both of us. It was too late to back out now, but for the first time since I agreed to it, I desperately wanted to.

*

Clients have a knack of grabbing my full attention when I'm least expecting it though and Julian was no exception. Right from his first sentence, I was engrossed.

"Will you go to court with me next week?"

"Er... wow, I wasn't expecting that Julian. Can you say a bit about why you want me to?" It wasn't just a play for time or the stereotypical therapist trick of turning questions back on the client: I genuinely couldn't answer the question without knowing more.

"I don't know... it doesn't matter... you don't have to."

Shit he's embarrassed, I didn't mean to do that!

"I'm not saying no, I just want to understand a bit more."

"I don't know... I just thought..." he tailed off.

"You just thought...?"

"I just thought it might be easier, you know, if you were there. It doesn't matter. Forget it."

"I don't want to forget it, it sounds important. If I was there, how would it make it easier?" *Careful, I don't want him to feel bad for asking, but I can't make any promises either. There are boundary issues to consider here too. I need time to think.*

"I don't know. I just think having someone on my side would help."

"It feels like a battle?"

"It is a battle. It's a battle to be believed. I'm going to say he's a paedophile, he's going to say I'm a liar. His army is going to try to pull me apart."

"And your army can't protect you from that?"

"My army has its own agenda. The generals are not really on my side. Yes, they want to win, but that's nothing to do with *me*. It doesn't help *me*. They want to win to further their own careers and I'm just a pawn in that. None of this helps *me*, it's not for *my* benefit. I get nothing out of this."

"Is that true?"

"My life was fine before. I was OK. Now look at me, all of this raked up, having to face all that happened, having to tell people, convince people, having to face not being believed. Everything would have been better if they'd left me alone."

"He'd have got away with it, though."

"He's seventy-five! He's already got away with it. He's had forty years of living a wonderful life, thank you very much. It's too late for justice. What can they do to him now? Take away his last few years? So what."

His voice got louder, betraying a new but understandably bitter edge. I knew he was deeply afraid of going to court and everything that entailed. It really had been a terrible day for him when all of this came back into his life, and I totally understood that it might have been better left alone, buried deep. I didn't necessarily conform to the usual therapist view that trauma must be dealt with rather than buried. Sometimes buried works just fine.

If he went to court, Julian needed to go for himself, not for everyone else. I needed to help him find his own reasons to attend court – or support him in refusing to if that's genuinely what he wanted.

"So why go through with it then?"

"… I don't know."

"There must be some reason you're even entertaining it. There are so many reasons not to go."

"I just don't want him to win again. They've made it clear that if I don't go the case falls through."

"And if that happened?"

"I can just see him smirking like he used to. I don't

think I'd be able to get that image out of my head, and I don't think I could live with it."

"You might go and lose and he would still smirk." It was a tough thing to say out loud but I knew Julian was already thinking it; it was his biggest fear. We needed to talk about it, not skirt around it.

"I know." Julian fell silent and fiddled absentmindedly with his wedding ring. Eventually he said, "But at least then he would know that I wasn't afraid to stand up to him… the thing is though, I am. I am afraid to stand up to him. I feel just like I did back then, weak and powerless. I'm just as pathetic as I was then."

"You think you're pathetic?"

"Yes, pathetic!" He spat the word. "I should've fought then and I should fight now." He looked away. "I just don't know if I can."

"You couldn't fight then, you were a child, and you had no one." And suddenly there it was; an inkling of what it might mean if I went to court with him. "Not fighting then was actually a good survival strategy. Back then, you had no one on your side. It's highly likely you wouldn't have been believed and saying something would have made it all so much worse. We usually make good survival decisions in childhood. It's only with the resources and knowledge of adulthood that we sometimes think we can see another way, but often that way simply wasn't available back then. You weren't pathetic Julian, you were surviving."

"I never thought about it like that."

"But I'm right, aren't I? That you had no one? That you wouldn't have been believed? It would've made it worse?"

"Absolutely, there was no one. Mum was a waste-of-space alcoholic, which was why I was taken away in the first place. I never ever saw her. She probably could've visited thinking about it now, but she never did. I never expected her to. There was no one. The word of a delinquent that no one gave a damn about versus a respected teacher? Telling would've been suicide, I knew that. I knew I mustn't tell."

This was exactly the kind of reinterpretation I was hoping for. I decided to press it home. "So, was it really pathetic?"

"No… no I guess not, not back then. But now? I'm a grown man and I'm trembling in my boots at the thought of facing him again."

"That makes perfect sense to me. You haven't seen him since childhood, it's bound to bring back all the feelings you had back then. You haven't met him as an adult. Your brain only has your childhood reaction to go on, and when you were a child he was very, very dangerous. He's coded in your head as an extreme threat, whether that's rational or not. Your brain will continue to react to him as dangerous until you re-write the code."

"By meeting him as an adult?"

"By having a different experience of him, yes."

"So, I should go to court? Is that what you're telling me?"

"I'm not ducking the question Julian, but it's not as simple as whether you should or shouldn't go. My job is to help you weigh up the pros and cons and for you to make that decision based on what's best for you. You could go and win and feel better for standing up to him. The risk is that you go and lose and feel... what?"

"Devastated! Humiliated all over again."

"So, you don't take that risk. You don't go at all and you feel, what?"

"Worse! Then I do feel really pathetic! Weak and feeble, and... like I'm saying it was OK."

I was desperate to guide him at this point, to tell him what to do, but I knew that I mustn't. It was crucial that he got there himself. I forced myself to stay silent.

"This is my only chance to tell isn't it?" he whispered eventually. "I couldn't do it then, but I can now."

"Yes, it is. You can't control who they believe, but you can control whether or not you tell. You have the power to choose at least that this time."

"I'm going to go." He sounded truly resolute.

Maybe I thought this would be my best chance to offer a reparative relationship, that if I could provide some kind of emotional protection this time around it would undo some of the damage of his past.

"And I'm coming with you," I heard myself say.

I don't know who was more shocked when the words came out of my mouth. I'd been planning to go away and think about it, talk to Sue maybe, weigh up the therapeutic and practical issues involved, but I was too moved at that point. I wanted to be there for him.

"I think you need someone there who's on your side this time." I answered the unspoken question written in his eyes. "And whoever they believe, you and I will know the truth."

*

After the session, wrapping my hands around a warm cup of tea, I wondered what had got into me. I didn't regret agreeing to go with Julian – I still really wanted to – but I knew I hadn't thought it through, and that was out of character.

Boundaries are always an important consideration in any therapy, but how tightly they should be held divides therapists. Purists would be appalled at me doing something with Julian outside the therapeutic hour. Although I did make exceptions and step outside rigid boundary 'rules' occasionally, it was only ever after careful thought about the therapeutic implications and the impact on me.

As I thought about it now, I realised that it was possible that I was acting out some kind of rescuer role with Julian and I should've thought first about what that meant for him. I kicked myself for missing it. To act so impulsively wasn't like me and I worried about it. I also secretly quite liked it. To go to court felt like a very human response to Julian's request. It also felt like a satisfyingly maverick counsellor response. This was the bloody 'real relationship' in action; messy and imperfect! *Get over it, therapy police!*

The trouble was, maverick was becoming a bit of a theme for me lately. Why on earth had I lied to Sue about being able to cope with what Robyn was about to talk about? I wasn't up to it. I knew I wasn't.

Robyn! Fifteen minutes to go! My stomach flipped as I was jolted out of my contemplation of the session with Julian and into the reality of her imminent arrival. I went to the loo again. I didn't need to; it was nerves. This really was crazy and beyond unethical! It was dangerous, for both of us. I could do real damage to Robyn by not being able to cope with her pain. What was I thinking? Was it too late? Could I tell her when she arrived that I couldn't see her? Would that be more or less damaging than seeing her and breaking down? Or worse?

Ten minutes to go. Was there time to make another cup of tea? I couldn't sit still so I made one anyway just for something to do. I knew I probably wouldn't have time to drink it but I warmed my hands on the cup again and tried to stop them shaking. Did my fear show? Would Robyn be able to tell? Would she assume I was scared of her pain? That it was too much for me? Would she think that she had to hold back like I had? She wouldn't know that it's not her pain but mine that's too much. Much too much! *Fuck! This is the most stupid thing I've ever done!*

Five minutes to go. I took a seat in my counselling chair and tried to breathe my way into relaxing. A money spider was hanging on the end of a long thin strand of web, the other end invisible against the window. I watched as she climbed slowly up about three inches and then fell all the way back down. Instantly she started off up her invisible route again, driven by some important motive only she knew, and fell back down when she reached the exact same point. And again. And again.

Suddenly, strangely, I felt calm. I was resigned to my fate, like an animal playing dead when it's finally caught by a predator. Calm was wrong; it was more like numb. There was no point in fighting it anymore. My time was up, so I gave in and accepted whatever was coming. My story, Julian's story, Robyn's story, the spider's story: none of it mattered, maybe none of it was even real. I was lost.

Robyn knocked on the door and stepped inside.

Chapter 16

We exchanged subdued hellos and I offered the ritual glass of water, which she accepted. The preliminaries are always awkward when the content is going to be highly emotionally charged. Add in our history and the way it ended and what could I say? 'It's so good to see you again, Robyn'? We both played the etiquette game anyway but kept the required pleasantries and social niceties to a minimum. This wasn't going to be easy and we both wanted to get on with it. Robyn dived in immediately. There was no other way.

"It was the 28th May, bank holiday weekend. We'd been camping on Shell Island..."

I can see the dunes in the distance, white with random tufts of sharp green grass. Harry is running towards me, desperate to show me something he's found and put in his little red bucket, sunlight bouncing off his fine blond hair. His nose is red from his cold but he's bright and happy. Sam is squealing at the feel of the still cold sand between his toes. It's an infectious sound and Mathew and I grin at each other and then laugh out loud as Sam gets more and more excited by it. Harry wants the attention back, he's excited too, he's found a crab's leg.

"Look Mummy, look!" *He tugs repeatedly at my skirt to make sure I'm looking and that's funny too.*

Robyn's story, not mine. Focus!

"And I knew then, I think, that something was seriously wrong. They tried to say in the hospital that it was a febrile convulsion, but I knew it wasn't…"

I knew too. Why didn't I speak up? Harry would still be alive if only I'd spoken up. What kind of mother puts her own need to be thought well of above the wellbeing of her child? If only I'd stamped my feet, asked for a second opinion. It shouldn't have mattered what people would think if I made a scene. Only Harry should've mattered. I should never have taken him home. Those vital few hours cost him his life.

Mathew didn't argue either. Curiously, I've never thought that he should have. Only I should have. I alone bear the responsibility for the death of our child. I've never even blamed that doctor. I can see him now, checking thoroughly, examining every inch of Harry, taking care. He'd probably seen many more febrile convulsions than meningitis cases, so it was a fair call. But I knew – call it a mother's instinct if you like – I knew and I did nothing, and so my child died.

How could therapy help? I don't actually want to forgive myself. That's the minimum suffering I deserve. Only, I don't suffer anymore. Not really. I don't think about it. At some point I realised that I was still Sam's mother and that he deserved more. Or was that my excuse; that I had to push my own punishment to one side in order to function for Sam? And despite my intention not to, I moved on, in a fashion, and despise myself all the more for it whenever I do remember.

Focus!

"When the second consultant arrived, he shook my hand formally and asked me to tell him what had been going on. He didn't look at Daniel at all, he just listened to me. When I'd finished, he checked Daniel's notes but he didn't re-examine him. I was getting ready to argue with him when he said the most unexpected thing."

I struggled to catch up. Had Robyn got a second opinion? Had she done the very thing that I should've done? The thing that would've saved Harry's life.

"He said, 'Mrs Carter, all of Daniel's vital signs are good and I'm sure that Dr Reed has made the right call and there's nothing to worry about'. I opened my mouth to argue but he held up his hand to stop me and then he said, I'll never forget it, he said, 'But when Mum is worried, I'm worried. Medicine isn't an exact science'. He said, 'We get it wrong sometimes, but I've learnt over many years that a mother's instinct is important information too and we do well not to ignore it'. I couldn't believe it. Someone was taking me seriously, without me even having to stamp my feet. He admitted Daniel for overnight observation as a precaution."

So it was a very different story after all. Robyn asked for that second opinion and Daniel stayed in hospital, in the care of the professionals. The doctor listened to a mother's instinct. The mother's instinct I hadn't even voiced. And Daniel had lived.

I wondered what else had happened that had left her so distraught, unable to get on with life. She looked broken, pale and gaunt, like she hadn't eaten or slept properly for weeks. It would be painful to listen to the rest, to hear about the happy ending that followed from her doing what I should've done. It would be like listening to the alternative reality I had played in my head over and over in the early days, but I was also curious now. What on earth had happened to her?

"I should've been reassured, and I was. But there was also a more sinister feeling. He was telling me my instincts could be trusted, and my instincts were that this was bad – really bad. I didn't want them to be trustable; I wanted them to be ridiculous."

Her voice was empty, sad yes, but also weary and devoid of intensity. I looked at Robyn properly then. Her eyes had filled but they were still somehow dead, fixed into the middle distance, re-living some terrible nightmare. She looked like a hollowed out version of a human being, a parody of a person. She looked like I felt deep inside. What had happened? Did the trauma destroy her relationship? Was Daniel traumatised? Disabled even? What was it?

"Later that night the fit started again, but this time it

didn't stop."

But Daniel was in hospital where Harry should have been. Daniel lived.

"When it was obvious the fit wasn't going to stop someone must have pressed a big red button somewhere because people came flying in from everywhere. I play that scene over and over in my head now. It was so efficient, so obviously well-rehearsed. Everyone knew what to do. They must've spoken to each other but I didn't hear them. Crazy, but I was awestruck by it all. It should've been terrifying but it didn't seem real. Or I wouldn't let it be real."

Why not? Where is she going with this? Why does she look like that? I don't understand, Daniel lived. He lived because she insisted on a second opinion.

"He'd had Ribena..."

Everyone's relieved, it's just Ribena. They catch each other's eyes. Mathew's arriving now...

"... needed to transfer him to another hospital..."

The transfer team are so calm, so efficient. It's so quiet, all the panic has died down. The fitting has stopped and Harry looks peaceful. He could be sleeping apart from all the tubes coming out of his mouth and limbs.

"... passed an ambulance at the side of the road..."

Wait! What? She was there? She saw Harry's ambulance? Not Harry's – that's ridiculous – Daniel's, she saw Daniel's. Maggie, focus! You're not listening, you're remembering. Listen to Robyn's story. Separate what's yours and what's hers.

But I began to hear her voice as though from somewhere deep inside me. It became muffled and distant, like listening through a door. I couldn't catch the whispered words, they ran and hid from me and so my brain disobediently filled in the gaps, and separation became impossible.

"… double doors to intensive care…"

No, that's a memory, she didn't say that! Parents' room off to one side.

"… school tables…"

Orange plastic chairs.

"… clock…"

Tick, tick, tick,

"… couldn't stop pacing…"

Mathew unnervingly still.

"… orange plastic chairs…"

TICK, TICK, TICK.

The room is swimming. I'm going to faint. Is that a memory or is it happening now? I can't do this. I want to run! I want to run and never stop. What was I thinking? 'I trust you to know what you're doing, what you can cope with and what's ethically right'. Shit! I can't see Robyn. She's out of focus; swirling, fuzzy, grey. I feel sick. What the fuck am I doing?

"… a woman came in…"

Tense and dishevelled.

A dirty cup, scrubbing, scouring. It's fine, everything's fine.

"... footsteps..."
Orange plastic chairs
"... I knew..."
I knew!

I had no idea what Robyn had actually said, what were really her words and what were in fact my memories. When she stopped talking and I woke from my own personal nightmare, we looked at one another for a long time and it felt like we were holding each other. Our eyes were brimming and both of us had wet cheeks. I knew only two things with absolute clarity: Daniel had not been sent home, and Daniel had died anyway.

"So how do I live?" she asked. "How do I ever live again?"

"Do you really want to?" I asked gently. I was on autopilot and still thinking of Harry.

She looked up, shocked and puzzled, before sighing and visibly deflating. She slowly shook her head. "No. No, I don't really."

"Why don't you?" I knew the answer but she needed to say it out loud, to acknowledge it, or anything else we talked about would be a waste of time.

"Because it would be a betrayal," she whispered. "A betrayal of Daniel."

"It may *feel* like a betrayal but that doesn't make it a fact." It was a challenge, but that feeling would shackle her to guilt if it wasn't challenged. I was under no illusion that she would instantly abandon it, but I needed to start the process of implying that there was an alternative. Whatever had just happened to me, my responses now were instinctive. I knew what I needed to do.

"No... maybe not." That was enough of an acknowledgement for now. I wouldn't labour the point.

We both sat quietly for a while. She seemed to have run out of words.

"You said you had another son?"

She nodded. "Spencer, he's nineteen months now."

I thought of Mathew, of how he'd had to do the parenting for both of us for a while. How he'd pushed his own grief to one side and cared for both me and Sam in the early days. I thought of how tenderly and sensitively he had led me back to Sam and my reason for being.

"Have you ever heard of Viktor Frankl?"

She shook her head but looked curious.

"He survived Auschwitz. But he not only survived, he emerged from the camp relatively psychologically intact. He later said that he'd held onto an image of himself in the future, lecturing on survival, on why some people did and some didn't survive the camp. He made it his mission while he was there to understand what made the difference. He went on to invent a therapy based on finding the meaning in suffering. He said, 'He who has a *why* to live for can bear almost any *how*'."

"Spencer is my *why*, then?"

"Doesn't he have to be?"

"Spencer is my why to *exist*, to go on functioning, but *living* is a whole different thing."

I understood. She didn't yet realise that Spencer needed her to *live*, that existing and functioning aren't enough to nurture a child, to be there for them through all their childhood trials. And as that thought crystallised, I started to wonder again whose therapy this actually was.

"Even if I wanted to," she continued, "I can't imagine how it would be possible. I can't imagine ever feeling anything but this, this blackness, this excruciating…"

"And you won't feel anything but blackness for a long, long time. You will feel tortured and desolate and… in agony."

Robyn closed her eyes and screwed her face up as though my words caused her physical pain but I continued anyway.

"You will feel isolated because you will see the world as it really is: cruel and unbearably painful, whilst everyone else still sees through a filter of delusion. Even Andy will be going through something different to you because he's a father and you're a mother. You may be together in grief some of the time but at other times you will also be very, very separate and you'll wonder why you don't understand each other."

Robyn was looking at me curiously now and I knew it was an accurate description for her too. I ploughed on.

"People won't know what to say to you. Some will

stay away rather than face you. It will be too much for them, too close to home."

"That's already happening," she nodded.

"You will be lonely and you will miss him so much that you think you will break in half. You will actually feel it physically and you won't believe it's possible to miss someone so much and for your body to go on functioning. Your arms will ache to hold him."

Tears started to roll down Robyn's cheeks again. And mine.

"And there will always be that hole. Many years from now it will still be there." I'd stopped looking at her now and was focusing on an eternity of memories. "And then one day, there will be a moment, it might be a sight or a smell or a thought, and you'll suddenly realise that what you just felt was joy. It will be fleeting, there and instantly gone. You might feel guilty the first time. But gradually you'll have more moments. They'll never be any longer than a moment, but eventually there will be several a day, if only you know how to look for them, if you allow yourself to look for them. And slowly you'll come to realise that that's all anyone has, isn't it? Moments – if we're lucky. Moments of joy punctuating a muted background of something else. And by then the something else won't be this, it won't be blackness, and it will be bearable."

I didn't mention crushing guilt. I didn't mention being unable to forgive herself. I didn't mention how secret shame would make it unbearable to remember.

Those things wouldn't apply to Robyn; Robyn got a second opinion.

When I looked up again, she was staring at me in disbelief.

"You too," she said. It wasn't a question.

Shit!

"Robyn… this isn't about me…" I swiped a tear away and tried to back pedal out of the corner I suddenly found myself in.

"You did though, didn't you? You lost a child too?"

"Robyn…"

"Please Maggie! Don't go all therapist non-disclosure on me. I nearly didn't come because I thought no one could possibly understand, I thought *you* couldn't possibly understand. Andy made me come. I thought it was a waste of time. How can anyone understand if they haven't been through this? Nothing comes close. Please Maggie, I have to know."

Her eyes pleaded with me. I looked out of the window to block her out while I attended to the competing thoughts. I couldn't make this about me and therapist non-disclosure was important, rules and boundaries are there for a reason. And yet…

After a long silence, I looked back at Robyn and held her eye. "I understand," I said quietly.

And there it was; we both knew. I felt vulnerable for just a moment and more tears threatened to engulf me. We sat there, eyes still locked, this time like two drowning women clinging on to one another. And in that moment, I realised for the first time that I could swim.

*

I was glad I deliberately hadn't scheduled anything for the rest of the day; glad it was Friday and I would have two full days before I had to focus on any other clients; glad that Mathew and Sam were both out of the house for a few hours. I needed time to absorb everything that had just happened and to focus on me. I needed to understand what it all meant and get my head straight.

We had lost the dogs years earlier, and on days like this I really missed them. I needed to be outside and moving in order to think straight and so I set off on one of our old walks. It was another crisp autumn day, cold and sunny. The trees were incredible shades of gold and orange that seemed to transform the whole landscape into a reddish hue as the low sunlight bounced off them. I noticed the colours briefly before I was lost in thought, and walked the two-mile circuit without seeing a thing.

I knew that I would never know the detail of Robyn's story now. I would never know exactly what happened to Daniel that night because we would never talk about the whole of it like that again. I didn't listen properly so the chance to know was lost forever.

Robyn, on the other hand, would remember every moment of it, every word, every gesture, every expression. They would be engraved on her heart and she would re-play every second of that horrendous night over and over. The slightest thing would trigger a small part of the memory and then the whole thing would play from there, like someone pressing play from some random point in a DVD.

I knew that I hadn't heard the detail of her story, that I'd been lost in my own, but I really didn't think that it would matter as far as Robyn's therapy was concerned. I tried to be objective, to challenge myself on that point, but I honestly didn't think it would make a difference. Daniel had died, suddenly, unavoidably, tragically and she didn't know how to live with that. That was what mattered. I knew exactly what that was like, I knew better than anyone what that was like. Identification was a huge hook into deep empathy and at least Robyn wouldn't feel like an alien living in a parallel world that no one understood. She would know that at least I understood and that would make such a difference. Robyn wouldn't feel isolated. That was much more important than me knowing the details.

I thought about what I had said to Robyn about moments. I hadn't realised, until I articulated it like that, what had imperceptibly happened over the years. I hadn't realised that I had slowly learnt to live again. I hadn't realised that the joy I felt around Sam and his friends, the meaning I had found through him, even the sadness I felt at the thought of him leaving, were all signs of life. I could give Robyn hope.

It still felt like a betrayal of Harry when I thought

about it though. There was still that familiar twinge of guilt, a feeling that I didn't deserve to be happy. I should have insisted on a second opinion.

But Robyn did get a second opinion and Daniel died anyway. Maybe Harry's death was inevitable too. In seventeen years that thought had never once occurred to me. It had never crossed my mind that Harry might have died even if I had stood up to the doctors that night and told them about my intuition. In my head, Harry died precisely because I was too weak to speak up. To consider another alternative was mind-blowing. Was it possible that my child didn't die because I was a people-pleaser, after all? Was it possible that I couldn't have saved him? That thought, if I could allow it, would change everything. It would mean I could remember.

An image of Harry as a baby popped into my head. I could see him sitting in his highchair in his little yellow cardigan with the teddy bear buttons. My mind skipped to Robyn years later choosing that button to represent the side of her that yearned for a child, and felt an overwhelming pang of sadness for her. All those years ago she had wanted a child so badly, just like me, and now he was gone, snatched away from her. Just like me.

I shivered at the thought. All those coincidences. It was spooky even back then, all those similarities; the wise whisperer, people-pleaser and adventurer, our philosophy and search for meaning and life, Andre and Andy and the identical relationship dynamic we wrestled with at the same age. But now there was this too. This was a coincidence too far. We each had a child, a son, who had died suddenly aged three from meningitis.

I desperately tried to remember what Robyn had actually said in the session. Did she say that they'd told her that Daniel had just had a febrile convulsion too? I'm pretty sure she said he had to be transferred to a different hospital. Did she actually say they passed Daniel's ambulance stopped by the side of the road too? Those things can't have happened to her as well; that would be too weird. I had got her story completely mixed up with mine, and had dissociated more than I thought.

The things I did definitely know about were simply statistically plausible coincidences. Although vaccines had been introduced since Harry died, saving hundreds of lives, many children did still die every year of meningitis. And hey, I was a counsellor, people came to me to talk about trauma and tragedy so I was more likely than most to come across those cases. Her boyfriend hit her once and so did mine, that's sadly hardly unique. We had a similar relationship dynamic but, again, so what? It's not an uncommon dynamic. And a similar outlook on life in our early twenties – who doesn't identify with that? It's a common idealistic view at that age, I see it in Sam sometimes now. John even said that at the time. I was being crazy, and yet something still niggled away at me. I couldn't shake the feeling that there was more than synchronicity at play here.

I shook myself and laughed and told myself to stop being silly. What else could it possibly be other than coincidence? Anyway, all that would have to wait. I had bigger, much more life changing thoughts to attend to, namely: what if I never could've saved Harry? What if his death had been inevitable too?

Chapter 17

Mathew watched me like a hawk for the next few days and Sue even phoned me to see how the session had gone. She never did that, it was a breach of boundaries after all, and I interpreted it as an indication that she'd had second thoughts about allowing me to go ahead. I told neither of them about the dissociation and reassured them both that I was fine. And I was. I was sure that I wouldn't dissociate again now that Robyn had told me about what had happened to Daniel, and whilst I knew it would be painful, I was equally sure that I could cope with what was to come.

I was aware that I was being very quiet and withdrawn at home and I knew that didn't help Mathew to be any less concerned about me, but what could I tell him? I couldn't say that I was re-evaluating the guilt that I'd carried for seventeen years about our son's death because I'd never told him about that guilt. It had been a secret even from him. I had never told him about my sinister intuition because I couldn't bear the thought of him blaming me too. I couldn't bear to confess that I'd known Harry was seriously ill and I'd allowed them to send us home anyway. What if he couldn't forgive me for that? I wouldn't have blamed him; I couldn't forgive myself.

I couldn't talk to Mathew about it yet because I was still trying to work it all out. I needed to block him out, to withdraw in order to think about what it meant and how it changed things, but I was OK. I genuinely felt OK. He didn't need to be concerned, I was just distracted; distracted and hopeful. Hopeful, in a vague hard-to-get-hold-of sense, for the first time in seventeen years.

It felt bizarre that the rest of my life carried on just as it had before. I cooked, I did the weekend jobs of washing and ironing, I functioned as though I wasn't re-assessing the validity of a belief that had haunted me for years.

Part of that functioning involved making practical arrangements so that I could go to court with Julian. I needed to contact other clients to tell them that 'due to unforeseen circumstances' I was going to have to cancel their sessions that week. Julian didn't know which day exactly he would be called to the witness stand; it could be any one of three. Over the weekend I decided to cancel my Tuesday and Wednesday clients and leave those on Thursday for now. I would cancel them on Tuesday night if it looked possible that Julian wouldn't be called until then.

When I wasn't lost in the past, I was preoccupied by

the ethics of going to court. It wasn't just the impact on Julian, for better or worse, that I hadn't considered, I hadn't thought about the practical implications either. I was prioritising Julian's needs over the needs of my other clients and I knew that wasn't right. I would've agonised about it much more if it had been Robyn's session on Friday that I'd had to cancel though, and that made me feel even worse. The truth was that I didn't really feel bad about letting any of the others down. I wanted to be there for Julian and that felt more important than the needs of the others.

What was happening to me? All the professional rules and boundaries I'd lived by for so long were going out of the window and a big part of me didn't care. A small part of me did though and that caused a lot of soul-searching. I did genuinely care about my other clients. I didn't want to harm them and I definitely didn't want to harm Julian: it was the rules I didn't care about. It felt like the right thing for Julian that I went with him, intuitively right, whether I could justify it or not. There were theoretical arguments for and against – a reparative experience or me rescuing, and therefore reinforcing, a victim position. Which one you favoured was subjective, a matter of opinion. I couldn't call it, it just *felt* right to go.

In the end, Julian called me on Tuesday evening to say he would be first on the stand on Wednesday morning. We arranged to meet in the lobby at 9.00 a.m. When I got there he was standing next to two other women and looked petrified. He introduced us.

"Maggie, this is DI Hammond who I've told you about."

DI Hammond had put Julian under a lot of pressure to attend when he had been unsure, and she was one of the people Julian had been referring to when he'd said that his team were doing this to further their own careers rather than to help him. I was predisposed to dislike her and judged her limp handshake as proof of my opinion.

"And this is Wendy. She's with... er..."

"Victim support." Wendy smiled and extended her hand. She had a firm steady grip I noticed.

"You can't be on your own with Julian," DI Hammond explained. "It's about ensuring no one steers the witness. Wendy will be your chaperone."

How ridiculous, I thought. If I was going to steer him, I'd have done it by now surely, in the hours and hours we've spent behind closed doors talking about what happened. Julian caught my eye, anxious to make sure I was OK with that.

I smiled reassuringly. "OK," I said brightly.

We were taken to a special witness room, a small shabby box of a space with just enough room for a table and four chairs plus two low waiting room style armchairs squeezed in against one wall. A window high up on the opposite side made it feel a bit like a cell; you'd have to stand on one of the chairs to see out of it. Court was due to reconvene at 10.00 a.m.

"How are you feeling?" I asked Julian.

"Nervous," he replied, looking at me pleadingly.

"I bet. A few more hours and it'll be over," I said and smiled at him again, trying to reassure him with a calm presence that I wasn't really feeling. His nerves were contagious and I was battling not to show it.

It was awkward being here and I didn't really know what to say. If it had been just me and Julian, it would have been natural to explore his feelings and unpick what exactly he feared right now. With DI Hammond and Wendy watching us conversation felt stilted and I didn't want to put Julian in a position where he felt exposed. The next few hours would be exposing enough.

"Oh, you'll be fine," DI Hammond said breezily, and I felt a flash of irritation.

You have no bloody idea, do you?

"Tea anyone?" she asked.

While she went to get some drinks, Wendy tried to chat to Julian. "Have you had to come far today?" She was clearly trying to distract him but Julian couldn't really focus on small talk so she gave up. "You'll be OK, love. Really. I do this job every day and witnesses are always nervous. You got Judge Harding though and he don't stand no nonsense from them barristers. He'll look out for you. You'll be fine."

It was a platitude but it was said with such warmth and sincerity, based on so much experience, that it was oddly reassuring. I was grateful to her for trying to help Julian who was now looking pale and wringing his hands. I felt useless. I couldn't help him.

A barrister dashed in, robes billowing out behind him.

"Julian." The barrister shook hands distractedly with Julian and nodded at me before demanding to know where DI Hammond had gone.

She came back in just at that moment.

"I need a word," he said brusquely, and hurried out again, leaving DI Hammond to deposit the Styrofoam cups on the table and scurry out after him.

Whatever was so urgent, it was something about Julian's case and we were just left sitting there in the dark as though it didn't concern us. It was disempowering. Julian caught my eye again and a look of dread passed over his face this time. I held his gaze and tried to silently convey reassurance. This was why I was here. I was here simply to be here, to know what he was thinking and feeling and to just be with him; to show him that I cared enough to be with him. It didn't feel like nearly enough though and I wished I could do more.

The barrister dashed back in and grabbed one of the table chairs, swinging it round to face Julian who was sitting in the armchair. DI Hammond sat on the other side of the table and I instinctively moved to stand behind them so that Julian could see my face.

"OK, so slight problem Julian, but nothing to worry about. Two of the other witnesses haven't turned up. They were due on after you anyway so we have a bit of time to find them. DI Hammond has got people on it now and if the worst comes to the worst we'll ask for an adjournment after you've testified."

"Who were they? I mean, were they victims too?"

"Yes."

"How many others have you got?"

"There are just the three of you."

"So if they don't show, it's just me?"

"We'll find them," Hammond interjected.

"That's why I'm telling you," the barrister continued, ignoring her. "Your evidence will potentially be more crucial. I'm going to add in a few more questions for you. I need you to paint a fuller picture of him, just in case."

"So it'll come down to my word against his." Julian's shoulders sagged. He looked beaten already.

I wanted to spirit him away, whisk him out of the whole sorry circus and protect him from having to face a defeat that suddenly looked a lot more likely than it had just a few minutes earlier. He looked at me like he'd lost already and I knew that he was wishing that he hadn't turned up either. This was why I was here, to telepathically know what he was thinking and, more importantly, for him to know that I knew so that he wasn't alone this time. I held him with my eyes, willing him to know that I was with him, come-what-may. *I am here and I will be here as long as you need me.*

"We'll find them," DI Hammond repeated.

It sounded like she was trying to convince herself as much as the others.

*

When Hammond and the barrister left, we sat in silence for a few moments until Julian said out of the blue, "I told Chloe last night."

"Really? Gosh, I wasn't expecting that. What made you decide to tell her now?"

Wendy discreetly melted into the background and we talked as though she wasn't there.

"Last night it was all suddenly very real. I hadn't decided until last week that I was definitely going to go through with it, but I don't think I'd really accepted that I actually was, until last night. Then it felt too big to keep from her."

"How did she react?"

"Not like I expected at all. It was like she wasn't even surprised. She held me and cried a bit and said she was sorry that I'd had to go through that on my own, but that she'd always known deep down that something really bad had happened to me. I thought that she'd at least be mad about all the lies, you know, not just about my past but, I mean, how long have I been seeing you for example? How many meetings have I had with Hammond? But she just said that she understood, that it was okay."

"Is she coming today?"

He shook his head. "She works on Wednesdays."

It was typical of Julian to have not asked her and to assume that something as pedestrian as a normal day's work would prevent Chloe from attending. Once again I was reminded of what a big deal it had been for him to ask me. We'd talked in the past about Julian never asking for help. As I thought about it now, I realised just how damaging it could've been to turn him down, how he could have experienced that as yet more rejection or abandonment from the first person he asked for help, ever, the *only* person. I'd had to say yes.

Soon enough, Julian was called to the stand. This was it. As we left the witness room we were each steered towards different doors by the ushers.

"Maggie and I will be sitting right behind you love," Wendy reassured him.

I could see him shaking as he turned and gave me one last terrified look over his shoulder before he disappeared into court. I felt like they were leading him to the gallows.

The actual proceedings passed in a blur. Julian turned around once as we sat down, just to reassure himself that we were there, and from then on his eyes never left the barrister questioning him, except to turn occasionally to the judge. He didn't look at the jury or the gallery once and studiously avoided looking at his abuser. We'd talked about that. He couldn't bear to see disbelief in the faces of the jury and he knew that the accused would have plenty of supporters in the gallery.

As for the guy himself, Julian didn't want to be reminded of the childhood power imbalance. He needed to be the powerful one today, so he focused only on whoever was asking the questions, and on the judge.

I looked around though. I looked at the jury and the accused and the gallery and I didn't like what I saw. I heard Julian's whispered voice spelling out the graphic details he'd dreaded articulating and I watched the jury. Some of them were clearly sceptical. Others were obviously finding Julian's words distasteful and I couldn't read what they thought. Some were shocked. I glanced at the man in the dock. He looked very respectable, like an archetypal decent, upright citizen, and he looked equally shocked, saddened even, by Julian's testimony.

In the gallery I watched a man of about Julian's age getting more and more agitated. He was clearly very angry and upset but I couldn't tell if that was because he was a supporter of the accused and therefore angry at Julian or something else. He left part way through Julian's testimony, clearly unable to bear it any longer. As I watched him shuffle along the row of seats to leave, I spotted a woman alone at the back, dabbing at her eyes with a tissue. I knew instantly who she was and wondered what Julian would make of her being here when he found out. I was glad she'd come.

The judge allowed an adjournment, during which our barrister and Hammond patted Julian on the back and patronisingly told him he'd done well, but the other witnesses still couldn't be found. The defence called Julian back to the stand. With only one witness, they now had license to challenge the forty-five-year-old memories of just one man. Obviously he wasn't going to imagine being raped but how could he be sure, after all this time, that it was actually the accused who had committed that heinous act? It was a masterstroke. They weren't disrespecting Julian – some of the jury clearly had sympathy for him now – but they were casting enough doubt to get their man acquitted.

I glanced at the man in the dock who was now looking directly at Julian, and saw him smirk. I looked quickly at the jury but they were all watching Julian. The judge too was looking the wrong way. I wanted to shout at them all: *there, there's your proof of who he really is!* But no one saw. I glanced at Julian. Luckily he was still studiously avoiding looking that way and when I looked back the smirk was gone, replaced by a benign, concerned expression. I sat there, seething and powerless.

After Julian was dismissed, there was no point in us staying, he wouldn't be called again. Leaving without knowing the outcome was an anti-climax, although secretly I think we all knew that it wasn't looking good. As we said our goodbyes in the lobby, I looked around for Chloe but she didn't appear. Maybe it wasn't her after all. Julian looked exhausted and completely dejected and I wondered what this would do to him. It felt like a second abuse, humiliating and shaming. The defence had been careful with him but if the jury came back with a not-guilty verdict, they would be effectively calling Julian a liar

Thursday was a full day of clients with their own unique dramas and problems. Each successfully drew me into their concerns whilst I was actually with them (a feat that never failed to amaze me) but in between I couldn't focus on them at all. Writing up session notes felt impossible, my head was swimming with Julian, the court case and what it would all mean for him. Waiting for the verdict, I felt in limbo like I was living in brackets. I guessed it was probably a pretty accurate, if muted, mirror of what Julian was feeling. Intermittently Robyn and our ridiculously uncanny connection popped into my head to join the clamour and, when it caught me unawares, Harry too and my part, or lack of it, in his death joined the thought chaos. It all felt surreal and discombobulating.

I stayed tuned to the local radio in between clients. The court case had inevitably attracted local media attention although luckily they weren't allowed to name Julian. I learnt that on Thursday morning, the defence had called several character witnesses who painted Julian's abuser as the staunchest of community pillars. I thought of that smirk and seethed. By mid-afternoon the jury had been sent out and by teatime it was all over: the six O'clock news announced they had returned a not guilty verdict. It wasn't a surprise but my heart sank for Julian and I was glad I was seeing him the next day.

Chapter 18

Surprisingly I slept well and the next day felt really quite calm, given I would be seeing both Julian and Robyn that morning. I had a free afternoon again luckily as I expected to be emotionally exhausted by then.

I scanned Julian's face closely when he arrived for his session, but all I could see was incomprehension. I was expecting anger, shock, shame, humiliation or any variation of those things but instead I saw only bewilderment. Julian looked lost and unfocussed.

"He got off," he said.

"I heard. I'm so sorry, Julian."

"They didn't believe me." He hadn't looked at me yet.

"I guess not." I wanted to say more but my head could only come up with platitudes and I wouldn't insult him with those.

He sat quietly for a few moments. "Can I ask you something?" He still hadn't lifted his eyes.

"Of course."

"Will you promise to answer honestly?" He fiddled

with his wedding ring.

"Without knowing the question, I can't guarantee that I will answer at all, but I can guarantee to be honest with you." *The truth and nothing but, but not necessarily the whole truth.*

He looked up. "Do *you* believe me?" He'd never asked me that before. I don't think he'd ever had cause to doubt it before.

I returned his direct eye contact. "Yes. Yes, I do believe you Julian. I always have."

He nodded as his eyes filled. He looked studiously at his fingers as he tried to compose himself; a man like Julian didn't do tears. "So does Hammond."

I wasn't sure I liked being compared to DI Hammond.

"She called last night and actually she was really helpful. She said how sorry she was and that if only the other witnesses had been found, it would've turned out so differently. She couldn't tell me what they would've said but she said they absolutely backed up my testimony. The three of us together were watertight, she said. There was no doubt in her mind that a guilty man had just walked free. She even said she was sorry that she'd pushed me so hard to go through with it, said she never would've done if she'd known the others wouldn't show. It needed all three for us to win so she'd pushed us all… it really helped… to know that the police believed me. It helped."

"Do you wish you hadn't gone either though?"

"No... no, I know I would feel worse now if I'd chickened out and besides, something else happened."

"Oh?"

"Chloe was there." *So, that was her*. "She took a day off work. I hadn't thought to even suggest it. She said she wanted to be there. Why would she want to sit through that?"

"Because she loves you," I said gently.

"That's what she said. But it was horrible stuff to listen to. I wouldn't have wanted her to hear that."

"Maybe it was up to Chloe to decide whether she could bear to hear it or not."

"She said that she decided to go when I told her about it all the night before. She didn't tell me because she knew I would try to persuade her not to."

"She knows you well then."

"Actually, she said that was another reason she had to go; this was a part of me she didn't know about. And that's exactly why I wouldn't have wanted her to go."

"So now she does know about that part. Does it make a difference?"

"Yes and no. She says it doesn't to her."

"And do you believe her?"

"Yes, I do believe her. I do now, anyway. I believe that it makes no difference at all to her, and that fact makes the world of difference to me... I can't tell you what difference that makes to me." He stared at his wedding ring as though seeing it for the first time. "We talked for a long time on Wednesday night and into the next morning. She was adamant that she knows me, that she's always known me. She says she knows who I am and the fact that somebody committed a crime against me all those years ago doesn't change that. She says that who I am is the same person she's been living with all these years."

"The same person she loves?"

His eyes welled again. "I don't understand it," he said quietly, and I knew something important had shifted.

"I know you don't." My eyes filled too. "I know you don't *understand* it, but you do *know* it."

"Yes, I do… I do know it." Tears escaped then and Julian reached for a tissue. "Why though? Why would she?"

"Oh Julian," I laughed, and swiped at my own cheek.

For the rest of the session, Julian talked about the impact of the not guilty verdict. He wasn't surprised, it was normal for him to not win against that man so he'd never really expected that to change. Chloe, on the other hand, was furious. I guess that like me, she was angry on Julian's behalf, feeling his emotions ahead of him. I knew though that her feeling angry would help to cement Julian's new awareness that Chloe actually loved him, the real him with no hidden secrets. I was glad she was angry.

Just before the end of our hour he said, "Did I ever tell you about the day I was put into care?"

"I don't think so." I wracked my brain, trying to

remember.

"I was eight. I'd been staying somewhere temporary, for about a week I think. A social worker explained there was to be a big meeting with social services, school and me and Mum to decide where I should live. She said that if my mum got better I'd be able to go home but they all needed to decide where I should live in the meantime and how to get my mum well again."

He looked down, his hands twisting in his lap.

"Mum never turned up. I sat outside that room whilst they all decided what to do with me and my mum never even came. I remember sitting on that chair in the corridor – it felt like hours – swinging my skinny legs and watching the door, thinking she would come running in any minute now. When it was obvious she wasn't going to come, I couldn't understand it. But I knew then that I must be really bad if my own mum didn't want me, if she couldn't even come to a meeting. I also knew that it meant I would never go home and I remember feeling so scared. And angry. I was an angry little boy from then on, I think."

"I bet you were."

"I was sent to the home where I first met *him*. I tried to run away that night. I wanted to find my mum and promise to be good, to beg her to let me stay. I was caught and he beat me for the first time and locked me in a cupboard all night. When I ran away the second time, the police found me and took me back. I told them he'd locked me in a cupboard but they didn't believe me. He beat me so badly that time that I never told anyone ever again. Until now."

"And now people do believe you." *Apart from the jury! Shit!* I cursed myself for my clumsiness.

"Yes, yes they do. Apart from the jury… but the people who matter believe me. I mean the jury matter too obviously, I am really disappointed they didn't believe me, but I didn't expect to feel like I do about you and Hammond and Chloe believing me. It changes something… and you going to court with me, and Chloe going, that changes something too. I can't explain it."

"Yes, you don't need to explain, I can imagine it does change things."

*

After Julian left I only had the usual twenty-five minute gap before Robyn was due to arrive. I had planned to prepare for the emotional challenge of it somehow, to steel myself, but I didn't know how. I didn't expect to dissociate again, though I did wonder if I was being naïve about that. I also wondered what not dissociating would be like, how I would feel witnessing her pain and knowing exactly how that felt. I did feel very anxious just thinking about it.

My mind kept flitting to Julian though and I smiled inwardly each time. Reflecting on his session had a calming effect. With a not guilty verdict it could all have been so very different, but this would be life changing in a very positive way for Julian. His wife loved him and he finally felt it. For the first time Julian had stopped hiding, stopped behaving as though he was the bad one, and so he could actually feel loved because he finally allowed himself to be known. If our identity is determined, at least in part, by seeing ourselves reflected in others, then Julian's sense of self had just begun to change for the better.

I wondered briefly about how mine and Chloe's attendance in court changed things. His mother didn't go to the meeting that determined his future but we did go to court. Maybe it was a kind of re-enactment that would undo some of the maternal abandonment. And of course, this time the police believed him too. I thought of Jung and his assertion that development doesn't just take place in childhood and infancy but continues through midlife as we interact and relate to people. Growth isn't uniform, it happens in fits and starts throughout our entire lives, unless we happen to live in a social vacuum of course.

*

When Robyn arrived, I was struck again by how pale and drawn she looked. She sat down and didn't speak for a while.

"I've been wrestling with what to say about you losing a child too."

"You don't have to say anything. This is your

therapy, I had mine years ago." *Damn! I should never have said anything.* I worried that she was going to ask questions about Harry and that I would struggle to balance her need to know with the importance of keeping the focus on her.

"The thing is, I'm glad you understand. That doesn't mean I'm glad you went through this, but I realise that it sort of inevitably does mean that and then I feel guilty."

"It's OK. I know what you mean."

Robyn smiled at me weakly, grateful I wasn't upset by her comments. The thing was I did understand, I understood it all, including how isolated she would be feeling. That's why I wanted to be here rather than someone else. I knew her knowing that I *really* understood was important. Robyn fell quiet again.

"I sometimes think that feeling guilty is the worst bit," she eventually said.

"Guilty? About Daniel?"

"I should have been able to do something. I keep going over and over it, wondering where I went wrong, wondering what I should have done differently."

"Do you ever come up with anything?"

People often ask themselves painful rhetorical questions but *seriously* asking them and actually trying to answer is often helpful. I was also acutely aware that I didn't know the detail; I didn't know if Robyn did or did not do something that might have made a difference.

"No. I just know that I failed him and that kills me.

And then I think that I deserve that. The pain is my punishment for failing so catastrophically as a mother."

You too?

"You didn't fail him Robyn."

"Why is he dead then? Sorry." Her anger was leaking out.

"It's OK. I get it... he's dead because he got meningitis and no one could save him." I spoke gently, although I was unsure who I was actually speaking to now.

"I should've been able to. I should've been able to stop him getting it."

"It seems to me that meningitis strikes pretty randomly."

Randomly taking Daniel. Randomly taking Harry.

"I know it's not rational, but it just feels like I should've done something more."

"I think that's biological. As mothers we're programmed to protect our young and when we can't, we *feel* like we've failed but that doesn't make it true." *Definitely not for Robyn and maybe not for me either.* "Sometimes random is really hard to accept. We need explanations so we look for someone to blame."

Is this what I did? I couldn't find anyone else so it had to be my fault? Unlike Robyn, I didn't speak up though... and Harry might have died anyway, just like Daniel.

"I do need someone to blame, someone to be angry with. Because I feel so bloody angry it scares me."

"I know you do." I really did and I didn't really know what else to say. "What are you scared of?" I probably already knew the answer.

"I'm scared I'll lose control, scared I'll lash out at someone who doesn't deserve it, scared I'll alienate everyone by judging their perfect lives and the fact that they have no bloody idea about anything!"

I didn't know what to say. I'd felt exactly the same for a long, long time.

Sometimes as a counsellor, even when I wasn't identifying this strongly, I ended up just sitting with a client because there was nothing I could do or say. I much preferred *doing* something. Sitting with them like this, whether I identified or not, made my empathy stronger somehow. I felt their feelings so much more vividly than when I was pursuing my own thoughts about what to do or say next to help. It was tough, empathising so deeply, feeling their pain too, much harder than fixing. And not fixing also made me feel completely useless. It was a double whammy.

Someone once said to me that the purpose of empathy in counselling is to make clients go deeper into the feeling. I had never agreed that that was the *sole* purpose of it, but it was certainly one of the effects of empathy. I often wondered whether that was actually helpful with some feelings, like those associated with depression. I feared that it made it worse. And it often did in the short-term.

I feared I might make it worse with Robyn now. But

what was the alterative? To not empathise, to not sit with her in this terrible place, to leave her feeling isolated? I couldn't bring Daniel back. That was the bottom line – I couldn't bring him back and so I couldn't make her feel better. This is exactly why people avoid the bereaved because they can't help. They can't make it better and that feeling of being so utterly useless in the face of such pain is unbearable for many people. And so they stay away. I wouldn't do that to Robyn, no matter how much empathising with her hurt me too, and no matter how useless I felt.

"It's easy to be naïve when you have a perfect life, when you know nothing about pain like this," I agreed.

"They are naïve! They talk about new kitchens and the soaps on TV as though those things in any way matter! Those things aren't real and those people disgust me. They're like Stepford wives! They know nothing!"

"They disgust you?"

"Even now, even knowing what happened to Daniel, they still think those things are important enough to talk about! How stupid and facile and blind! They don't talk about them to me – they know that it wouldn't be well received – but they still talk to each other about rubbish, I know they do!"

"Did you talk about things like that with them before Daniel died?"

"No… well, not soaps. I got a new kitchen a few years ago. I suppose I must have talked about it at the time. I don't really remember. Maybe I did. Maybe I was naïve too."

"We're all a bit naïve, aren't we? We busy ourselves in trivia and pretend that we aren't mortal, pretend that the trivia actually matters. I seem to remember you used to talk about this kind of thing quite a bit the last time we met."

"Yes, I did… I don't think I ever lost that perspective in some ways. I never got into makeup and designer clothes and competitive dinner parties and stuff I still think is superficial… but in other ways you do kind of get swept along with the norm of the crowd you're in. I got a job, I wore the right office clothes, I said and did the right things to fit in.

"Then when you have kids, it's worse. Everyone has an opinion on feeding on demand or weaning or how many playgroups and activities they need to do to develop. It's all consuming and you desperately want to get it right, for them to be OK. So at what age they hit certain milestones, and whether they are bright or developing exactly as some nameless official thinks they should be actually becomes important. And you forget to celebrate the fact that they're healthy and happy… and alive and part of your life… until they're not… and then you realise that what age they fucking walked and talked is irrelevant! What's relevant is that they're here… they're with you… they're breathing and laughing and… making you laugh."

She wiped her cheek absently with the back of her

hand and her expression lightened, so fleetingly that I almost missed it, as some memory of Daniel popped into her head.

"Tell me about him," I said. "Tell me about him making you laugh."

Robyn smiled weakly as more memories came and she started to tell me about Daniel.

*

Later, sitting cradling a cup of tea, I thought about what I'd said to her about guilt and feelings of failure being biological. It was clear to me, at least in her case, that the biological instinct to protect our young could very possibly lead to unfounded feelings of failure when a child dies. In my case those same feelings had felt very much founded, but what if they weren't? What if it was just biology in my case too and I wasn't actually to blame?

I thought of Julian, of how mine and Chloe's attendance in court might have accidently been a therapeutic re-enactment of a pivotal moment in Julian's life. I wondered if observing Robyn wrestle with her thoughts and feelings would somehow be like a sideways re-enactment for me too. Would I undo the destructive conclusions I had come to by going through it again vicariously with Robyn? She had had a different experience and yet the outcome had been the same. It all felt so much more random and inevitable seeing it through her eyes. As I thought about that, the world suddenly felt more cruel and unpredictable and I shivered. Yet it was still easier than thinking that I was solely responsible.

I thought of Julian and wondered if it made any difference that he had consciously made up his history; the rest of us subconsciously do the same thing. I vaguely remembered something I'd once read about some philosopher, Kant I think, saying that each of us sees the world through filtering spectacles. My memories had been inevitably distorted because I saw the world through the filter of my own beliefs. I believed that I was a people-pleaser and that that was bad, and I made sense of the world through that lens. But it wasn't *the* truth of my past. I'd made up my history as surely as Julian had, just not consciously. Was there even such a thing as the truth of the past or is there only ever the past as it's currently construed?

My tea had long gone cold and it was starting to get dark but I hadn't noticed. Mathew and Sam were still out and so I just sat in the counselling room, lost in thought. We need explanations, we need to know why, and I knew that. I had needed an explanation of why Harry died and I had felt so very guilty so I had come up with the plausible explanation that I could've saved him. I clung to my narrative that being a people-pleaser caused Harry's death because it fitted with my filter. Maybe it was another wrong story, another distorted memory of my own past. Stephen jumped into my head again.

Maybe, I thought, we continue to be egocentric long after childhood. Maybe we like to think that we can control and affect much more than we actually can. Maybe that gives us an illusion of safety. Random is so much more terrifying. Again, the thought made me shiver. This is why we need an explanation for things because thinking that anything can happen to any of us at any time, no matter how wise or good or kind we are, is almost unbearable

I thought about what Chloe had said about knowing Julian even though he'd lied about his past. Could that be true? Is Julian the kind, wise, good man she's always believed him to be? Who was the thieving, angry, 'bad' lad he was before she met him then?

Attachment theory and other child development theories suggest that our brains and characters are formed in relation to people very early in life and are largely fixed from then. I'd always believed that but now, for the first time, I wondered. Attachment theory is just a theory, even though most people treat it as fact. What if it's wrong? There are plenty of historical theories that we laugh at now. What if some of our current cherished theories are laughable in the future?

We know so very little, I realised. In reality, we only guess at much of what we think we know. It was a sobering thought. Neuroscience is still in its infancy; we can't pinpoint the bit in the brain that correlates to an insecure attachment or a character trait such as kindness. How do we know who we really are? Are we who we see reflected in others? Are we our memories, our experiences or our faulty interpretations of those things? Would the re-enactment – if that's what it was – really change Julian? Would working with Robyn change me? Do we have a core that is unchanged by experience? Is Julian's core good, bad, wise, kind? What about mine? Are they even the right questions?

Mathew and Sam arrived home and, my head still spinning, I went out to greet them. I put dinner on, listened to stories of their day and functioned exactly as I had done for years, as though nothing had changed. In reality, nothing had.

Chapter 19

The work with Robyn progressed slowly and mostly all I could do was be with her as she went through it all. She voiced her anger and railed against the unfairness of her son's death. She shared memories of Daniel, talking about how much she missed him. And as she grieved for Daniel, I grieved for Harry. As my guilt loosened its grip and I allowed myself to remember, I was free to miss Harry too. It was painful but also strangely freeing and, for the first time, I started to enjoy the memories of the time I did have with him. I increased my supervision with Sue to weekly and as Robyn talked about Daniel, I shared with Sue the memories that stirred up in me.

October slipped into November and then December and Robyn had to face the first Christmas without Daniel. She was dreading it of course; he would've been at such a lovely age for Christmas. I remembered how that first Christmas without Harry had passed in a blur for me. I'd bought presents for Sam and cooked a basic Christmas dinner but there was no festive spirit.

Sam was too little to understand and was just excited by his new toys, but I spent most of the day watching him while thinking about Harry and all the things he would've been more excited by – the whole Father Christmas thing, stockings left on the end of the bed and a carrot for the reindeer. Sam went along with it as Mathew did those things with him, but he didn't really understand. Harry would've been jumping up and down and squealing with delight.

The year Sam was three had been even harder. Here was a living, breathing example of what I'd missed. Sam did squeal and jump up and down but all I could think of was how much I'd missed Harry doing that. Then as the years went by, Sam was less easily fooled by any act on my part and I had to get my head together. He could sense my emotions with uncanny accuracy and he didn't deserve to have a miserable mum every Christmas. By then I had developed the skill of not directly remembering Harry and so the only change needed was to stop going through the motions and genuinely engage in Christmas again. I gradually focused more and more on trying to make it a special, fun day for Mathew and Sam and on creating lots of smiles and laughter. And as I noticed and registered each smile, I began to live in the present again.

"I just wish I could cancel Christmas altogether," Robyn was saying.

"You don't want to go through it at all," I paraphrased.

"I just don't see how I can. How can I do all the happy, jolly, fun stuff that goes with Christmas when Daniel's not there? Christmas is for children and he's not there."

"But Spencer is."

"Spencer's too little to appreciate it all, apart from the toys obviously, and I'll make sure…"

"But you're not," I interrupted.

"Sorry?"

"You're not too little to appreciate it all."

"I don't understand."

"You had two boys Robyn, one of them isn't here and that's going to be awful for you, but don't miss the other one too."

Robyn's eyes welled and she looked away.

I carried on. "If Daniel had lived, both boys would have been doing things on Christmas day that you and Andy would have looked back on sometime in the future and smiled about. Spencer will be fine. As you said, he'll love the toys and the excitement. It's you I'm worried about. Precisely because Spencer will be fine, there will still be things he does on Christmas day that could make wonderful memories. Don't miss them too just because you're missing Daniel and that hurts like hell. I'm not saying you should be happy and jolly, it's obviously going to be a really, really tough day. I'm just saying notice. Notice the moments Robyn, notice Spencer and enjoy him. Spencer didn't die."

It was a deliberately challenging set of words.

Talking to Robyn, I'd realised how much I'd missed of Sam's childhood. By shutting down, by trying not to feel the pain of Harry's death and the guilt surrounding it, I'd also shut out the joy. And for too long, I'd shut out Sam. After Mathew had nursed me back to him, I'd mothered Sam and nurtured him and tried to give him as normal a childhood as possible so Sam hadn't missed out on me. At least, I hoped he hadn't. But I'd missed out; I'd missed out on him.

*

Christmas came and went, my last Christmas with Sam living at home. Robyn coped and even shared a few stories about Spencer's antics over the holidays in amongst the tales of the furtive tears she had inevitably shed over the festive period. We eased into January and as the days edged gradually longer, Robyn slowly began to talk about things other than Daniel. I learnt that Andy had never hit her again and that together they had found a healthier way of relating. She had eventually learnt to voice her feelings, in the moment, whenever he was being unreasonable or sulking. Gradually, aware now of the effect he was having, he had changed too. As in any healthy relationship, they argued, but they were each able to hold onto themselves during arguments and to be real and honest with each other.

I wondered again about Andre. Would he have learnt too? What would my life have been like if I'd stayed with him? I'd assumed that Robyn had been able to hold onto her free spirit too. After all, Andy had first brought out that side of her and they had stayed together, unlike Andre and me. When I asked though, she said that after a few years it had gradually been taken over by other concerns.

"I do miss that side of me so I've thought about it a lot, about where it went, whether it was ever a real part of me."

Me too!

"I have this theory that the maternal side and the free spirit are in some ways at odds with each other."

"Really?"

"I think there was a kind of nesting that I got into, long before I was pregnant. I got a good job, we bought a house and a car and then a better house. It was important to keep them, it was important that the house was a nice one. And so it was important to follow the rules at work, even if I didn't agree with them. It was important to play the game, to conform, to get promoted but not out of any sense of competition. I was preparing you see. I was preparing the nest for my future children. And eventually I just forgot that I didn't agree with the rules and they became my norm."

"That seems a shame somehow."

"Maybe. As I said, I did miss the free spirit side of me occasionally, but I was happy too. Especially when the children came along. I knew I could do all the adventurous stuff later but for now they needed stability and security. And a mum who's not so wild she's embarrassing!"

Robyn smiled at some hypothetical image of an embarrassing mum. I joined in but was also distracted. Had that happened to me too? Was it the maternal side, nesting and building something secure and stable, that had pushed out the free spirit rather than the people-pleasing side of me? Somehow that was easier to live with.

"I loved it," Robyn continued. "I didn't really think about the philosophical meaning of life stuff when I had the boys. They were my meaning. We just had fun and played, and adventures became collecting bugs in the woods or building dens out of sheets in the back garden. It was enough… it was more than enough. It was all I ever wanted." Her eyes brimmed with tears again.

"I know." I wanted to say more, wanted to challenge her to hold onto that way of being with Spencer, but that would've missed where she was in that moment. In that moment, she was missing the life she'd had with *two* boys, not one. My challenge would wait for another time. It was good that she could remember the happy times and that she was no longer drowning in anger all the time.

"Of course, Daniel dying has made me think about all of those questions about meaning all over again. I keep asking what the point of it all is. I don't mean it in a suicidal way, just in a why-are-we-all-here-anyway kind of way. We're born, we suffer and then we die.

That's about it really, when you stand back from it all. Does that sound depressive?"

"Yes and no. I decided a long time ago that our problem as a species was the fact that we could think about our own situation. We have an observing self, a part of us that reflects on our own lives and thoughts and feelings. That's the part that is difficult to live with. If we didn't think about it all so much and just got on with living, it might be easier."

"Careful, Socrates said that the unexamined life is not worth living remember," she teased.

"I'm not so sure. I don't think that it's a coincidence that in the Adam and Eve story, God's punishment was self-consciousness. Whether you're religious or not, it's a great metaphor for the human condition. They were blissfully happy in the Garden of Eden and then they ate from the tree of knowledge and their eyes were opened to their nakedness. It's a parable that tells how self-awareness creates shame and fear and gives us a terrible sense of separateness. Self-awareness comes with an awareness of our own solitude, smallness and mortality. It's part of the package. When we engage in self-reflection, we often think about how the past should have been and feel disappointment or anger or regret. Or we think about the future and feel anxiety or despair. Without the ability to self-reflect, we would live simply in the present moment just like the other animals in the Garden of Eden. Sorry, I'm rambling."

"No, no, it's interesting. So, we should live in the

present? Is that what you're saying?"

"We should try to, yes. I think it's probably the best we can do. It won't alleviate the suffering, but it will allow the joy in too."

"Easier said than done though."

"Definitely!" I agreed. "It seems it's almost impossible for us to stay in the present for very long, like we can only do that in a very transitory way. It seems to be the way we're made."

We both fell silent for a while. It was one of those awkward silences; I'd talked too much and left her behind. Robyn wasn't thinking about what I'd just said, she was wondering what to say next. I should've made a process intervention, asked about what was going on for her and I knew that, I knew that this was my stuff now. I was fully aware of what I was doing but I was still contemplating my own healing and continued anyway. I could only hope it would help Robyn too but I doubted whether it would actually count as therapy.

"If you were the director of your own life and could start again, would you avoid this pain by not having Daniel in the first place? Would you sacrifice the time that you did have in order to not go through this?"

It was something I'd been asking myself as memories of Harry had begun to surface and I'd begun to enjoy them again. I was genuinely curious, not knowing if I could only enjoy those memories now because time had dulled the pain. I didn't know if Robyn could enjoy hers yet or if they just hurt.

"No, of course not!" she responded immediately before the implications of the question sank in. "Well… no…" There was a long pause. "I suppose the thing is, the memories are both good and bad at the same time. I see a photo of a happy time and I know it was a happy time but it makes me cry. It physically hurts. Still, seven months on! I've put all the photos away because I can't bear the pain of looking at them."

I sat and waited; waited whilst she considered how her grief was robbing her of the time she did have with Daniel as well as the time she never got to have. I knew exactly how that felt.

"What did you do?" Robyn threw me by asking a direct question about my experience for the first time. She had avoided asking me anything until now and we'd both stuck religiously to the rules on boundaries. It would've felt disingenuous to avoid this question now though, and I decided on honesty.

"I put the photos away too. For a long, long time… maybe too long," I replied.

*

That weekend, I waited until Sam and Mathew were out at a rugby match and then hesitantly pulled down the loft ladder. I'd thought long and hard about facing the memories hidden away up there and I knew that it was time now, but I was still nervous. I couldn't remember what was stored there and hadn't been up once since

Harry's things had been moved by Mathew about a year after he died.

The loft ladder scraped and clanked into position and I checked the pins had jumped into the correct holes before tentatively climbing the steps. A waft of cold, musty air hit me as I flicked the light switch at the entrance that illuminated the entire space. There was room to stand upright providing you were directly under the peak of the roof and in the middle of the walkway that ran along the entire length. The walkway, boarded and solid, had been kept clear of the myriad of infrequently used items that were relegated to this space; the suitcases, summer duvets, Christmas decorations, the fake tree, and numerous bags, bin liners and cardboard boxes containing unknown hoards lined either side.

I walked slowly along the length of the walkway, letting my eyes sweep over the bags and boxes. I didn't know where to start. Towards the far end, where all the stuff that wouldn't be needed again was stored, several see-through storage boxes with lids were stacked three high. My eyes landed on one that had a fluffy yellow duck squashed against the lid. I smiled – Sam's 'Ducky'. He had loved that duck.

Opening the first two boxes was like opening a slideshow in my mind, but it was a slideshow of Sam: teddies, cowboy hats, plastic guns, jigsaws, a game called Pop-up Pirates, Kerplunk and more were crammed in with no fewer than three toy guitars. Toys ferreted away up here and left for years. I smiled at the memories and imagined grandchildren playing with these treasures. Mathew had presumably chosen to keep these particular ones and not others for that very reason.

Another box contained a huge wooden train set, a set started for Harry's third birthday and built on each birthday and Christmas for several years with Sam. It was the first memory of Harry I'd found. Sam had loved the set and it'd been a feature of the living room for years after Harry died, but now I remembered Harry getting the first few bits; enough track to make a figure of eight with a bridge over the middle, a *Thomas the Tank Engine* and a carriage for it to pull. Harry had been so excited and so determined to build it himself with no help. I remembered his face, screwed up in serious concentration, his tongue sticking out as he tried to work out how the track should join back on itself. In the end, I'd shown him but then he'd insisted on taking it apart so that he could do it himself. I smiled at that memory too and then noted that I was okay, that this was indeed a happy memory, a memory no longer twisted by pain and grief.

I came across a box of books and slowly took them out one by one. Immediately the tears started to fall. Oh the books, full of memories and emotions, a reminder of the unbearable sense of loss I'd felt every evening at not being able to read to Harry anymore. Mathew had to take over story time after he died; I had been unable to face these books and the memories.

I pulled out a thin paperback and was instantly transported back to sitting on Harry's bed, one arm around him as he snuggled against me, the other turning the pages of the book. *'Ho ho for the robbers, the cops and the robbers ho ho'.* Harry loved that book, and it was my favourite too. I pictured the blue walls of his room and the sky I'd painted on the ceiling complete with clouds and stars that lit up at night. I remembered how his head had felt against my chest, the weight of it, getting heavier as he struggled to fend off sleep. I remembered the soft clean smell of his newly washed hair, fresh from bath time. I remembered how soft and fine it felt. I remembered how he looked in his *Postman Pat* pyjamas and how lean and lithe his growing limbs were.

I'd loved the peace of story time, his little body worn out from a day playing, curled into me, finally still and quiet. He was such an active little boy, into everything, bright, curious, questioning; we'd called him the 'why bird' when he was two. I smiled through my tears as I remembered. His days were spent moving – chasing, tumbling, running, climbing, building – it was only during story time that he would be still and cuddle like this. It had been my favourite time of the day.

'Not much young man,' said the criminal gran...' I laughed as I read. Harry had loved that bit. I remembered him doing Grandma Swag's voice:

'Ho ho for the robbers, the cops and robbers ho ho'.
Still weeping and smiling, I lifted the box of books

off the stack, revealing a small white label on the lid of the last box. In Mathew's handwriting, it simply read: 'Harry'. Tears and smiles instantly dried. I could feel my heart pounding in my chest and hear the blood in my ears. Was I going to do this?

Slowly, hesitantly, I removed the lid. This box wasn't transparent; the lid was a solid blue plastic that completely hid the contents. As they were exposed, I gasped. Tears flowed instantly and unchecked. I reached for Harry's 'blankie', held it to my face and started to sob, then stopped suddenly as I realised that I would spoil it. I pulled the blanket away, not wanting to taint it, not wanting my tears and snot all over it. I wiped my nose and cheeks on my sleeve and when I was sure I'd stemmed the tears, I tentatively held it up to my face again, hoping to smell Harry on his special blanket, the blanket that went everywhere with him. But I couldn't, I couldn't smell Harry. All the blanket smelt of now was the mustiness of the attic. The tears flowed again and I physically ached as I held his precious comforter to my stomach and rocked, feeling the loss, the grief and the pain all over again. Time hadn't dulled it at all.

Eventually the feelings subsided a bit and, sniffing and wiping my eyes, I cautiously peered into the rest of the box. Harry's favourite teddy, the hospital wristband he'd been given when he was born that read 'Baby Fenton' because we hadn't decided on a name, the quilted blanket from his cot, his first shoes. I took them all out one by one, each causing fresh tears but also smiles as the memories came flooding back. I pulled out his wipe-clean *Postman Pat* apron. How he loved to bake. I pictured him getting flour all over himself and the kitchen. *Oh my goodness, his little red wellies!* Tears and smiles simultaneously erupted once more as I pictured him jumping in every single puddle all the way home from nursery.

When I got to the bottom of the box, I spotted something I didn't recognise: a blue leather book sporting the same small, white sticker as the box lid. This one too just read 'Harry'. I'd never seen it before but I knew instantly what it was. Oh Mathew.

I put everything else back in the box and carefully carried the album down the clanking loft ladder. I pushed the ladder up, closed the hatch and took the book downstairs, placing it unopened on the coffee table. I shivered, cold now, after an hour and a half in the attic. I found a fleece, added logs to the fire, made a cup of tea and stole a box of tissues from the counselling room. When I was finally comfortable, I knelt in front of the coffee table and opened the album.

Mathew had done an incredible job. How had he done all this without me knowing? *When* had he done this? Where had I been? Page after page of photos of Harry, all in date order, month by month, a chronicle of his short life. I cried and laughed in equal measure; Harry in his hospital cot, me cradling Harry, Mathew cradling Harry, Harry in the tree house, Harry with chocolate all over his face and in his hair, Harry holding new-born Sam, Harry and 'blankie' curled up sleeping with the dogs in their basket, Harry with his pants on his head laughing hysterically. Page after page, my beautiful boy; his whole life in pictures, all three birthdays, all three Christmases. Precious memories sealed behind acetate covers. At the end of the album Mathew had left several empty pages. It seemed appropriate.

I was still sitting there, cheeks still wet with tears, when I heard the front door. I heard Mathew and Sam tumble in and deposit arms full of kit and warm clothes in the hallway. They were still full of tales of the match. Sam was insisting that the referee had made several outrageously bad decisions. Mathew's response sounded soothing and sanguine but I couldn't hear what he said.

As I heard Sam go through to the utility room, I blew my nose and wiped my eyes but made no attempt to move or close the book. Mathew called my name as he came into the living room, looking for me.

"Ah, there you... oh." He looked from the album to me and back again, scrutinising my face, looking for clues.

"It's okay," I assured him. "It's okay... really."

He sat down next to me and pulled me to him, wrapping me in his arms.

"It's beautiful," I said. "Thank you."

We sat like that for a while, listening to Sam banging

around in the utility room.

"Mathew?"

"Hmm?"

"How would you feel if we put some photos of Harry up around the house?"

He pulled away so he could search my face again. "Are you kidding? I'd love it," he said. "I still have the framed ones we had up when…"

"When he died," I finished for him, letting him know that it was OK, we could talk about it now. We should've talked a long time ago.

"I'll go and get them," he said, dashing off as though I might change my mind if he wasn't quick enough.

I had started looking through the photos again when Sam bundled through the door, still mad at the referee. He stopped mid-sentence, looked at me and then at the book. I smiled at him, an invitation.

"Is this him?" he asked, instantly squashing himself next to me and grabbing the album. I laughed at the ability of youth to be completely unfazed by the mood and emotion of the moment.

Sam was eagerly turning the pages, peering at each photo and asking about it when Mathew came back in with a box. He sat down and started pulling the framed pictures out of the box and piling them on the coffee table. As he did so, a bunch of unframed photos fell from their hiding place between the framed ones.

One caught my eye and I plucked it from the carpet, unable to take in what I was seeing. Mathew stopped unloading the box and watched me, horrified.

"I'm so sorry, I had them developed after… and forgot they were here."

"No, no, it's all right. It's not that."

The photo had been taken on the beach that May bank holiday weekend, the last weekend of Harry's life. I'd never seen it before, but that wasn't what had shocked me. In the photo, I was holding Harry, my hair pulled back in a ponytail. I remembered how the wind had whipped my hair around my face and into my eyes and, irritated, I'd tied it up out of the way. It wasn't a style I ever normally wore. With my hair like that, the resemblance was uncanny; I couldn't imagine why I hadn't noticed before. I stared into my own face in that picture but it was the first time I recognised that Robyn's eyes stared back at me.

Chapter 20

I kept the picture stuck on the fridge door with a magnet and puzzled over it every time I walked past. I could recognise myself – I knew that I had once looked like that – but it seemed to look more like Robyn than me now.

When it had been taken, I'd been on a diet for months, trying to lose the baby weight after Sam was born. That day, I'd felt really good, having finally reached my target weight. I was a tall, lean looking size ten. Then after Harry died, food had felt irrelevant and I'd become gaunt and ill looking before Mathew eventually coaxed me back to eating. There were no pictures taken of that time but I remembered how concerned family and friends had been, how many comments were made about my weight and reluctance to eat. I went through the motions for a while until my appetite finally returned and after that I just ate what I felt like. I never did regain an interest in how I looked or dieting, and my weight had eventually settled at around two stone heavier than when that picture had been taken. My hair was very different too; dark brown before, it had become grey very quickly after I lost Harry. I had cut it into a short bob soon afterwards and had worn it that way ever since, now complete with what I hoped was a chic long fringe swept off to one side. Seventeen years had also added plenty of wrinkles!

I scrutinised Robyn when she arrived for her next appointment. She'd put on weight since the previous October when she'd arrived emaciated and drawn, but she was still very slim. Her hair was long, and although I now saw that it was actually flecked with grey, it still appeared uniformly dark. She generally wore it tied back in a ponytail as I had in the photograph. The resemblance was uncanny.

I puzzled over it for ages, remembering once again all the remarkable coincidences we shared and now this physical similarity too. I desperately tried to make some kind of sense of it while at the same time telling myself that there was no sense to make, that they were just coincidences. I couldn't quite believe that though. What were the chances of so many of the same things happening to both of us? Even taking out our existential views on life and the fact that we'd each had a boyfriend who'd hit us once when we were the same age, even removing those things that were likely to be statistically quite common, the rest was too remarkable to be just coincidence. We'd both lost a child, a son, aged three, to meningitis. It felt like the details of that horrendous event had been similar for both of us too and I had to consciously remind myself that I didn't actually know the details surrounding Daniel's death, that I was mixing up my experience with hers. The odds had to be so small though even so. And we even looked like each other!

Eventually, head spinning, I had to let it go and accept that it was coincidence. After all, what else could it be? Although the picture did remain on the fridge door, I stopped seeing it.

By March, Robyn decided to end therapy. I wondered how she would cope with the anniversary of Daniel's death in May, but did nothing to dissuade her other than assuring her she could return at any time. I didn't want her to end though; Robyn would always be special to me. I felt bound to her in a way that was rare with other clients. I knew it came from our many shared experiences, but I also knew that I couldn't let *my* feelings of such a deep connection get in *her* way. Robyn needed to go and I needed to let her. She had the rest of her life to get on with and sometimes in bereavement counselling you reach a point where the counselling itself was the main thing still holding you in the shadow of the bereavement. Ending therapy was an important part of moving on.

On her last day, we had both cried. Robyn brought me flowers and a card that read 'You'll never know how much you have helped me. Thanks to you I can now see a sliver of light in my darkest moment'.

"Thank you, I'm glad it helped. I know how much even a sliver of light means," I smiled.

She hesitated. "I know you do. To be honest, that's what's been the biggest help. We haven't talked about what happened to you and that's quite right, I get that, but knowing that you have been through this and seeing you now, still standing, looking okay... I mean, obviously, I don't know that you're okay but you seem okay... well, somehow that gives me hope. I don't think it's possible that you could be still carrying *this* intensity of agony."

She looked concerned that I might be offended by that so I smiled to reassure her and shook my head. I didn't want to say anything. I was still wary of any explicit discussion of my stuff although I admit that that was a rather moot point given the number of times I had actually been absorbed in myself while working with her.

"I know we're obviously not the same person," Robyn continued, "and our experiences and what we make of them will be different, but I really did feel that you just understood this so completely. There were things I didn't have to say out loud; I just knew you knew them anyway. I know it's probably because you've been through it too, but it felt more than that. It was like you were in my head, under my skin somehow. Like you'd lived my life too."

The hairs on the back of my neck stood on end. *Robyn feels it too!* In an instant I assessed all my options: should I tell her about the other coincidences? Tell her that I felt a weird connection too? Show her the photograph and let her see that we even looked the same? I immediately dismissed each of them. Even thinking about saying any of it out loud made me aware of just how ridiculous it sounded, of how ridiculous it actually was. Robyn was simply voicing the experience of many clients about how it feels to be truly known. It's by no means universal but it's a common enough experience in therapy. *Maggie, get a grip!* I couldn't let it go though. 'Like you've lived my life too' she'd said. It felt exactly like that, like we were each repeating almost the same story seventeen years apart.

We hugged goodbye, appropriately initiated by her, and I wondered if I would ever see her again. I couldn't help thinking of the last time we'd said goodbye and how very different it had been. I often felt bereft when clients ended, but this time I knew that there would be a Robyn-shaped hole in the pattern of my week for some time.

*

Julian had oscillated between railing against the unjust verdict and marvelling in his new relationship with Chloe. In between, we continued the slow, painful work of unscrambling the subconscious messages of his abusive childhood. The verdict hadn't helped at all in this respect and Julian often fell into the old pattern of blaming himself. If his abuser wasn't guilty in the eyes of the court, then it must all have been his fault after all. At those times, he struggled to accept that Chloe loved him, struggled again to accept that he was loveable and fell back on his belief that she had fallen for his act.

Gradually though, Chloe's anger at both the court verdict and his abuser couldn't be ignored. As she and I steadfastly refused to blame him for any of his past, including his own misdeeds, Julian slowly came round to a different perspective. A turning point came with something Chloe had found in the library. She had done some research and, in a book on the history of the area, found an old black and white photograph of the home where Julian had been placed. A dozen or so small boys had been scrubbed, polished and arranged on the steps leading up to the big oak doors of the main entrance, the entrance that ironically they were never allowed to use.

On the left-hand end of the front row, an eight-year-old Julian squinted at the camera. His head was cocked to one side, one eye closed against the glare of the sun. His arms hung loosely by his sides as though he didn't know what to do with them if he couldn't ram them in his pockets. His extremely skinny legs stuck out of a too-big pair of shorts, gathered tightly at the waist and held up by what looked like a piece of string. Someone had clearly tried to tame his hair but it still stuck out at strange angles over his ears and collar. He was tiny, even for an eight-year-old.

At the other end of the group, on the back row, stood

his tormentor, then a stocky twenty-three-year-old. He was barely recognisable as the apparently respectable and now slender man I'd seen in court that day; barely that is, apart from the smirk.

It was that photograph that finally helped Julian accept that he was blameless. Everything his abuser had told him about being bad and deserving the 'punishment' withered under the truth of that picture. It was impossible to see anything other than a vulnerable, lost little boy and the all-powerful bully in the back row who had assaulted, beaten and eventually raped him. That photograph proved to Julian, in a way that words never could, that he had been completely innocent.

"So, what do you reckon then? Am I fixed?" he asked one day in April.

We'd been meeting fortnightly and then monthly as he'd adjusted to his new world view.

"Were you ever defective?" I challenged.

He smiled. "Fair enough. He was the defective one, wasn't he?"

I nodded.

"I think I was a little bit broken by it though."

"Maybe. It's really up to you to decide when you're ready to end though. What do you think?"

"I think I am, to be honest." He looked at me searchingly, concern etched across his face.

I smiled and nodded, reassuring him that it was okay to leave. Clients like Julian, who had spent a lifetime looking after everyone else's needs, often worry about the therapist when they end, worry that the ending will be perceived as rejection. There was a long pause. Now decided, Julian looked emotional at the thought of leaving.

"I've been wondering what my life would have been like if I'd never gone to that home, if I'd never met him. I suddenly realised that if I hadn't been going off the rails, I would never have gone into that shop to nick trainers and so never would've met Chloe. Maybe I have him to thank for that in a strange sort of way."

"Who knows? There are so many different paths our lives could take, so many different junctions where events set us off down one route or another. It seems pretty random to me and all we can actually do is choose how to respond to the circumstances we find ourselves in. However you ended up in that shop, you have yourself to thank for making it work with Chloe."

"Yes, I realise that now." Having decided this was our last session, Julian seemed in a reflective frame of mind. "It's weird isn't it, to think of all those random junctions and how your life might have turned out if you'd taken a different path at some point."

"A philosopher called Nietzsche had this theory of eternal return. He said that because the universe is infinite, each of our lives must be repeated an infinite number of times. That's the nature of infinity, you see. In an infinite universe every single event that makes up a life must be repeated in exactly the same order an infinite number of times. By that argument though, all the different possible versions of our lives would be repeated infinitely too. Every time there was a choice point, a junction, there would be a version of you that took the other path, do you see? At least that's his theory. So, maybe there's a Julian out there somewhere who just nicked the trainers and ran," I said playfully.

"Blimey! That's a bit deep Maggie. Not sure I can get my head round that one, but more fool him I guess!" He laughed. After a moment's pause, he added more seriously, "I like where I am now, but I'm not sure that I'd want to live all of my life again, over and over an infinite number of times."

"I'm not sure many of us would. I guess the Nietzsche thing is about encouraging us to at least make the right choices when we do have a choice."

We lapsed into an awkward silence. It was often like this in last sessions, everything that needed to be said had been said. There was no work to do and I didn't even feel inclined to review where we were and how we had got there. That was appropriate when the work had been more cognitive, more about challenging and changing concrete thoughts. It hadn't been like that with Julian. He had embedded a new way of communicating honestly with Chloe that didn't need pointing out and if he ever fell back into shame, he simply got out the photograph. He had adopted strategies and new ways of being without us ever calling them that.

I was about to suggest that we didn't need to fill the

last ten minutes if it felt like we were done now, when Julian tried to fill them anyway.

"Who comes up with something like that anyway?" He was still talking about Nietzsche. "I get it, I do understand that's what infinity means, but crikey! An infinite number of Julians running round the place! What if two of them somehow ended up in the same time and place and actually met?"

I felt the colour drain from my face, a shiver race up my spine. I felt suddenly too hot as though I might faint. *Robyn! What if...?* Julian was grinning at me, wanting me to join in his fanciful philosophising but I was struck dumb. *No, it couldn't be.*

"Maggie?"

"Sorry." I shook myself. "You just reminded me of something. I am listening, go on."

"It's okay, I obviously watch too many sci-fi films. I was just messing about... I was actually trying to avoid having to say goodbye, I think."

That certainly pulled my attention back into the room with him! Julian's eyes filled and I mirrored him.

"I can always come back if I need to, can't I?" For all his fifty-one years, he looked just like that lost little boy again.

"Yes, of course. The door is always open." I said that to all clients as they left but I didn't want Julian to use it as an excuse to avoid a sad ending. "And maybe you won't need to."

"Maybe I won't." He looked at his hands, awkward

and unused to this kind of relating. "I'll miss you Maggie," he mumbled.

"I'll miss you too."

He looked up, sceptical. I'd seen it before. Clients assume that as they're one of many, I don't feel anything for them. Or at least I don't feel as much as they do and, being brutally honest, that was often the case. Occasionally though, clients like Julian really did get under my skin and lodge there. How could he not? We'd been through so much together. I met his eye.

"Truly. I will really miss you Julian."

*

I wandered round feeling lost all afternoon. My emotions were a myriad of conflicting responses to that last hour. I was proud of the work Julian and I had done together, and smugly satisfied that everything had turned out so well for him – that verdict could've made it all so very different. I was also incredibly sad that I wouldn't see him again, that everyone's favourite uncle was getting on with his own life now and was no longer any part of mine.

Those emotions were a familiar part of the counselling landscape though. I'd felt them before and I would feel them again. I was trained in how to handle them, but then there was the Nietzsche thing. I really didn't know how to handle that. I pulled the photograph down from the fridge door and stared at it for a long time. The face on the now dog-eared print seemed to morph into Robyn and then me and back again. In the end, I could no longer tell who it was I was looking at. What if Nietzsche's thought experiment was actually possible? What if we really were the same person? Robyn had even said it herself: 'It's like you've lived my life too'. I laughed out loud at myself as the thoughts coalesced, but then looked at the picture again. *It can't be.*

*

"So, let me get this straight Maggie." Sue was trying valiantly to maintain a respectful, curious attitude. "What you're saying is…" She shook her head, confused. "Actually, tell me again what it is that you are saying?"

This was a bad idea but I'd already said too much to back out now. "I'm saying that I've felt for a long time that there are too many coincidences between me and Robyn for them to be just coincidences. Then Julian came up with this idea: he said what if two of Nietzsche's infinite recurrences overlapped in time and space and met and… I thought…" I tailed off as I felt my cheeks starting to burn. On what planet did I think sharing this crazy idea with Sue was a good idea? What would she think of me? *Ground, swallow me up! Now!*

Sue was looking at me like I had completely lost the plot. All credit to her though, she stopped gaping and closed her mouth quicker than I probably would've done and rallied with a standard, "Say a bit more," line. It was a trick I used too when I needed time to think.

I decided to back pedal. "Well, just think if it *were* possible, what we could learn from each other." *It is possible, I know it is. It's the only possible explanation.*

Sue visibly relaxed, obviously relieved that she didn't have to have a difficult conversation about my fitness to practice and wonder which psychiatric ward would have a bed.

"From each other?" This was a conversation she could join in with.

"Yes, well, it felt like I learnt an awful lot from Robyn as well as, hopefully, the other way round."

"Definitely the other way around," Sue interrupted.

"If we were two versions of the same person," I continued, choosing my words carefully now, not implying that I actually thought we were of course. "If we were two versions of the same person, then her learning from me is like the classic 'letter-to-my-younger-self' idea, isn't it? But me learning from her, well maybe that's just as important an idea. Maybe it's something we should think about with clients."

"Go on." Sue was genuinely interested and I found myself on a roll.

"Well, I did learn a lot from her, especially when I first met her. Somehow she reminded me of a wisdom I'd lost. We have a different kind of wisdom at twenty don't you think, a wisdom that is nothing to do with experience? Everything just seems clearer at that age, simpler, perhaps because of the lack of experience. It's easier to hold onto our values. I often found myself thinking about what my younger self would say when I was working with her back then.

"And, of course she put me back in touch with that existential view of life, the adventurous side, the side that wanted to live rather than exist. It's funny, that side of me is around much more now as Sam is about to fly the nest and I can make plans without having to factor in what he might need from me. Robyn said that she thought the adventurous side and the maternal side were incompatible and I think she's right."

Sue nodded and smiled, happy now that I wasn't going mad. "We learn from all our clients. There are even whole books dedicated to just that phenomenon, but it's true that we do learn from some more than others."

"Outside counselling, I think that elders like us have a lot to learn from youth too though. Young people have so much to teach us, they have this unbounded energy and a sense of justice." I was thinking of Sam. "It's like their black and white thinking style takes you straight to the heart of the issues, issues we muddy as we get older by adding in the grey. They see things more clearly somehow, like the little boy who pointed out that the emperor had no clothes."

*

Driving home, I wondered again about Nietzsche's eternal return and the idea that Robyn and I were the same person. Nietzsche never suggested that the eternal return hypothesis was actually a scientific possibility, it was just a thought experiment he proposed to make us think about whether living our lives again would be a good thing or not.

If it were possible, would we still be the same person now? Robyn had made a different decision about Andy than I had about Andre. Why was that if we were the same person? At what point did we become different people who make different choices? When Robyn came for counselling? No, it was too egotistical to think that counselling can fundamentally change who a person is. Counselling certainly helps people listen to themselves more fully though and that sometimes helps them to make different decisions. It's those different decisions at key choice points, at those junctions, that then change the trajectory of their lives and the experiences they have, and *that* might change who they are. If we are who we are because of decisions we make and what happens to us as a result, then that's the mechanism by which counselling makes a difference; it helps us to be assertive, to know and express our needs, to believe in ourselves and reach for our dreams.

Robyn and I weren't the same person. Robyn had learnt to believe in herself and trust her inner wisdom early in her life while I felt like I was just getting there, that I had learnt that from her only very recently.

I wondered if I would ever see her again and then suddenly realised that I could actually engineer that. I knew that I could both test out this crazy idea, confirm once and for all that she and I shared the same story, and see her again. And I was pretty sure when. And I was pretty sure where.

PART THREE
2014

Chapter 21

"I tell the story that I can't cook, but it's not the truth." I was speaking to a room full of counsellors at a conference. "I have two hands that work. I have two eyes. I can read the instructions in a recipe as well as the next person. How could it possibly be true that I can't cook? There is no reason that one person can cook and another, with all the physical requirements needed for cooking, can't. It's just a story I tell myself about myself. I even have a backstory that I could tell you about the *reason* why I can't cook, but it's still a belief, it's not a fact. It's only the repeated telling of a story, keeping the belief alive, which actually makes it true. I believe that I can't cook and so I don't. I don't practice and hone the skill, I don't learn how to adapt recipes or make up my own, and it becomes self-fulfilling. Somehow my belief, and *only* my belief, actually causes the fact of it."

I scanned the room. Yes, they were still engaged, still listening. I still had them.

"Counselling is about hearing stories, interpreting

stories and re-writing stories. We each interpret our own stories before we have the requisite tools for the job, before our brains are wired for the task. Then that interpretation becomes our truth, but it's no more the truth than the fact that I can't cook – although my family might have something to say about that."

Polite laughter from the delegates. *Good, this is still going well.*

"Everything that happens from then, happens in the context of the 'truth' we originally made of our stories, a 'truth' we arrived at when our brains were still a long way from formed, possibly less than fifty per cent formed. Belief is built on belief, while we blithely imagine that we are actually self-aware, that we know ourselves well. We don't know ourselves at all, we only know our version of our own truth. It's impossible to hold and believe two conflicting ideas at the same time – that's called cognitive dissonance – and so we filter out any evidence that contradicts our 'truth' and that 'truth' becomes entrenched.

"We think we have conscious control of our actions, but we don't. We use our stories to explain what we do and who we are, but neuroscience is now showing that the part of the brain that explains our actions, the conscious part, is not even running the show, it's just a narrator. And in many ways that narrator is stuck in childhood. It's stuck in the interpretations and stories we made up, often when we were very young. Our sense of self is actually based on stories that are fundamentally wrong.

"What I'd like you to do now is to work in threes. There are two parts to this exercise: first, think about the stories that you tell to explain who you are. Keep yourselves safe, don't go for anything too deep or likely to provoke strong emotions and definitely stay away from any trauma in your past for this exercise. Think about where that story came from and how you know, or think you know, that it's the truth. Challenge each other to really explore if there is any evidence for its accuracy."

Several people nodded, acknowledging that the brief was clear.

"For the second part, I'd like you to think about whether there are any stories from your past that no longer feel like they belong to you. Maybe they are something to do with a part of you that you've now lost, for better or worse, something that you've moved away from." I scanned the room again. People exchanged glances and there were one or two looks of confusion this time, but I didn't care. It was important.

They duly shuffled chairs anyway, and a low hum of discussion started to fill the room and gradually got louder. Nothing I had said would be new to them, but I hoped that perhaps I'd presented it in a way that made them think. I wanted one person in particular to be made to think.

*

At the end of the workshop, as the delegates were gathering papers and filling in feedback forms, a few came to ask questions and thank me for the course. A solitary figure hung around at the back of the group that surrounded me. With head bowed, looking at a phone, I couldn't see a face but I knew who it was. Eventually the group of questioners drifted away, leaving just the two of us. I was standing with my back to her but sensed her there before she spoke.

"Hello Maggie, remember me?"

Yes! I inwardly fist pumped and outwardly smiled before turning around.

"Robyn, of course I do, how are you?" I was genuinely delighted to see her again, and to see her there, but it wasn't proof. I had met my old counsellor again eight years after Harry died at a conference just like this. But I'd had eight years to think about it and I knew that plenty of clients go on to become counsellors, and that all newly qualified counsellors in this area come to this conference. It's like a rite of passage. This wasn't the proof I was looking for though. Not quite yet.

"Good thanks. Yes, really good I think. I'm a counsellor now... well, obviously."

"Yes, so I guessed." *You'd be surprised at the things I've guessed Robyn.*

"I was wondering if it would still be against the rules for us to go for a coffee?"

Perfect! I wouldn't have to initiate it now.

"Possibly. But what the heck? Stuff the rules! I'd love to go for a coffee and catch up with you."

We wandered off in search of the nearest coffee shop. When we had bought drinks and found a seat in the corner, Robyn started talking about the workshop, not realising the part she had played in its conception.

"It's interesting to think about whether our stories are actually the truth or not. I mean, the things that happened to me definitely did happen, but it's when I use them to explain who I am now that we enter the realms of fiction isn't it? I thought that I became a counsellor because Daniel died but, thinking about it, I was inspired by the counselling we did before that too. And maybe neither played the part that I think they played. Maybe I'm just nosy and like to know about other people's lives."

I laughed. "Yeah, me too possibly."

There was an uncomfortable pause. I should have expected a degree of awkwardness but I hadn't completely thought that bit through. I had been too pleased that she'd actually shown up and, of course, I did need this catch up. Even if I had thought about it, an expectation of awkwardness would never have stopped me. I had to know for sure. How was I going to steer the conversation where I needed it to go though?

"I found the question about 'stories that no longer feel like you' interesting."

Bingo!

"I find myself telling Spencer stories about my life before he was born and it doesn't feel like I'm even talking about me. I know I did the things I'm telling him about, but they are so far away from the life I'm leading now, that it seems like I'm talking about someone else."

It worked! That question had been meant for her, and her alone, precisely because I felt the same way. I'd thought long and hard about what would constitute proof. Robyn was one of the very few clients with whom I hadn't discussed her childhood. I knew proof would lie there and could've engineered a question that would've got her thinking about her childhood. But then I wasn't sure that she would discuss it with me after the workshop. And I didn't think that it would be easy for me to bring the conversation round to her childhood now that we were in a non-counselling scenario.

The fact that we looked so alike wasn't proof either. I'd researched that. Apparently human DNA is so limited that we each have six or seven *doppelgängers* around the world. No, proof would be something very different, details so precise that they couldn't possibly be coincidence.

I'd thought about simply sharing some of my stories with her but, although we weren't counsellor and client anymore, the ethics of our old relationship still seemed to apply. And if I was right? Well, that would require a whole new set of ethics that I couldn't even begin to unravel! What ethics could possibly be applied to this situation? I'd decided a long time ago that if this meeting happened, then it was better to say nothing to her.

"You're thinking about stories from when you were travelling?" I prompted.

"Yes, how did you know?"

"Lucky guess." This was so much easier than I expected. With hindsight, I think that I was sure then, before she told me the rest.

"I've been thinking about them a lot lately. I'm quite proud of the part of me that did those things. What did we call it? The free spirit?"

"We never really talked about your travels. Where did you go? What did you do?"

"Oh you don't want to hear about all those things. It feels self-indulgent to talk about myself now. I'm not a paying client anymore."

And that, in a nutshell, is why it's hard to transition from counsellor and client to a friendship.

"I know, but I'm interested. Really. Go on, tell me about them. You see, if I was still your counsellor I wouldn't be able to be nearly so directive." I grinned to encourage her. Of course, I wanted to know about her travels but not for any reason that she could possibly have imagined.

"OK then," she grinned back. "Well, my biggest adventure was in Myanmar, Burma as it was then. I was snuck…"

…into the country from Thailand… I smiled

inwardly.

"Hidden under a tarpaulin…"

… on the back of a truck.

"A guest of the Karen Freedom fighters."

It felt like finally acknowledging something you've known for a long time. I was no longer amazed or stunned or sceptical, it just felt okay, comforting somehow.

"I have a photo at home," Robyn continued, "of a fourteen-year-old boy…"

… he's sitting on the back of a truck. I could visualise the picture, still hanging on my spare room wall.

"He's holding a Kalashnikov…"

… and his eyes, oh how his eyes haunt me.

"He looks so scornful of the westerner taking photos."

The westerner who knows nothing… I remembered the embarrassment I'd felt taking it.

"He's on his way to the front line and he looks…"

… defiant and terrified at the same time.

I simply smiled and tried to look suitably surprised and impressed. What could I possibly say?

Acknowledgments

I had no idea, before I wrote a book, how much of a team effort it is getting it to this stage. Writing the manuscript in the first place is solitary but after that you need a community of generous people willing to give their time, effort, expertise and advice.

My support crew began with Catherine Taylor and Emma Skitt who encouraged (and pushed) me to write *The Wrong Story* in the first place, refusing to accept my assertion that I would get round to it 'one day'. Two years later, once I had a 'finished' manuscript, I congratulated myself – I had written a whole book, it had 83,000 words, a beginning, a middle and an end and a story line that flowed. For some reason that was enough and so no-one read it. Eventually, Jane Warner (author of *The Hartpury Horror*) persuaded me to dig it out of the loft and let her read it (which felt terrifying at the time). Jane was very positive and so I tentatively let Emma Skitt, Ralph Lewis and Kathy O'Keeffe read it too. To say their praise was glowing is an understatement and they really pushed me to take it further. Without their effusive encouragement and support, we really wouldn't be here.

Next to step up were a wonderful team of volunteer beta readers; some I knew and some I didn't, but all answered the call to read the book and give me honest, objective feedback. Lynda Robson, Lynne Dare, Lindsey Martin, Janet Hiscocks, Alison Carmody, Issi Lammas, Julie Halliday and Edward James were incredibly positive about the book whilst also being completely honest about the one bit that they felt didn't work as well as the rest. Edward James gave me a dynamite idea of how to rewrite that bit and here we are.

Yvette Holborough went above and beyond our agreement for her to proofread the manuscript before I submitted it and gently and collaboratively suggested edits too. Undoubtedly these all enhanced the book and made a publishing contract more likely. Nick Pease (author of *Revelation*) guided me through the submissions process, helped me with my submission pack and was absolutely key to me getting a contract with Cranthorpe Millner.

As a new author, I had no idea what working with a publisher would be like; would the book now be taken out of my hands and edited in ways I didn't like? The team at Cranthorpe Millner have made the whole process a joy. Vicky Richards has been an incredible senior editor, tolerating my prevarication over cover ideas and ensuring I felt in control of everything to do with my book at all times. Nothing was too much trouble. She clearly wanted me to be delighted with the final product and I am. Shannon Bourne and her team came up with a very special cover that I instantly fell in love with and Lauren Barnes has, and is still, doing a wonderful job on the marketing front.

Finally thanks go to my amazing husband Richard Jenner, who literally kept me alive throughout this whole endeavour. As I repeatedly got lost in the world of Maggie, Robyn, Stephen and Julian, he reminded me that in this world I did actually need to eat and drink and endlessly replaced cold, forgotten cups of tea with hot ones. His attention to detail also made him the perfect final, final, final proof-reader before I eventually agreed to stop searching for flaws and signed off the final edits.

It may be my name on the front cover but without a wonderful group of people behind me, *The Wrong Story* would never have made it into your hands.